lost in static

CHRISTINA PHILIPPOU

RBANE
Publications

urbanepublications.com

First published in Great Britain in 2016 by Urbane Publications Ltd
Suite 3, Brown Europe House, 33/34 Gleaming Wood Drive, Chatham, Kent ME5 8RZ
Copyright ©Christina Philippou, 2016

A CIP catalogue record for this book is available from the British Library.

ISBN 978-1-910692-70-7
EPUB 978-1-910692-71-4
MOBI 978-1-910692-72-1

Design and Typeset by Julie Martin
Cover by Julie Martin

urbanepublications.com

The publisher supports the Forest Stewardship Council® (FSC®), the leading international forest-certification
organisation. This book is made from acid-free paper from an FSC®-certified provider. FSC is the only
forest-certification scheme supported by the leading environmental organisations, including Greenpeace.

For James

Ashes ...

RUBY

I can't believe it's Juliette.

The crumpled form at the bottom of the stairs. The body lifted onto the stretcher. The blood.

Why won't they tell me if she's OK?

'... drugs ...' I heard the ambulance people say.

Seriously? It's just weed. She wasn't taking anything else. I'll vouch for that. Even if it lands me in a world of trouble.

I rested my head on the wall. It was cool, made my cheeks burn less. This was not how term was supposed to go. First year of uni was meant to end on a high. Just not the drugs' variety.

The police walked past, continuing their conversation about 'pills, some coke and a rolled up note'.

Juliette's? But surely the only thing she had in her room was leftovers of an eighth?

I patted my pockets as our hall tutor brushed past me. *Nothing. Where are my fags?*

Breathe, Ruby, mate. Breathe. She'll be OK. Matt was. But then he collapsed on the spot, not at the top of the stairs.

They shut the ambulance doors and the sirens wailed.

What's happening? Where are they taking her? Can someone tell me please? Does anyone care?

I felt the brick against my face. It wasn't helping any more. I needed to cool down. *I need a drink. And a smoke. I need to move. Why can't I move? Help, someone. Help!*

But no one was interested. *All wrapped up in their own worlds. Making up stories. Oh yes, the rumours will be even wilder after this one.*

I caught a movement and looked over at the huddle by the grass. He grabbed hold of her hand. And then looked over at me. *Am I supposed to care?*

I sniggered, possibly out loud. *It's pathetic of him.*

But at least it shook me out of my trance. I felt my leg muscles twitch and was able to move again. I turned and headed up the hill to clear my head and start my hunt.

YASMINE

We all stood there, in a tableau of conflicting thoughts and shock. It was one of us in that ambulance, and the tension reverberated across the grass verge outside our halls of residence. We stood in a circle, roughly grouped into the cliques that had grown out of a single hall cluster over the last two terms, with only Ruby standing apart from the rest of the crowd, leaning casually by the building opposite and staring at the ambulance that held Juliette's comatose form.

The hall tutor indicated strongly that the authorities

believed drugs were involved. The drug paraphernalia found in her room had clearly helped form this impression, along with the fact that Juliette was lying unconscious at the foot of the stairs with nothing but a joint, a lighter, some pills, and a plastic bag with half a gram of coke in her pocket. None of the 'responsible' adults were forthcoming with any enlightening information.

I stood on the wet grass in the comfort of the main group. I felt his hand squeeze mine, and warmth filled what just a second before had been a void of feelings and thoughts. I smiled and looked up at him, expecting to see his caring, rich face peering down at me in concern. I couldn't have been more wrong; his gaze was firmly set on *her*, standing in solitude and guiltily patting her pockets every time a policeman walked past, wondering, paranoid, if she had any drugs on her person. It was truly worrying how close Ruby and Juliette had become, and I couldn't help but wonder how much Juliette had confided in Ruby prior to that ill-advised plunge down the stairs.

'Darling, this is horrible. Could we please go get a drink?' I said, pulling on his arm and steering him away from halls and *her,* toward the safety of the Students' Union.

Term 1:

OCTOBER
TO
DECEMBER
2000

Fresh

RUBY

I was scared. Dad had left earlier and I was alone in the tight, musty corridor of my new halls.

I can do it. I can face them by myself. It's the first term of first year and no one knows anyone else, so why be scared? Breathe, Ruby, mate. Breathe.

Behind the cream kitchen door I could hear Kylie Minogue's *'Spinning Around'. Great. Couldn't have hall mates with worse taste in music.*

I pushed open the door to the kitchen. 'Hi, I'm ...'

I stopped short in front of a god with green eyes. He was leaning against the wall, next to a small red fire extinguisher mounted in easy reach of the hob. *It really brings out the colour of his eyes. What are you doing? Don't stare.*

'I'm Ruby,' I tried again. *Congrats, mate, you almost sound normal.*

'Hi, Ruby,' said green eyes. 'I'm Callum, and this is Matt and Paul.' He gestured towards the two boys sat at the table drinking beer, then smiled. 'You're the first girl here.'

Is that a good or a bad thing?

'Beer?' asked Matt or Paul, taking out a bottle from the crate of Stella on the table and holding it out for me to take. 'Apologies, but we were discussing football.'

Of course, the need to apologise. Because no girls are interested in football.

'Cheers, mate. Talking about how long Keegan will last?' *Nooooo! Why say that? Boys don't like it when girls know about football.*

Green eyes smiled again. 'No, we're betting on the title. Keegan hater, are we?'

Or maybe they do like it. 'Not at all, mate. And it's Leeds all the way. Obviously.' *Stop talking now, Ruby, mate.*

'Leeds fan, are we?' asked the other half of Matt and Paul.

'Absolutely!' *Stop it, Ruby, mate. Now.* I looked down at the table and started playing with my keys.

'Interesting. Family into football then?' asked green eyes.

No, mate, don't ask about my family. Please. I really don't want to talk about them. 'Yeah. So what were those bets?' *Attention away.*

I breathed as the conversation turned back to football and far from me and my family.

It felt like minutes, but it took hours for the kitchen to slowly fill up. I couldn't remember all their names. But I remembered Matt and Paul with their beer. And Callum with his green eyes.

Then there was Yasmine. She was blonde and beautiful and confident. Just what I wanted to be. Well, apart from the being blonde bit. She was interesting, with hobbies ranging from fashion design to yoga. A bit girly, but in a good way – really sweet. I could tell we'd be friends. Well, I hoped so at any rate.

At sevenish, someone suggested we head to the Union. Most of the girls disappeared to do their makeup.

'Not going to freshen up?' asked Callum.

'Are you saying I need makeup?' *Me being cheeky? Where did that come from?*

He blushed.

Oh no – he does think I need some. Great. 'Fine – I'll go put some on.'

Off I went to change into my only strappy top and put on some mascara, eye shadow, and lip gloss. *Is that even in the right order? Who cares, mate? Callum does. And what chance do you have with him? None. Exactly.*

About half an hour later, we were all in the Union. Pints cheap and plentiful. Cheesy music. And Callum on the dance floor. Other than the music, what more could I ask for?

We all danced and sang at each other like we'd been friends for years. The drink helped, obviously. Although Callum kept ending up next to Yasmine. *Inevitable really.*

But I had fun.

I can do this university thing, I really can.

YASMINE

The carpets were grim, the walls peeling, and everything

stank of mould. The colour scheme, too, was in drastic need of an interior decorator. All in all, I wish I'd been allocated a room in the en-suite halls of residence, but, as luck would have it, I'd drawn the short straw. My room was tiny, with a single bed that creaked, a desk squeezed next to a wardrobe which could just about fit my underwear, and an armchair that belonged in a charity shop. At least there were two shelves for my books and stereo, a bedside table, and a lockable cupboard above the wardrobe, in which I placed my unpacked suitcase (with my valuables stored in the secret compartment I'd sewn into the lining), before heading out to meet the, hopefully hygienic, people with whom I'd be sharing toilets and shower rooms.

Pleasingly good music was blaring in the kitchen when I walked in, and I was cheered by the sight of ample cupboard space and multiple fridge-freezers. There were plenty of people occupying the kitchen already, a few of them huddled by the open window, smoking, and the rest scattered around the table, drinking beer and laughing.

I sat down next to a girl named Ruby who was desperately in need of a makeover, dressed in prehistoric Levi's and a shapeless, faded blue polo shirt, worn out trainers, and no makeup. She was, however, interesting, and seemed to have the potential to be useful to me during the course of the year, especially given the amount of attention she was receiving from Callum, easily the best looking boy in the room.

Conversation mainly consisted of small talk, but, at

length, it reached uncomfortably personal heights. It began, innocently enough, with discussions over home towns, and Juliette, the chain-smoking, faux-religious zealot of the group, asked me where I was from.

'Sevenoaks,' I replied, just as the news topic on the radio turned to the recent spate of robberies in Kent, all of which had started in Sevenoaks: the numerous break-ins at the homes of rich, prominent, and celebrity homes; the missing jewels and lack of clues; the incompetence of the police in hunting down the culprit(s); and the abrupt end to the string of thefts for no known reason a few weeks before.

'Sevenoaks? Been affected by the burglaries?' asked the probing Juliette, fidgeting with the cheap cross around her neck.

'Well, yes, our house ...' I had to admit it, though I felt my throat close up and my lungs collapse as I struggled to both catch my breath and change the subject; I successfully managed to turn the latter to travelling, a great topic for revealing people's background information.

It transpired that Callum was a seasoned globe-trotter, and my attraction to him grew throughout the afternoon as he revealed more of his hobbies, pursuits, and academic interests, all while effortlessly demonstrating his soft-spoken nature. He was a pleasure to spend time with then and throughout the evening that followed, something I hoped would become a habit for us both.

CALLUM

Sunday 01/10/2000 13:41
Subject: Uni

University. I'm finally here! Girls, alcohol and no-one who knows anything about me. Or you. Or the parents. I'm on my own. I can be me. Failures of the past be gone. Watch out people: Callum, social and academic god, here I come! (Yeah, you can stop laughing now.)

And the first day certainly wasn't a disappointment. Two guys – Matt and Paul – had arrived before me with a few crates of beer. Apparently their parents had supplied them – wish I'd thought of that. Even without the beer, they were good guys.

Then came Ruby. Ah, Ruby – the football-mad brunette – a Leeds fan from down South. A girl that knows when the next England game is, who manages Ipswich Town and that Leeds United are in the Champion's League. Which is about as much as I know about football – as you know – but I managed to blag it. And she's hot. My dream girl, actually. Shame I had to go ruin it all by making some joke. I don't even remember what I said. She clearly didn't take it well and then kept away from me the rest of the evening. Not cool.

There's Juliette – fit but very quirky and a smoker. She and our Spanish resident – Juan – hit it off, chain-smoking in the corner of the kitchen by the window, without asking if we minded. Quite disgusting really.

Then there's Yasmine – an eight or nine on the fitness

scale. And she wears very tight-fitting clothes, which is a bonus. She has the poshest accent I've ever heard – my mother would definitely approve of her.

There are a few other girls, but they're taken or not worth it. Although I could change my mind. Alcohol helps with that. A lot.

The boys are all great – we're already planning sporting and academic domination together and it's only been a day. And partying, socials and nights out of course. All integral parts of uni life. Wish you could've been here for it.

I just can't wait for term to start. Women and a first – it's going to happen. Come on!

Cal

JULIETTE

Well, firstly, thanks for this – although I know you've already judged me. But I had to come one last time. I feel it's my duty to tell my story. You may not want to hear it – I know you've already made up your mind. But I have to clear my name – or at least my conscience – and I want to explain why I'm leaving. I don't care if you don't want to hear it now – you promised to listen, and I'm telling you anyway.

It started that first day. Most of us moved in on the Saturday – the weekend before the first term of uni. I was excited, I have to admit. Life with Mummy had become more claustrophobic with every year – and that was before recent events – and I was looking forward to truly experiencing life and enjoying myself. I know you don't approve. I think it's funny how Jesus preached love and forgiveness even with his dying breath and yet that's the part most Christians conveniently ignore in their daily dealings …

Where was I? Oh yes, our corridor. I had a smoking room, which I'd asked for, of course. One of the few things Mummy and I share even today – smoking that is, not a room. But my room surprisingly smelt a lot better than the corridor, with its reek of cheap disinfectant, sweat, and God knows what else.

When I entered the kitchen, about half the people were already there. You'd approve of Matt and Paul – they were lovely and very generous, even if it was with their beer, and you probably wouldn't approve of that. Then there was Juan, the self-styled Latin lothario – he wasn't very good-looking – who was offering cheap Spanish cigarettes to those of us paying full UK duty. And of course Callum, your typical public schoolboy with average intelligence and above average looks. But no-one worth fainting over. Ha! I really do mean no-one.

There are two girls of interest to you from that lot. You haven't met her, but Ruby's your classic good girl – pretty, intelligent, low self-confidence – and a complete tomboy rolled into one. But she came across as sweet and interesting and I liked her right away. Yasmine on the other hand was – from the start – a pretentious, all-girls boarding school, overconfident, label fanatic. And yes, my view may be a little biased because of later events, but I didn't like her from the very beginning. I know forgiveness is sacrosanct in my religion – yes, even now – but, given what she did to me, it clashes with my nature.

Anyway. We did what your typical group of strangers would do – we talked and drank. And, amongst the chitchat, we managed to fit in current affairs, following on from the news on the radio. It transpired that Yasmine's home had been victim to the Kent Kleptomaniac. I pressed for details – knowing how much her type like to talk about themselves – but she smoothly changed the subject to travelling.

Most of us kept up, but poor Ruby was lost – she'd not left England for holidays since she was little. 'Before I can remember. Someday, maybe …' she'd said. That really struck me.

And so it went on. Snippets of information about who we were, where we were from, what we had done, and what we'd like to do. We were just a bunch of teenagers randomly thrown together and trying to fit in, each with our own agenda and ambitions.

Eventually, we all went down to the Union for the freshers' welcome night, which basically consisted of music, alcohol, and lots of terrible dancing. Probably the sort of night Mummy had in mind all those times she tried to convince me to go to the local poly and commute from home. Afraid of the debauchery. Ha!

Anyway, that night we all stuck together. We danced in a circle, and it became explicitly clear that Yasmine was after Callum. She kept moving over to dance next to him, almost pushing others out the way. She seriously thought he was as into her as she was into herself – vanity all the way with that one.

I should have seen it coming then.

Clubbing

YASMINE

On the Sunday 'morning' following the fabulous first evening of wine, dance, and flirtation with the increasingly handsome Callum, I walked into the communal kitchen to find it in a state that can best be termed 'shanty-town toilet style'. Besides the thick, stale odour permeating every corner, there were two bulging ashtrays on the kitchen table, a set of pungent empty kebab wrappers strewn on the floor, and a whole host of dirty plates, glasses, and pots and pans in the sink. I felt so nauseated, I couldn't face breakfast.

I was about to walk out when Juliette waltzed in, sat down at the table, and lit a cigarette.

'What are you doing?' I asked.

'Smoking?' She looked combatively at me.

'Some of us really don't appreciate eating in a smoky kitchen.'

'Oh, sorry,' she said, the sarcasm spitting poisonously from her reptilian mouth. She picked up an ashtray and moved over to the open window.

I tried to disengage, but couldn't stop myself from asking, 'Do you know anything about this mess?'

She looked around. 'What mess?'

I couldn't believe what I'd heard. 'The ashtrays, litter on the floor, and washing-up that needs to be done.'

'Ashtrays and washing-up are mine – I'll sort.' She continued to smoke her cigarette nonchalantly.

'When?' I asked, trying to contain my annoyance. 'You look like you've been up for hours.'

'I've been to church. I'm just having a cigarette and then I'll clean up. Relax.' She pretended to stare out of the window, a feat rendered impossible by the internal steam and external mud-spatter fogging the pane.

'Relax? All I want to do is eat my breakfast in clean surroundings.'

'I'm on it,' Juliette said, *still* sitting on the window ledge, smoking.

'You're so selfish,' I seethed, the hangover, nausea, and Juliette's rudeness finally getting the better of me.

'Not all of this mess is mine,' she said, exhaling dragon-like as she stood up and glared at me.

I stormed out, not waiting to see whether or not she actually cleared up the disgusting mess she had admitted to causing.

Luckily, the next time I entered the kitchen it was in pristine condition; unfortunately, it did not remain in this state indefinitely, and I found that I could walk into that same putrid scene on any given morning. The chain-smoker and I had a large number of arguments over it, and the hollow excuse of her being at church in the morning came up more than once as a reason for not clearing up the previous night's chaos, a clear case of hypocrisy and not loving thy neighbour in my view.

❯

The first few days following that initial encounter disappeared into an indulgent mist of booze, extensive partying, and detrimental hangovers. Term was suddenly upon us, bringing with it the much-anticipated freshers' fair and the unanticipated, dull, and dragging Chancellor's welcome to new students.

I found myself spending a lot of time with Ruby who, despite her cheap and non-chic dress sense, proved herself both interesting and useful company, especially when she seemed as desperate as I was to gain wilful employment to run alongside the academic schedule. We both registered with the temping agency on campus, applied for bar (and, in her case, waitressing) jobs at both the Union and university outlets, and scanned the student press for any other part-time job possibilities, applying for anything and everything that wasn't too demeaning.

Between short trips to numerous lecture theatres to endure a vast variety of equally dull and uninformative welcome speeches, I wandered around the stalls at the pretentiously named freshers' fair, each stacked with students seemingly keen to convert you to their cause, all the while hoping you'd just pay your enrolment fee and never turn up again. Hundreds of first-year undergraduates lapped it up, ignorant that any involvement in clubs, societies, and their related activities would be peripheral to academic and hall life.

Despite my misgivings, I did submit and join the jewellery-making society, as it offered a miscellany of courses, information, seminars, and come-and-play sessions. Unlike loutish sports clubs and naïve societies, they positively fuelled my artistic temperament, and I left their stall dreaming up art projects, some in combination with the fashion accessory designs I'd begun at home. I had always wanted to read an art subject at university, but realism had prevailed so that I had ended up reading business as a way to ensure the funds flowed post-graduation. I not-so-secretly hoped that taking classes of creative interest and dabbling in the arts in an extra-curricular manner would, in combination with my business degree, allow me to start my own company doing things I loved while simultaneously giving me the recognition I deserved.

The week came and went quickly, lubricated by generous alcohol consumption, but it was obvious that trouble was brewing where Juliette was concerned. It wasn't just the messy state of the kitchen or the way she pretended to be pious. It was something else, something I couldn't quite put my finger on. Something very wrong and very dangerous.

RUBY

My stomach was churning. Archers and lemonade followed by Juliette's Baileys was clearly a bad idea. *Head stop hurting, pleeeease!*

I stumbled into the kitchen. Juliette was there smoking. It reminded me that I'd smoked last night, which explained why my mouth felt furry. *Ugh!*

There was no music playing. *Good.*

I rested my head on the kitchen table. It was nice and cool and made my head feel better.

'Here,' said Juliette, passing me a glass of water.

Just the ticket. 'Cheers, mate,' I said, holding the glass to my temple without lifting my head. *Feels even better than the table.*

The door opened and in strode Callum. *Oh no. Nowhere to hide.*

'Can you please smoke by the window?' he asked Juliette.

Yes, that's it, speak to her. Don't look at me. Please.

'Of course. Sorry. How was your run?'

'It was great, thanks.' He turned to me. 'How's our Leeds fan feeling this morning?'

'Fabulous,' I said through the table.

He pulled out a chair and sat down next to me. 'You don't look it.'

Of course not. I look terrible. And smell terrible. And feel terrible. So please stop staring. If you are staring. Are you staring? Stop it, Ruby, mate. Why would he be staring?

'Always quick with the compliments, Callum,' said Juliette. 'Everyone looks amazing with a hangover and three hours' sleep.'

'I didn't mean it like that, actually! Are you OK?'

Great. Now I'm a victim that needs to be pitied.

'Fabulous.' *Just stop staring at me.*

'Right – off to bed for me,' Juliette said, walking out. 'And be nice.'

No, Callum, please don't. Just ignore me. It's for the best.

We sat there in awkward silence for a bit. Obviously, we had nothing to talk about. Even if we had, I didn't care at that moment. I just wanted the table to stop moving.

'Would you like some more water?'

'Mmm.' I couldn't really talk. I needed to gag.

Why now? I just stood up and ran out to the toilet. *Smooth, Ruby, mate. Very smooth.*

All I remember of Monday is that we drank. Lots. And the next day. And the one after that. Complete with stomping hangovers every morning. In fact, Britney Spears' *'Oops I Did It Again'* became the hall motto. Crap song, but rather apt.

Somehow I made it to Freshers' Fair that week, all on my own. *I know!* I started with the women's football stand, which was packed high with pint glasses. There were two girls sitting on the table, one with a cigarette in her hand and the other with a pint of snakebite. *Great advertising.* Well, I was sold, at any rate. Apparently, the club was mostly made up of beginners, which explained why the club photos were 25% football to 75% drinking and socials. *I can handle that.* Trials were at the end of the week. *Trials. I can do that, right? Right.*

Then back to halls. Matt was there with a beer. 'Hello. Been fairing it up, have you?'

'Yup.'

'You join football?' He slid a beer across the table to me.

'Yup.' I caught it and took a sip. *Warm but nice.*

'Any other word in your vocabulary?'

'Nope.'

We both laughed. *I'm being cheeky. Me! It feels great.*

'When are trials?'

Oh no, not trials again. Why is everyone pushing? I gulped down most of the beer. 'End of the week.'

'Don't look so scared. You'll be fine. The men's is on Friday evening too, so we can head over there together. If you like?'

I tried not to look so relieved. The idea of just showing up to trials was scary. Making it most of the way there with a friend or two wasn't.

So I made it. Both to trials and the first team. And then to the bar with my new sweaty friends for some mild drinking. Which turned into heavy drinking. Which turned into a night out. Which turned blank.

JULIETTE

I know you're going to disapprove, but – to tell you the truth – that first night didn't really end for some of us. After the Union event finished, we headed back to our corridor, some via the dirty campus kebab van that always seemed to appear when you needed it, like something out of *Harry Potter*. Maybe she'll include one in her next book – can't wait.

So … Ah, yes, I cooked a drunken fry-up and we sat up eating, smoking, and talking. It was refreshing to hear other people's views on life, the universe, etcetera. It got me thinking about my own beliefs. The ones I've held since I can remember. Well, since Daddy died and we started going to Church. They … well, other people's views were interesting. Maybe it was the alcohol, maybe it wasn't. But … well, my beliefs suddenly seemed a little archaic, I'm ashamed to say. Please don't look at me like that. You might prefer to call it traditional, but … I'm just going to go on with the story.

So, anyway, when the last of the stragglers went to bed, I refreshed myself and headed to Church. Apart from it being my duty, I hoped I'd find solace there. Guess that's why Mummy started going in the first place. I have to be honest with you – I didn't find answers. But I found peace. Until I got back to our corridor that is.

Yasmine was in the kitchen and ready for the kill. She – of course – had gone to bed on our return the night before, probably because Callum had. No late-night kebabs, drinking, or socialising with the neighbours for her.

I admit the kitchen was in a bit of a state that morning – the wind had blown the kebab wrappers from the overflowing bin to the floor and no-one had picked them up – and there was a lot of dirty washing in the sink. But it was student halls the morning after a huge night out. What did she expect? The maid to have cleaned it all up at six in the morning?

Apparently so.

She started yelling at me to clean it up. Me! The pretentious madam blamed me for the lot. I calmed my nerves with a cigarette. I even moved to the window when she complained about the smoke, even though we were in smoking halls. Well, that hardly helped. She screamed at me for finishing my cigarette before clearing up, tossed her hair in a threatening manner, and stomped out of the kitchen. She even tried to slam the door behind her which was hilarious 'cause it's fitted with one of those hydraulic door closers which just made the door creep shut. Ha!

Anyway, I cleared up everyone's mess and was just relaxing when Ruby walked in looking like death warmed up. She'd surprised me the night before by both staying up and opening up. Behind that unsure exterior was a very interesting, intelligent, and fun girl that had led a difficult life. You know I can relate to that.

That's when the boy-wonder, Callum, walked in and started teasing her. Admittedly, he was doing it in a flirty manner, but she wasn't taking it that way, so I needed to step in. I felt I had to. The first of many. Hmm.

Anyway, from that first Monday, life basically consisted of more communal drinking in the Union, more partying, and more drunken cooking and trying not to set the kitchen on fire at two in the morning, setting the theme for the rest of the week, month, year – and for more behaviour of which Mummy would disapprove.

Sorry, I'm off course again … I wanted to talk about freshers' fair, which was where I took those first steps that led me here. It was brilliant – rowdy, colourful, and full of fascinating characters. There were so many stands for clubs, societies, and the like, all touting their greatness and begging us to join them. I obviously joined the Christian Society, though I have to admit that it was more for Mummy's sake than mine. But Saturday night's conversations had inspired me and added to my desire to experience life. Throw off the claustrophobic existence. Forget the pious, boring boyfriends of yore. Stop regretting all the good times because they didn't fit into someone else's ideal. *Live* life. Like in Mummy's favourite Psalm – 118 – 'This is the day which the Lord hath made; we will rejoice and be glad in it.'

And I was rejoicing and being glad. So I took control and spent all my free time at the fair. Talking to people. Letting myself be persuaded to join clubs I'd never imagined I would. I even decided to join mixed hockey. Not that I've ever been any good at sport, but there was a gorgeous man holding the fort at the stand and all the hockey folk I spoke to didn't say a word about actually *playing*. It was all about the socialising, the parties, and the friends they'd made – perfect. And, to be fair, I've never been disappointed on any of those fronts.

I can go on for ages about all the clubs and societies that I joined or almost joined, but by far the most formative decision – in hindsight at least – was picking a sociable club and actually getting involved. Because that kind of wholehearted involvement – both mine and Ruby's – was at the root of the events that unfolded. And why I'm here.

Absconders

It all went from bad to worse, commencing with the mundane start to the academic year and followed swiftly by the unbelievable social events unfolding within the bastion of our residential halls.

Ruby and I had been getting along very well. I wouldn't have considered her a friend as yet, for I was far too wary of anyone I'd known such a short period of time, but I was definitely warming to her. She seemed to be fairly easily swayed into anything, given enough peer pressure and, as followers were always useful to have supporting you in life, I did my best to woo her over from the dark and dangerous path being paved by Juliette. I thought I had succeeded, too, as she escorted me on my grocery shops, shared work-related highs and woes with me, and confided in me in a way I didn't think she did with others. I confided in her too, at least with regards my feelings toward our gorgeous fellow resident, Callum.

It therefore came as a great surprise, and further reinforced my lifelong belief that you cannot trust anyone other than yourself, when a shamefaced Ruby slunk away for a run with him. They clearly had only one thing in mind, and it wasn't running pace. Callum had suggested joining her, with a keenness that resembled a bumbling schoolboy, and had made it evident from his blushing cheeks and shifty gaze that he would not welcome any others on this particular expedition. Unfortunately, I had no excuse to join them, what with having trumpeted my dislike of any form of exercise other than yoga and Pilates to all my fellow hall residents over the course of the previous week. Besides, I would have been outrun within the first minute and left panting ungracefully like a Labrador if the speed with which the two of them raced up the hill and out of sight was anything to go by.

I waited in the kitchen for them to return, but to no avail. I didn't see them through the window, unsurprising though that was given darkness had fallen, and I didn't hear them return, assuming that they did so. After over an hour, I gave up my fruitless and increasingly pointless wait and headed to my room to re-read the final chapter of my favourite book, Raffles, which always cheers me up. The good, clean, and moral don't always win.

RUBY

I had no idea where I was. My arms felt heavy, my pillow hard. My bed stank and there was a wild animal roaring in the room.

I opened my eyes. I was on a carpeted floor. Someone

– something? – was snoring on the bed. *This isn't my room. What on earth?*

The bedcovers stirred. A head with impressive bed-hair popped out through the covers. 'Morning,' it groaned.

My brain wasn't working. 'Morning.' *Where am I? And who are you?*

'Smithy.' She giggled, holding out a hand attached to a wrist tattoo.

Am I thinking out loud?

'Ruby, obviously.' I shook it. 'Where am I?'

'My room. You were slurring last night and had no idea where you lived, so I offered my bed but you passed out on the floor. Better for me!'

Makes sense. 'Sorry. And thanks, mate. Better be going,' I mumbled and staggered out of her room. Quickly.

On the way back to mine, the blurred memories resurfaced. Smithy was also a fresher. She'd been good at the football try-outs and up to all sorts of hilarity at the Union social afterwards. She'd kept up an impressive drinking speed. She'd dived behind the bar and poured herself a pint. She'd stolen some bloke's team tie. She'd danced what she'd said was her goal-scoring routine on a table. She'd flirted with one of the women's football committee. And then we'd carried each other back to her halls, conveniently right next to the Union. *Great night.*

Back at our halls, the boys were all in the kitchen. As was Yasmine, sitting next to Callum. *Of course.*

He turned to look at me disapprovingly. 'Walk of shame?'

Making fun of me again? Not really in the mood for that.

'I slept on some footie girl's smelly floor.' *Go on, laugh at me.*

'Niiiice.'

Oh, sarcasm. Even better. I got some water and sat by the window.

Juliette came in. She lit a cigarette. 'Do you want one?'

Not sober I don't. I shook my head. *Bad idea.* I started to say something.

'She doesn't smoke,' Callum interrupted.

Juliette just smiled. I was glad. I wasn't in the mood for this conversation. Or any conversation for that matter. I excused myself and went to my room to study before heading out to work. I even missed the England game – the last one at Wembley. Hardly a crazy Saturday night.

○

We'd had a huge communal Sunday Roast, and dinner was out of the question, so we spent the afternoon and evening sat in the kitchen, chatting. Most of us were drinking water. We'd officially gotten freshers' week out of our system.

But some things hadn't changed from day one. Juliette and Juan smoking. Matt and Paul being indivisible, sipping their beers. Me sitting quietly in the corner. And, of course, Yasmine and Callum flirting. *Enough already!* I got up.

'Going somewhere?' asked Callum.

'For a run.' *Feel the fresh air. Sweat out the week's alcohol. Get away from everyone for a bit.*

'Good idea. Mind if I join you?'

What? Why? So you can see me sweaty and horrible? And mess up my pace? 'Sure, mate. Anyone else?'

No more takers. *Good and bad, I guess.*

'Lap of campus OK with you?' asked Callum.

Why not break a proper sweat? At least he looks great after exercise: the upside. Let's not think about the downside: how I'll look.

Off we ran. Our pacing was very similar, which was surprising but felt good.

At the top of the hill, Callum slowed to walking pace. 'Stitch?' I teased.

'No, but look at the view.'

The view?

But he was right. Darkness had fallen and the lights from campus below looked wonderful. It felt like we were in a park looking down on a sleepy, Disney-lit city below. The Union and halls were all lit up, as were the main roads and the canal. And in between were patches of black with the occasional glitter – the fields and lake. All adding to the beauty.

Callum sat on a bench and patted the wood next to him. 'Two minutes to take this in?'

Next to you? Anytime.

We sat. For more than two minutes. And talked. About life back home, school days, and everything else. The only minor blip was when he became quite cagey about his background.

'My parents enjoy their privacy.'

Don't we all? Just don't want to share? Please share.

'But not with you. Right?'

Callum turned and looked at me strangely. 'No, not with me. Despite their jet-setting lifestyle, they wouldn't even send me to board.'

Never thought that the two could be connected. What different worlds we come from! 'That a good or bad thing?' I asked, intrigued.

'Good. But sometimes I wonder if school life could have been different, you know?'

'Yeah, I know what you mean, mate.' *People remembering I'm female, maybe?* 'I got bullied by girls at school.' *Oh my god! Why did I just say that?*

'So did I.'

Well, that was unexpected.

He put his arm on the top of the bench. I felt the warmth of it on my back. Saw sweat, like grass-stains, running down his face. And wanted to reach out and wipe them away. I couldn't breathe. I had to say something or he might notice.

'By girls?' I asked quickly. *Oh Ruby, mate, is that the best you can do?*

'No. All-boys school.' He smiled at me. 'But people used to tease me about my parents' erm situation.'

A droplet of sweat slid down the back of my neck.

I shivered. *Not now.* This was actually interesting, a side to the confident and gorgeous Callum I never thought existed. Plus, his arm had dropped to my shoulder. *Stop beating so damn loudly, heart, mate, he'll hear you.*

The cold metal of his watch touched my neck, but I didn't want this moment to end. My body didn't care what I wanted. I shivered again.

'You're cold. Shall we get on with our run?'

No.

But I got up. We ran down the hill. Round various halls of residence. By the lake. Round department buildings. Along the canal. And, eventually, we were on our way back across the waterlogged fields to our halls.

That's when Callum slipped and fell head first into the mud.

'You OK, mate?' *Turned an ankle?*

'Fine.' He snorted, amused.

How does he manage to look gorgeous even with a faceful of mud? It's completely unfair.

I laughed and held my hand out to help him up. He pulled a little too hard and I landed on top of him. He started laughing harder. I wasn't sure what to do. He rolled over me, pushing my back, hair, and side of my face into the mud. It was wet, cold, and slimy. *Ugh. Good thing mud doesn't feel like this when I'm on the pitch.*

'Thanks,' I said, spitting out brown particles in the direction of his face and pushing him off me. *He thinks I'm one of the lads. Typical.*

He got up and pulled me up. 'Good face mask! No need to stop half-way on my account.' His piss-take grin filled his face.

I slapped his head playfully. 'Don't be rude.'

'Sorry.' He put his arm around me and started to walk me back to halls.

More piss-take. I shrugged it off.

When we got to the front door, we took our shoes off and crept up the stairs. Then into the bathroom to wash the mud off our trainers, which were dripping by the time we were done. As my room was closer, I offered to take his shoes there to dry. He agreed, then followed me in.

'Nice room.'

'It's the same as yours.' *Crap. Apart from the underwear I threw in the corner when I changed. Definitely not my best bra. But better than the one I'm wearing now.*

'How do you know?'

Huh? Know what? Oh, room. Yeah, good question. 'I don't. But I need to go get this mud off me. Ugh.' It had started to cake on my arms, hair, and face, and was still squidgy on my back. *The post-match feeling. Yuck.*

'I can help.'

What? Are you joking?

He smiled and reached out to touch my hair. I held my breath. *Stop beating so damn loudly. Stop now.*

I looked at him and smiled back. His hand gently traced a line of mud down my face. *What's going on? What's happening?*

He brushed his thumb across my lips. I felt earthquakes throughout. His hands moved to the side of my face, pulled me roughly towards him, and kissed me. Me! *But surely he likes Yasmine? Is this a joke? Or is he serious?* He continued to kiss me. *Maybe he's serious.*

At any rate, he helped me out of my clothes and into the shower. And then into my bed.

I'm still confused. Did that really happen? And, since I'm pretty sure it did, how the hell do I face him again?

CALLUM

Sunday 07/10/2000 16:27
Subject: Re: RE: Uni

Hello! Glad to hear you're having a great time out there.

I am too. Term is going absolutely to plan. Academically, socially, personally.

The nights out have been great: We've drunk, we've flirted, we've danced. It's freshers' week after all. That's what the start of uni's all about, right?

The welcome lectures have been good for meeting people, too. Subsequent lectures have been interesting, although most won't start properly till the second week of term. Some of the subjects are clearly more challenging than others. But the course as a whole – based on the summaries and reading lists – exceeds my expectations.

Life in halls is great too. The boys and I have hit it off: we've hung out in the Union, played pool, had a few kick-abouts. And then we've bought crate after crate of beer and drunk them dry.

And of course there are the girls, adding to the party atmosphere. Especially Juliette, who can always be counted on to get the party going – though she continues to smoke out the kitchen and make the air odiously unbreathable.

Yas is a calming influence on all the drinking. Every evening she slowly sips her glass of wine – sometimes two – and then just sits there talking. No chucking trips to the bathroom, no slurring, no passing out in the corner and drooling on her arms – refreshing really. Added to the fact that she sits next to or opposite me every night in her nice tight tops and dresses – no complaints there!

But Ruby – still my number one – Ruby remains distant. OK, so telling her she looked terrible with a hangover the other day has clearly not helped. But even that doesn't explain why she ran out of the kitchen last time we were alone there and never came back. (Stop laughing.) Or why she's never around. Maybe I'm being paranoid – maybe it's because she's balancing a job, football and academia. Hardcore and so cool. At least she's around most evenings for drinking in the kitchen or nights out in the Union. Oh yes – she's definitely around for most of those.

But things aren't always happy and tranquil – the first feud of term came to a head yesterday morning. Ruby had turned up at eleven in the morning in the previous night's clothes – man that hurt. Although apparently she'd been sleeping with a girl – forgiven! And then

Juliette walked in and offered her a cigarette. The cheek! As if a footballer would engage in that kind of filthy behaviour! Ruby declined and then not-so-subtly left the kitchen, feeling deeply insulted.

Juliette sat down on the window ledge and started smoking.

Yas asked her not to. Then Juliette snapped at her with something like 'What? Smoke in smoking halls? I'm by the window' and Yas replied appropriately.

Juliette just rolled her eyes and kept smoking. She asked around to see if anyone else was bothered by her behaviour. I said something, obviously, and she looked over at me and said 'Anyone other than Yasmine and Callum?' Yes, she said that, actually!

That was followed by silence, obviously – the others didn't want to upset anyone. Juliette smiled at Yas and kept smoking.

That was the moment that Juan chose to walk in. He smiled at everyone and sat down next to Juliette. Then he lit up.

Yas lost it – understandably. She started yelling at Juliette, calling her pretentious and selfish and all sorts of nasty names. And Juliette responded with sneers and cutting remarks – it was ugly. And this time I – along with everyone else – decided to stay out of it. Eventually Yas stormed out and Juliette followed, although she did mumble a 'sorry' in the general direction of the table as she left. Juan just sat there with his mouth wide open and his unsmoked cigarette between his fingers. It was awkward.

Later, when it was just Matt, Paul and me left, Matt asked me if anything was going on between me and Yas. I was genuinely surprised – I didn't realise there was something happening. Is there? We've flirted a bit, but there's nothing more there. Paul called me dense and Matt teased me and I had to concede that she's hot – which she is. According to Matt, she's been pawing at me since we first got here. Who knew?

But the general consensus was that although Yas is definitely hot – she is – it's Ruby that we all seem to be after. Yes, that's right – I'm not the only one. I'm not the biggest fan of competition, as you know, but it is what it is.

Let me know how you're getting on on the woman front – I know you'd have made a move by now if the roles were reversed. Maybe I should take a leaf out of your book …

Cal

Monday 09/10/2000 11:53
Subject: Scored

Hello. You haven't replied or called. I've been trying to get hold of you, actually. Something's happened – I pulled Ruby! Yes, that's right – shag and all. Get in! (No pun intended, though it is funny in that context, don't you think?) And since you're not answering your phone and I have time on my hands, I'm going to tell you all about it.

I'd been in the kitchen with everyone, thinking about that conversation with the boys – the one about how we all put Ruby top of our list of girls in halls – when Ruby stood up to leave. So I pounced – I asked to join her. She looked like I'd just spoiled her party, but I'd already stood up and was making for the door. She was cornered, but too polite to refuse – I had counted on that. (See? I can be sneaky too – maybe it's in the genes.)

She made quite a show of asking everyone else – she smiled invitingly and everything. I held my breath to the point of suffocation while looking round the group of potential takers. Luckily, everyone else was quite protective of their Sunday evening rest and didn't even look like they were considering the offer – they all kept their heads down.

Ruby went off to change and I followed, but not before I caught Paul smirking through his beer bottle and Matt winking at me. The pressure was on.

We decided on a lap round campus, which took us up the hill overlooking the main grounds. Ruby was powering on ahead and I didn't want her to notice that I was struggling – courtesy of the shaken roast and beers that were suddenly weighing down my stomach – so I eased up at the top.

'Stitch?' she joked.

I used your 'just taking in the view' line. I stopped and spread out my hands to envelop the lights and water below. Not quite as well as you do it, but she bought it, actually. She sat next to me at the smallest of prompts. You'd be proud of me – I was on fire!

And so we started talking. It's been a while since I talked like that with anyone, actually. To my horror – for lack of a better word – I found myself opening up completely to a girl I've known for just over a week. About important things – school and holidays in every nook and cranny of the world. But not you. Not yet.

She – in turn – told me things I suspect she hadn't shared in a while. About her family – she 'doesn't' have a mother (no further information was forthcoming) – and she'd been bullied at school, which I could – of course – relate to in some way. But at least you were there.

When she started shivering, I knew that it was – unfortunately – time to move on. Even though her shoulders felt comfortable and snug under my arm. Yes, I'd used the old 'stretch and casually drop' move on her – she hadn't even noticed.

And off we went, this time downhill and on the flat. It was liberating running with someone like her – we kept apace. And the pain in my stomach had now gone. It was great. Until we got to the field near our halls, where I tripped not-so-gracefully in the boggy ground and landed flatly and face first in a pile of mud.

She peered down at me, looking concerned. But when she saw I was OK, she started laughing uncontrollably and held out her hand to help me up. I pulled her hard, deftly landing her on top of me. Perfection – you'd have been proud. I then couldn't help myself and rolled over her lovely body. Her breath was warm on my face, the cut grass and sweat smelt surprisingly sweet, and her tits looked great from that angle – well they look great from every angle, actually. She laughed again but then pushed me off hard. I have to tell you, I felt defeated, so I relented and helped her up. Failure, I thought.

We walked slowly back. You should have seen how well she pulled off the crusty muddy hair – it was unbelievable. Her boobs were staring hard at me through her soaked England shirt. And that ass ... I tried my luck again thinking maybe I'd misread her actions – maybe she was just uncomfortable in the mud? I put my arm round her, but she shrugged it off. Epic failure, I thought.

But when we got back to halls, I don't know what came over me. Well I do, actually – I couldn't stand it anymore. I went for broke and made an excuse to keep the conversation going so she couldn't leave. This time she didn't blow me off. Or resist my following her to her room, the showers and her bed. And so the night ended in success after all.

Which brings up the inevitable post-shag questions. Now what? And who to tell other than you, if anyone?

I need advice. Help me!

Thanks,

Cal

Smoke

YASMINE

The night before's sweat had been showered away, but I could still feel it burning cigarette holes in my skin. True to the Victorian plot my life had become, I almost collided with a sleep-walking Juliette on my way out to an early class.

'Morning.' She smiled a sickly sweet, hypocritical smirk.

'Good morning,' I said, matching her tone and, I prayed, her expression.

'Seen Callum this morning?' The smirk stretched into a full-blown sneer.

'No.' I smiled through the naked scenarios my imagination was modelling, and made my way to a lecture I was destined not to focus at.

I had no idea what it was that had turned Juliette against me in the first place, but it was becoming increasingly clear that she was not planning to engage in civilities on any level. What had started as a difference of opinion had turned dramatically into a permanent state of outward hostility. As such, it was with trepidation that I returned to halls after my afternoon stint in the bookshop and walked into the kitchen.

My nemesis was nowhere to be seen, and, instead, I walked in on a few of the boys, including the luscious Callum, sitting in the kitchen sipping beers and discussing academics while the radio howled.

'Hello, boys.' I smiled my widest and, I hoped, most inviting smile.

'Hi.' Callum's face was unreadable, his usual cheeky smile remarkably absent.

'Everything alright?' I asked.

'Absolutely. Why wouldn't it be?' his reply came, a little too fast.

The radio hissed static at us, so I turned it off. I poured myself some cereal and sat down to eat, just as Ruby walked in wearing a very bland waitressing uniform of black trousers complete with an unnecessarily tight and somewhat transparent white shirt.

'Looking good,' said Matt, raising a suggestive eyebrow.

Ruby blushed, smiled awkwardly at him, turned and opened the far left cupboard by the sink, pulled out a chocolate bar, nodded at me, and left the kitchen, managing to complete all the aforementioned tasks without once speaking to or, more tellingly, looking at Callum.

'What's going on with Ruby?' I asked.

'What's going on with her?' Callum echoed softly in an unconvincingly innocent manner.

'Anybody else notice she didn't look at Callum?'

Paul chuckled. 'Callum? I thought she was ignoring

me, following that silly incident this morning.'

'What silly incident?' I was unamused at how quickly and successfully Callum had managed to avoid the subject.

'Oh, she was taking your shoes out of her room this morning and I cracked an unwelcome joke about you two. Almost made her cry.'

'Callum's shoes?' I asked, my desperation for full details of the seemingly not-so-innocent relationship coming across more evidently than I'd hoped.

'Yeah, she took them into her room last night to stop them dripping mud all the way down the corridor,' said Callum. 'The hall tutor doesn't seem a particularly compassionate chap. He'd probably have charged me for carpet-cleaning.'

'He's not really the understanding type, is he?' Matt said sombrely. 'Charged Mike twenty quid for setting off the fire alarm the other day.'

The conversation turned to Mike's raucous and constantly immature behaviour, especially after a few drinks and at ungraciously insensitive hours of the night. It was frustrating not knowing what was going on between Callum and Ruby, but I'd run out of excuses to probe without looking desperate, so I sat with the boys and hoped the conversation would eventually turn to juicier subjects, which, inevitably, it did not. Bored, I retired to practice the Primary Series before going to bed, only to be woken by the fire alarm.

'Mike!' I thought, throwing on a jumper and running out of the door.

We all gathered in the grassy courtyard and shivered, despite being huddled together in the cold dark, and watched the hall tutor admonish a man that clearly was neither Mike nor one of our hall residents while Juliette stood by them, attempting to skulk. They had, in all probability, returned drunk from the Union and decided 'smiley potato faces were the way forward' or something to that effect and had, instead, been left with burnt crisps and a grill on fire. Bringing a random individual back to your residence with you is one thing, allowing him to set off the fire alarm is quite another. None of us were particularly amused when we were finally allowed to return to our beds or, in our 'arsonist's' case, Juliette's.

The next morning, Ruby and I sat alone, tired, and silent in the kitchen, breakfasting before our nine o'clock lectures.

'Were you also woken by the fire alarm?' I asked.

She blushed and stared silently at the table, unconsciously playing with her keys in a noisy and irritating manner.

'Everything OK?' I probed, dreading a detailed answer.

'Oh yes, just tired,' she replied quickly, flashing me a sheepish grin and rising to wash up her bowl and spoon as she diligently did after every meal.

'Something going on with you and Callum?' I asked with a bluntness that surprised even me.

Ruby looked positively frightened by that, dropping her bowl into the sink then jumping as the door opened and Juliette sauntered in, and, seeing her opportunity, making a run for it. Juliette took one look at me and sauntered back out and, thankfully, I didn't see her again for the rest of the day. Unfortunately, though, I did hear her and a couple of boys singing at the top of their lungs at midnight. Sticking my head out into the corridor, I hurled abuse at them. A very good-looking individual smiled his apologies and proceeded to futilely attempt to quiet the rest.

The week continued in the same vein, with Ruby and Callum avoiding my questions, and Juliette bringing raucous, immature, inebriated, and thoroughly random, unkempt men into our halls. At first I felt it wasn't my place to raise the latter issue, given our constant and very public battles, but eventually I had to share my concerns with my fellow residents.

The next time we all found ourselves assembled in the kitchen, I cleared my throat and jumped in at the deep end. 'Anybody else finding Juliette's parties a little extreme?'

'You do seem to have a constant stream of male guests, don't you?' Matt looked at Juliette with a thoughtful and, I thought, somewhat bitter expression.

'What,' asked Juan, predictably taking her side, 'does it matter?'

'Other than the fire alarm incident, what have they done to bother you?' Juliette looked combatively down the length of her nose at me.

'They do make a lot of noise,' said Mike, looking first at me then into Juliette's cold eyes, 'but then who am I to talk?'

'We're just having a good time.'

'At other people's expense,' I said, not quite believing the lack of verbal support I was getting on this issue, particularly given the tired and angry faces I had seen at the fire safety point a few nights earlier. 'Loud parties in the middle of the night and setting off the bleeding alarm …'

'I can't be held responsible for other people's actions!' she snapped.

'Of course you can! People don't let themselves in and party in other people's corridors at four in the morning of their own accord!' I could hear my own volume rising but was unable to control it, despite my stuttered attempts at lateral thoracic breathing, Pilates-style.

'Well, maybe, if you try to keep your boys in your room and away from the fire alarms, then it would be less disruptive,' said Paul.

'I will.' Juliette smiled at him and took out a cigarette and then said, unconvincingly, 'Sorry.'

'And while we're on the subject, can you not smoke in here?' Perhaps this was not the ideal moment to head down this much-trodden path, but my tiredness and frustration had gotten the better of me.

She sighed loudly. 'I'm not going to smoke outside and, if that bothers you so much, may I suggest you put in for a transfer to a non-smoking hall and leave us all be.'

The room was silent. Most were staring, shocked, at Juliette.

I stood up abruptly and left before I said something I'd really regret. Her malice was acutely painful and I so badly wanted her to feel the same that, at that moment, I decided to do something very stupid indeed.

JULIETTE

And this is the part of the story that you'll definitely disapprove of. But please, please hear me out. It's important. And it all revolves around Yasmine – the personification of sin.

But I'm getting ahead of myself. The second week of term involved getting to know my hockey teammates better. It started in training, where the club president gave a little speech and basically told us freshers that the hockey team had one rule – that every member of the team had to know every other member properly. And so we were given 'homework' – spending the next week with a number of different groups within the team. So the first two days I spent with some second years from the first team, the next two with some third years from the seconds and so on. It was effectively a week-long social to get to know everyone in small chunks. And it worked a treat, if not for reading.

Of course, it did mean that I had to have a number of mainly off-campus residents squatting in our corridor on a semi-regular basis. But as it was only for a few days at a time and we were due to go out clubbing every night – and therefore wouldn't be hanging around much – I didn't think it would be an issue.

I hadn't thought that things would get *so* out of hand. And – to be honest – I got lost in the fun. I wish I could say that it wasn't brilliant, that I repent. But I don't. It was worth it – worth the fights, worth the guilt, worth the consequences. All of it.

And yes, I did do things that Mummy would disapprove of. Which – of course – means that you'd disapprove too. I did drink too much. I did kiss boys. Not all of them that week, of course, but there were some that term. Which is funny, given the reason I'm here and you and Mummy have turned your backs on me. No, don't protest. I turned my back on you too – the chicken or the egg, same end result.

Anyway, where was I? Ah yes, Yasmine. Now, people have tried to excuse her actions – well, her actions that term at any rate – and, in all fairness, there were a few things going on. Maybe I was just the straw that broke the camel's back? Who knows? But she was definitely unhappy about the Callum situation. And I certainly did the un-Christian thing of rubbing salt in the wound.

Sorry, have I lost you? Basically, Callum fancied Ruby. And off they went for a run that poor Yasmine was none too pleased about. Even less pleased when it transpired that something had happened and nobody was sharing. To be fair, Ruby and Callum didn't share what had gone on with anybody, not until a few weeks later. But it was clear that something *had* gone on, you know? And it was clearly eating Yasmine up. So she kept indiscreetly probing and kept being batted off. Ha! Must have been frustrating for her. Sorry – am I enjoying this part of the story too much? Well then, let me get back to the less amusing bits.

We're back with the hockey boys and girls partying in our corridor, OK? Still with me? Good. So, every afternoon, we went out to the Union for a meet-and-greet session, had some beers and spirits, went out clubbing, and then came back to mine to eat hangover-prevention grub and theoretically get some sleep. Only – inevitable really – we continued to party.

And that did have some unwarranted side-effects. Like this boy, Liam, setting off the fire alarm – he was doing an impersonation of his namesake, Liam Gallagher, singing '*Wonderwall*' at the top of his lungs with a cigarette between his lips in the non-smoking section of the corridor under the fire alarm. Very funny, but maybe not ideal in the cold light of day.

And then there was the Wednesday evening where we had initiations and all non-campus players were distributed between the on-campus hockey team. So I had six bodies to pack into my little cell block. Instead of sleeping, we decided to have a rave in my room, which spilled out into the corridor and may have woken up a person or three. Again, not ideal in the cold light of day. But an inevitable consequence of the mix of teammates, alcohol, and not enough space. And – like I said – I was swept up in the general chaos.

I'd never been so free to do whatever I wanted without the need to answer to somebody other than Him. And I have to admit that, for a while there, I even forgot He existed. Don't look at me like that, please. The truth is I took full advantage and partied like I should have done for years leading up to uni, instead of knitting sweaters for the local charity shop and praying between ciggie breaks with Mummy.

Sorry, that was harsh, though – unfortunately – true.

So, anyway, back to Yasmine. At the end of the week we were all chilling in the kitchen – most of us nursing hangovers and dealing with personal mini-dramas – when I suddenly got verbally whipped by her for Liam's actions.

I snapped and told her I couldn't control people setting off the fire alarm.

If it had been a cartoon strip, you would have seen her steaming at the ears. She shouted something along the lines of 'But you *can* control bringing them here and setting them loose in the corridor at four in the morning.'

Paul tried to mediate and suggested I keep – or at least try to keep – my team in my room and away from kitchen ovens and fire alarms, which – of course – would be less disruptive. I could see that I had affected more than just Yasmine and truly meant my apology.

Then Yasmine blasphemed. Apologies for repeating it here, but I have to get you to understand what an evil person she is. She spat, 'And for God's sake, can you not smoke in here?' at me.

I looked up from the empty cigarette packet I had been playing with. I should have ignored the comment or pointed out that I wasn't actually smoking just then. But I'd had enough of her cursing. I told her we smoked in the corner of the kitchen – leaning out of the window – and not when others were eating, and how it was unfair of us to be going to smoke outside in this freezing cold when we were living in smoking halls. Then I may have overstepped the line and suggested she put in for a transfer to a non-smoking corridor and leave us all be.

The room fell silent as Yasmine stood up, scraping her chair on the floor so loudly I thought she was taking a run-up to come punch me.

Instead, she stomped out and we all breathed a sigh of relief. It had been a scary confrontation and – in retrospect – the signs of madness were there and building. But – despite the obvious seething anger – I never anticipated her next move. Or how much it would cost me.

Drowning

RUBY

I was having a bad game. This sort of thing had never happened to me before. *I'm living with him! And I have to see him every day. Or avoid him every day more like. Plus, there will be gossip. Inevitable, really. Sexiest man in halls pulls resident tomboy for laughs. Maybe I should avoid everyone, just in case.*

But that's clearly impossible. I'll just have to put up with it. The whispers. The jokes. Like school all over again. Nothing really changes.

Yasmine was the first to pounce. Then Paul. Then Hannah. Then Matt. I pretended not to know what they were on about. I ignored the snide references. I knew how to handle this: water off a duck's back and all that.

I did increase my shifts at work though, which kept me out of halls and away from the rumour mill. Refreshing. For a whole three and a bit days at any rate.

Then, on Thursday night, none other than Juliette walked in with a bunch of her hockey team. *Successful avoidance: Game Over.*

'Hey, Ruby. How're things?'

I like her. No probing. No insinuations. Just friendliness and fun.

'Good, thanks. What are you having?'

'You on the menu?' asked one of the blokes.

Great. More jokes at my expense.

Juliette slapped him hard on the head, and I liked her even more.

'We'll have ten pints of lager – what do you have on tap?'

They were the last to leave. Three courses. Countless pints of Stella. Constant booming hilarity worthy of a radio laughter cue button.

I wasn't on clean-up duty that evening, so I caught them at the door. Or they caught me. Same difference.

'Where're you going?' asked the bloke from earlier. He held his elbow out for me to take.

More jokes at my expense. Keep them coming.

'Home,' I told him.

'Booooring. We're headed to the pond for a smoke. Come along.' He held his arm out again.

Give the poor bloke a break, Ruby, mate. He's just drunk.

'He means the lake. And do come.' Juliette clapped her hands and danced around me like a loon.

'It's not big enough to be a lake.' He held out his arm a third time.

Maybe it's well meant after all?

'Twinkle's from the lake district.'

I didn't ask about the nickname. I just grinned and took his arm. 'OK.' *Why not?*

And so we sat and smoked and talked. And swigged vodka out the bottle. We even lay back and stared at the stars. *Stars put everything into perspective, don't they?*

But the next day was dire. I missed my morning lecture. I struggled to get out of bed. I had to drag myself to work where I hoped not to throw up. A hope which lasted less than an hour. *Not the best of shifts.*

At least there was a big event on at the Union that night, so halls were quiet. I walked into the kitchen expecting it to be empty. I'd already sat when I saw Callum. He didn't look happy, but he did look gorgeous as usual.

Those deep green eyes. Stop it, Ruby, mate. Don't think about it.

'Hi. How was your shift?'

No need to be polite on my account.

He slid his beer bottle across the table at me. I was too exhausted not to accept. I felt the blood surge in my fingers as his brushed mine.

Stop blushing, Ruby, mate. Stop it now.

I noticed the books. 'Studying?' *Top notch on the observation front, genius.*

'Yeah, I'm having issues with my course. Bloody hard. Need to brush up on my basics.'

He looks very down. And sexy. Very sexy.

'If you need any help from me ...' *Why say that? Now he thinks you want an excuse to spend time with him. Don't act like you're so desperate. And the best way to do that is to stop thinking about his abs. You're never going to see them again, mate.*

'Don't make promises you can't keep.' It was a flat statement. No sexual innuendo. No flirtation. He was genuinely pained.

'I mean it.' *Careful. Just because he's unhappy doesn't mean he won't take it the wrong way. But then maybe I can be of help, even though it's complicated. I don't want him thinking I have ulterior motives. Although I obviously do have ulterior motives. I want to run my fingers through his beautiful Eighties' curls again. Run my hands down those stone-hard abs once more. Oh, plenty of ulterior motives. I just don't want him thinking that I have any.*

'Hmmm?' He'd said something I'd totally missed.

'Do you want to talk about what happened?'

What? No, I don't. I'm trying very hard to forget your abs. And upper arms. And whole body generally. Stop blushing, Ruby, mate. Breathe. Control yourself. Remember you don't appreciate being gossiped about. That's better. Steady voice now.

'I haven't said anything. Yas has been after details. She's got them from the boys, I guess.'

'From the boys?'

Yes, you know, your friends that you've been blabbing to. Oh, and don't crack your knuckles, Callum. It's a horrible habit, mate.

'I haven't said anything. Figured we had to work out what was going on first,' he said, eyes shining.

That got me. *He hasn't said anything? Was the sex that bad?*

'Really?' I paused, inhaled deeply. *OK, I'll bite.* 'OK.

What is going on?'

He smiled at me and held out his hands. 'I don't know. Maybe we can work it out over a video? My room?'

Lust does strange things to people. I took his hands. 'Why not?'

It was a good night, despite the lack of sleep. As was Saturday night after the Union. And Sunday in the showers. And Monday both before and after the four Star Wars films' video marathon. Running my hands down those abs was becoming a habit. Not that I was complaining.

But, on Tuesday, he disappeared. Matt and Paul asked after him. I don't know why they were asking me. *Maybe he's told them after all? Or did someone see us?* I just shrugged in reply.

But when he still had not shown his face by Wednesday afternoon after football, I braved it. I walked up to his door in broad daylight and pushed it open.

He was slumped at his desk. Head in his hands. Papers everywhere. He looked awful.

'You OK?'

'Yeah, why?'

Did he just growl at me? I knew I shouldn't have come. He hates me now. I turned to leave.

'No, wait! Sorry. Just having course issues. It's a mess.'

Poor you.

'Need help?' I glanced at the assignment on his desk. *It's so simple.*

'Please.'

Are you that dim? But OK – more time with you. Hopefully between the sheets. Twist my arm.

It was actually hard going. He really was struggling. I had to be careful not to tease him, as I wasn't really used to teaching.

But at least I had the excuse of my football social. I wasn't even going to go. It was initiations and I had to dress up as a baby. I really, really hated dressing up. It was so embarrassing. Even worse, there would be other teams circling too.

But it was better than spending the night teaching primary school. I even gave myself half an hour to get ready when I really only needed ten minutes. I'd well and truly run out of patience.

I put on a pair of old pyjamas. Strung a dummy round my neck. Put my hair in pig-tails. And covered myself up in my coat. *If I'm the only one dressed up there, I just won't take my coat off. The pyjama bottoms can easily pass for silly trousers.*

But when I got there, I was clearly under-dressed. *Everyone* had made an effort. Smithy, especially, lived up to the occasion. She was wearing a nappy. An actual nappy. And a long bib. And that was it, excluding the trainers. A gust of wind and she'd be exposed. *The girl has guts.*

We drank to kill the inhibitions. By the time other people started filling up the Union, we were happily drunk. Hammered enough to be dancing on tables. Even me! It was great.

I bumped into Juliette in the toilets and dragged her to our circle.

'No speaking to people outside the circle!' yelled my captain. 'Two fingers.'

'No, you have to meet Juliette. She's awesome.' *Am I slurring? Yup, definitely slurring, Ruby, mate. Ah well.*

'What's so awesome about you, Juliette?'

My captain's intrigued. Brilliant. This means I can forgo the drinking penalty. Right?

'She's a social animal,' I said.

'Are you?' Smithy asked. 'So am I. Do you want to see my tits?' And she lifted her bib.

Another tattoo.

We all laughed as Juliette's jaw dropped and she turned end-of-game red. She turned away.

Then I remembered. 'She's also a little wee bit religious.'

'Oh, that's a relief.' Smithy looked down and groped herself. 'I thought there was something wrong with my tits.'

We roared. Juliette seemed to recover. 'I've never had a girl flash me before.'

I passed her my half-drunk pint out of self-preservation. I couldn't hack any more and it would go to waste otherwise. Either on the table or down the toilet.

'Drink through the pain,' I told her.

Juliette laughed, took my pint, downed it, and then joined our circle. She took out two fags and passed me one.

Smithy joined us. 'I didn't know you smoked,' she said to me.

'She's a social smoker,' Juliette said.

Of course I am. And by social she means in the absence of Callum. He's made his feelings on smokers very clear.

'Ah. One of them.' Smithy nodded at Juliette. 'Your friends keep looking over.'

The hockey circle were all staring in our direction.

Juliette clapped her hands together like a little girl. 'Let's join up. They're a good bunch. Besides, Twinkle would love another stab at you.'

At me? She's joking right? Besides, I'm sort of taken now, aren't I?

Before any of us realised what was happening, Juliette and Smithy had added a few tables and chairs, and the hockey team had joined us. Juliette had somehow taken control of both circles.

The night descended into chaos. Of the best kind.

But all I could think of was getting back to Callum's abs. Callum and his green eyes, waiting for me when I got back. *He's going to be waiting for me, isn't he?*

CALLUM

Thursday 12/10/2000 19:13
Subject: Re: RE: Scored

Hello you! Glad you're partying hard in the sun.

It's less fun here. Things have got too tricky too fast for my liking. One minute I've got a crush on a handful of girls and the next I wake up with one of them. I have to admit – at least to you – that I like her. A lot. She hasn't stopped being my dream girl because I slept with her. It was so good after all. By far the best sex I've had. (No jokes on how little sex I've had, please.) But how to act? We live together, along with others. And it's complicated.

It's been aaaages now and I haven't spoken to her. I'm talking about Ruby, in case you hadn't realised. She's avoiding me. And I'm avoiding Yas who was, according to Paul, 'having kittens' when Ruby and I went off for that run.

As for the boys, I keep having to change the subject. Luckily, there's always academia. That's what we are here for at the end of the day, right?

It's actually worrying though. The more we talk about it – the boys are on more or less the same course – the more I realise that they don't struggle in the way I do. They seem to think it's all straightforward. Am I too stupid for this?

I could really do with your help here, man, I really could.

Cal

Saturday 14/10/2000 14:04
Subject: News

I have news! I did it! Success!! Too many exclamation marks? Never! Ruby and I are no longer awkward.

It'd been almost a week, actually. The boys kept asking about my run with Ruby – tongue in cheek of course. But still, it was weighing on me.

'How long can she keep avoiding me?' I wanted to yell at them.

But it finally happened yesterday. I'd decided to stay in the kitchen and try to sort out my course mess, which was a bad idea as nothing made sense after all that drinking. Not even the simple things. So I just wrote out a list of tutors to email for suggested texts and then just stared at it for hours.

The door had creaked open and I remember looking up. Ruby was under the door frame, looking ever so hot in her waitressing outfit. Although obviously not as hot as she looks without it.

I asked her how her shift was – tried a 'winning' smile. She returned it with a superior version and sat on the chair across the table from me. I just wanted to grab her and kiss her right then and there. Troublesome, I hear you say.

I passed her my beer to make conversation. I didn't want it to be awkward. Our fingers touched – I wanted more. Is that a song?

We made small talk, then I opened up. I'm always opening up with that girl – there's something about her. We talked about how I'm having a few issues with my course – how it's harder than I imagined and the others don't seem to notice.

She asked if I needed any help from her. I told her something along the lines of not making promises she couldn't keep. She said she meant it, though she kept staring hard at the ash tray on the window sill that Juan and Juliette hadn't emptied. They stink the place up they do. It's a terrible habit. I don't know how the non-smokers that hang around them all the time do it.

I felt I had to say something – but I couldn't bring myself to broach the subject that was clearly on both our minds. I looked at her, but she kept nodding into her green bottle and I realised she hadn't once looked at me in the eyes like I so wanted her to. It unnerved me, so I jumped in and asked her if she wanted to talk about what happened, holding my breath and waiting for the slap of rejection. I was answered with silence. And there it was – it had been that sort of night. The silence stretched. It was painful – I felt stifled.

Finally – finally! – she broke it. She said she hadn't told anyone, but apparently Yas had been asking around about us and she'd hear 'all the gossip' from the boys anyway.

That's when I realised – Ruby was being testy because she thought I'd kissed and told. I shrugged – I'm doing that too often and Mum would disapprove – and told her I was waiting to find out what was going on first, then held my hands out to her across the table, like you do. I don't think I get away with the 'I want a shag' signs in the same way – no subtlety. But she took the hint and then dragged me to my room. Score!

Cal

Tuesday 17/10/2000 12:25
Subject: Re: RE: News

Hello. Glad you're good and having fun.

I'm not. Like, take yesterday. It was supposed to be a good day. I woke up with Ruby again and the sun was shining – all was good with the world, actually. And then I went to class to the seminar from hell.

I failed the test. So the tutor decided to add to my embarrassment by asking me to answer one of the questions I'd failed. As for the help I'd expected and the being pointed in the right direction text-wise, well, that didn't happen either. I got the distinct impression that I just wasn't worth her time. Maybe she worked out who the parents are and figured I was here just for the parties. And – to add insult to injury – the next assignment's been handed out and looks even more impossible than the previous one. I'm in over my head and I just can't understand why.

Any advice?

Keep having fun – one of us needs to be.

Cal

Wednesday 18/10/2000 20:32
Subject: More news

Hello! How're you doing?

I'm OK, actually. Earlier, just when all hope was lost, Ruby saved me – she came into my room and asked me if I was OK. I had to force a smile when I looked up at her, but I hoped she didn't notice as I didn't really want her to leave – nothing like a shag for alleviating stress.

I can still see her as she leaned against the door frame – it really accentuated her toned figure. In a good way – you should have seen it – it really made her breasts look great. Seeing them again properly would definitely improve anyone's day.

Anyway, after I explained how I was struggling, she offered to help – sat down and went through it with me. Life-saver! And it's not even her subject. But she was slow, methodical and patient and really explained the basics to me in a non-patronising way. We went through the previous assignment and my lecture notes and it all started to make sense – the girl's amazing!

Eventually she excused herself to go to a social. I was left to go through the last part of the assignment myself, with the promise of help later if I needed it. It was tough work, but I've got through it. I can't wait for my reward!

I'll let you know all about it.

Cal

Thursday 19/10/2000 15:54
Subject: Even more news

Hellooooo again. I've got mixed news. Some crazy stuff's happened! I've been trying to ring you but you're not about. Let me start at the beginning otherwise I can see you in whatever internet café you're in – shouting at the computer like it's the screen's fault without having the full story. So here goes.

Although I'd got a goodnight kiss before Rube left – bonus – I really wasn't in the mood when I walked into the kitchen after hours of work to find the others playing drinking games. Fuzzy Duck.

But at least there was Yas. Sober from abstaining but still sat at the table, wearing this tight-fitting red dress that showed off that excellent body. All dressed up and nowhere to go. She batted her eyes at me and smiled hello. I couldn't help but smile back. She has that effect on people. She was still looking intently at me, with that inviting smile highlighting those luscious red lips of hers, so I asked her how she was doing.

Matt answered for me with a sly smile I really didn't like but wish I could pull off myself. 'We're good,' he said. 'How about you?' That boy's such a joker.

Then Paul piped up. Mustn't be outdone, must he? Apparently I'd been spotted leaving Ruby's room at seven in the morning. Yes, the 'rumour conclusively stated' I was in yesterday's clothes. So much for keeping things secret.

I looked round the table at eleven pairs of eyes looking squarely at me. Yas', in particular, were not very friendly. Her right eyebrow was ready for lift-off. I kept up the pretence that I had no idea what they were talking about, especially as the frustration on Yas' face was priceless.

But after stringing the conversation along for a while, Yas lost patience and looked ready to strangle me – the accumulating amusement swiftly lost its appeal. So, when she said, 'For God's sake Cal – is something going on with you two?', I finally caved and said 'Yes'. Matt and Paul teased with some exaggerated clapping – I guess I'd deserved that.

But if I thought I was getting away that lightly, I was wrong. Yas – being the minx that she is – wasn't finished with me yet. She flat out asked – suggestively, of course – whether or not it was serious, then leaned over and patted the empty chair next to her. You could see all the way down her top. Not a bad sight.

I smiled again. 'Beer anyone?' I managed – and without drooling too!

Then I sat. She flicked her eyes at me in a way only girls can pull off and let her arm brush against mine. I was just pulling myself together when Matt burst in with his news.

Shit – got to go – ring me.

Cal

YASMINE

The plan had been formulated and was ready for execution, so that all I had to do was wait and get Juliette caught up in the aftermath. But fate had other plans, and that night dealt a blow that was so painful and gut-wrenching that it made me reassess my whole life philosophy and regret some of my past actions.

We were in the kitchen playing drinking games and

having fun, with Callum flirting away like Ruby had never existed. He had joined the soirée a little late, but his entrance had been enough to brighten an already luminous evening.

'Hello,' he said as he came in, smiling directly at me.

I couldn't help but smile back, what with Callum always making you feel like you are the centre of his world.

'How're you doing?' I asked him, ignoring the pointed stares I was receiving from some meddlesome parties.

'We're good. How about you?' Matt interrupted with a sly smirk that was like a line of ants creeping up the sides of his face.

Paul, never one to let an opportunity to embarrass Callum slide, piped up with 'We hear you were spotted leaving Ruby's room at seven this morning? And, before you protest, the rumour conclusively states you were in last night's clothes.'

I exhaled gently, using my best Sama Vrtti Pranayama technique to focus my breath and release my entrapped anger, then looked up at Callum through my damp eyelashes, but not before I took in the rest of the table. His command of the kitchen occupants' attention was unmistakable and complete.

'The rumour does, does he?' Callum joked.

'Ducky Fuzz,' Matt hooted. Then, looking around at the furrowed eyebrows he added, 'Not funny?'

'So?' I was succeeding in controlling my voice's pitch but somewhat less effective in keeping my eyebrows in their correct, structured place.

'So?' Callum was clearly aware, keeping up the pretence to further stab his gold-tipped dagger into my frustration.

'You and Ruby?' I wasn't going to let him escape, no matter how that made me look in the eyes of my hardened peers.

'What about me and Ruby?'

'Oh, come on! Is something going on?' I tried to control the exasperation, but Callum was a skilled artisan at emotional manipulation.

'Going on?'

'For God's sake, Cal! Is something going on with you and Ruby?'

I had reached the stage where I was both lacking in any semblance of composure and adopting a threatening body posture. Whether it was one of the two or a combination of both is irrelevant, the important thing was that it worked, and he relented.

'Yes,' he verified, a soft blush reaching his cheeks as he held my stare defiantly.

Matt and Paul broke out into theatrical applause, and the rest of the malleable lemmings at the table followed suit.

'It's not serious, is it?' I leaned over as I patted the empty chair next to me, hoping that my pleading eyes and inviting pose would sway the bookmakers' odds back in my favour.

He smiled that cheeky trademark smile. 'Beer anyone?'

Then he lowered himself slowly into the empty chair and I beamed at him, letting my arm brush against his. I felt a jolt, as if all energy locked in a Mula Bandha seal had been released, and I know he felt it too as he smiled back and struggled to pull himself both away and together.

It was then that the door slammed open. Matt, paler than the freshly white-washed wall and breathless as a marathon athlete at the finishing line, stood there for a moment before he broke his horrifying, pivotal news.

'I think we've been burgled,' he spat through sharp intakes of breath. 'My room's been tossed and there are some things missing. Some of the other doors also look open. I ... What do we do?'

I screamed.

Broken

RUBY

There were three police cars parked outside our halls. Well, technically there were two. The third belonged to campus security. But still.

And there was a security man at the front door. *What's happened? Is everything OK? Is everyone?*

I didn't know what to do. The severe drunkenness was shaken away, but I was hardly sober. *Am I allowed in?* The man looked at me standing there.

'Hi. Can I go in?' I asked. *Stop looking so suspicious, Ruby, mate. It's not a crime to be tipsy.*

'Do you live here?'

'Yes. What's happened?' *Fine, don't tell me. Just stand there and roll your eyes, fat man.*

He took forever to check my student card and motion me in. He wasn't very friendly. *If that was my job, I wouldn't be happy either, I guess. Checking drunk student IDs. Great.*

There were loads of people in the corridor upstairs, none of whom I recognised. Two people pushed past me without looking at me. The second one barged me a little and I hit the toilet door hard. I felt myself falling and the drunkenness was back.

Luckily, someone caught me and I looked up to see Juan's face.

'Thanks. What's going on?' *Am I slurring? Oh dear. Did I just say, 'Oh dear'? I must be hammered.*

'We've had a break-in.'

'What?'

'We have had a break-in,' he said slowly, looking like he'd been red-carded for someone else's offense.

Best not to try and explain what I mean. Given I'm not sure what I mean. What do I mean? Totally hammered. Just move on.

'Who? Where? How?' I asked.

'The rooms past the fire door. Thieves came up the other staircase. We were all in the kitchen and heard nothing.'

I heaved a sigh of relief. For the first time since we moved in, I was glad my room was next to the main staircase and opposite the toilets. But then I felt guilty. *The poor people affected!*

I followed Juan into the kitchen because I had no idea what else to do.

Juliette was smoking in the corner. She was talking to Paul and they both looked unhappy. Matt was talking to two policemen. *But where's Yasmine? Her room's on the other side too. And she owns a lot of expensive equipment.*

As I turned, I saw her. She was crying into Callum's chest. He had his arms around her.

I felt backwash in my mouth. *Should've known, Ruby, mate. Should. Have. Known.*

I ran out of the door before they could see the tears, but I heard his footsteps behind me.

'Ruby! Stop, please!' But I kept going. The tears were pouring. My heart was groaning. I couldn't stop.

He grabbed my arm. The alcohol had slowed me down.

'We have to talk,' he said, not letting go.

YASMINE

I'm not proud of my reaction. I screamed and ran, my heart ready to tear its way through my sternum, my mind repeating the phrase 'it's not possible' like a track on a scratched CD, and my body teleporting itself to my room. My door was closed, but opened with the pressure I applied while trying to get the key in the door with shaking hands.

The room was a mess. There were folders strewn everywhere, my stereo was gone, the limited contents of my jewellery box had been thrown onto the floor, and my cupboard was a mound of once-pristine, neatly-folded clothes clearly rifled through. The purple pouch containing an antique broach encrusted with precious stones, which I had taken out of my safe storage compartment to take to my jewellery-making class the next day, was gone. I screamed and punched my pillow with rage, breaking a nail as the hot tears stained my cheeks with riverbeds through the Clinique foundation.

I looked around my personal disaster zone then, making sure the door was shut behind me and the curtains drawn, checked my hiding place, relieved to find that the thieves had not uncovered it. Unfortunately, the purple pouch and its contents were still missing and, given that I was not supposed to have it in the first place, this realisation brought on the panic and despair.

I ran back into the kitchen and straight into the warmth of Callum's arms, and there I stayed, feeling the safety of his arms and, possibly naively, believing that it would all work out with a fairy-tale ending. Juliette arrived to add to the evening's festivities by screaming 'my bible!' and tearing down the corridor, then making continuously snide remarks about the value of friendship over that of possessions on her return. What did she know? She probably owned a handful of bibles and, let's be honest, those things are two a penny.

I couldn't even face the police. I felt empty, torn, like someone had stripped me of more than just prized possessions. I had never felt this way before and the pain of loss, the fear of facing my room again, and the consequences of it all conspired to haunt me.

'You OK? This stirring up old memories?' Callum whispered softly in my ear.

I hadn't wanted to raise the subject, as it had always been carefully boxed in my private and delicate 'off limits' pile, but grieved silence was hardly an option.

'Yes, it does. Except this time it really *hurts*, you know? I can't believe I've had my antique broach stolen!'

'Don't worry, they'll get it back. And if they don't, it was insured, right?'

'Of course it wasn't insured!'

I inhaled deeply then slowly released the heavy breath, knowing that it was not best to lose my cool at this particular moment in time.

'Don't panic, it's going to be OK.'

'You don't understand. I shouldn't have had it here in the first place.'

The policeman chatting to Matt turned and stared at me for a second, then resumed his chat so that I felt safe from his prying eyes, but I still turned down the volume as you can never be too careful. Callum also looked at me, with those jade eyes oozing concern and sympathy, and try as I might to fight it, I felt myself wanting to explain.

'It was never supposed to leave my house,' I said, carefully. 'I should never have brought it here. It was a stupid thing to do and now ...' I couldn't bring myself to articulate the horrific consequences of that piece falling into misguided yet calculating hands. I didn't even want to think that those scenarios actually existed. I started to cry.

Callum held me closer and, as a result, when the policemen came to take my statement, which basically consisted of my name, address, whether I had locked my door, if I'd seen anything, and an inventory of any lost items, I felt that I could handle it.

Then I was back in his arms, being held tight and credulously hoping that I wouldn't have to face my room alone that night, or the demons that dwelt within it. Instead, the peace was broken by Ruby's entrance who, upon seeing Callum with me, turned and walked out with a look that said 'follow me' and, unfortunately, he took the bait and sprinted after her.

That was the final straw. I had lived through and put up with a lot over the years and, particularly now that I had other things to worry about, I was damned if I was going to let some unkempt tomboy and a chain-smoker get in my way. Looking back, that was my biggest error: underestimating my enemy.

JULIETTE

I keep thinking back to the night of the break-in. I must've known then and I really should've acted on my instincts. But instead I let my lack of sobriety influence my judgement. I could've saved myself a lot of pain, loss, and suffering, but instead I just ignored the signs.

Hindsight is a wonderful thing, I guess.

Anyway, I returned early from the Union that night, mainly because I had managed to lose my team as well as Ruby and Smithy. There was a lot of noise coming from the kitchen, so I walked in to join the fun instead of trying to write a crime literature critique drunk. But there was no fun to be had – I found a frantic Yasmine with red eyes and blotchy makeup. And how she was pining for attention! She had Callum eating it up like nobody's business. Boy, did that girl have male manipulation down to an art form! I was glad Ruby wasn't there to see it.

I asked Matt what was going on and he told me to go check my room – the rooms down beyond the fire door had been broken into.

I ran. Possessions may not be the 'be all and end all', but I had some sentimental items there. You'd be proud of me – my first thought was Daddy's antique bible – you know the one with the engraved silver cover that had belonged to Daddy's family? Yes, he obviously never had any use for it.

At first I thought it was all fine, as the door looked normal, but the policemen in the corridor said otherwise. Under their supervision, I pushed the door open without a key – and I know I had certainly locked it. The room was a mess – clothes and books and papers everywhere. My minidisc player was missing, but that was it as far as I could tell. The bible was surprisingly still there. And it's not like I had much else in my room anyway – frugal living and all that.

I then headed back to the kitchen to 'give my report' and my fingerprints for 'comparison purposes'. I didn't even notice them looking for fingerprints, assuming they actually did so. They probably wanted my fingerprints for records, but I could hardly object, could I? Besides, it's not as if I'd done anything illegal yet. And it's hardly any use being paranoid now, is it? Exactly – glad we agree on something.

Anyway, back to the story. Yasmine had looked up at me as I entered and so I felt compelled to ask her if she was OK – you know, for appearances. I couldn't have the entirety of the corridor thinking I was the bad guy for being horrible to Yasmine. Well, obviously I couldn't care less now but back then … it was different, you know? I liked most of them and didn't want my feud with the manipulative bit– sorry, girl – to bring it all crashing down.

In response to my question, she turned on the waterworks big time. They were accompanied by screaming and hurled accusations. It was so extreme that I thought the police were going to arrest *me*! *So* over the top, you know? I mean, Matt, Anne, and I had lost stuff too, but we weren't acting like the world had ended.

I lit up to calm down. It felt like a bad dream. All I could hear was Yasmine sobbing 'they stole my broach' over and over again. According to her chat with the policeman, the broach in question was some artefact she'd bought at a *charity shop* and had been planning to remodel as her latest jewellery project. Ha!

It was all drama, drama, drama, but, at the end of the day, she couldn't describe it beyond 'a normal antique-looking broach with some semi-precious stones' that was 'worth a significant amount'. Of course, she was acting like the thieves had made off with her 5-carat engagement ring, not some insignificant useless item. Well, in retrospect it was hardly useless … But I'm getting ahead of myself – that comes later in the story.

Anyway, I just couldn't handle the amateur theatrics anymore. All I wanted was the strength to go back into my room and clear up the mess and then get on with life in our corridor. I managed the former, but Yasmine obviously had other ideas about the latter.

Stoned

The aftershocks of the break-in were felt long and hard into the night and with them brought a clarity of mind, though not, predictably, the peaceful variety. On reflection, my knee-jerk reactions were not particularly becoming, and the truth is that it had never occurred to me that anyone other than Juliette would be affected by my plan. Unfortunately, what started out as a way to get back at the girl that was making my life a living hell could easily have turned into a cause for guilt and ostracism. The break-in had inevitably affected my better judgement, so that the consequences of my actions were ill thought through at best. I had been hurt by the violation of my personal space and loss of my belongings as a result of the robbery, the pain and suffering caused by Juliette's constant attacks, the disloyalty shown by Ruby, and the conflicting signals beaming from my beacon, Callum.

The night of the robbery was eerily dark and quiet, and I spent it sat in Easy Sit Pose on my bed, by myself, listening to the stomach-churning rhythmic rapping of what could only be a bed knocking on my west wall, the one adjoining Callum's room. Not only had he been unaffected by the robbery due to the sheer luck of having a room on the busy side of the fire door, but he had made up with Ruby and ensured the entire population of our halls were notified of said fact.

My thoughts wandered relentlessly to the dark undercurrents of Juliette's actions and the long-term danger that lurked under that pious exterior. It scared me that someone with that much power could hoodwink so many into believing she was sweet, innocent, and caring, and that only Callum and I were able to see through the seemingly impermeable exterior to the deeply hypocritical interior.

The next day, I was inevitably under-slept, upset, and in a venomous mood, so when I heard Juliette and Juan creep into the latter's room, I jumped at the chance to set my plan into motion. I waited until the inevitable damp, rotting stench of marijuana wafted from under the door and then headed out in the opposite direction. I made my way down the corridor in a swift and silent manner, crossed the glass pane of the kitchen door with speed, and padded down the musty carpeted stairs. I did not want to be seen as, if I had, I would not have been able to go through with it.

Against the odds, I made it unseen to my final destination, a red door that contrasted horribly with the salmon-pink/vomit-coloured doors that unceremoniously lined the ground-floor corridor. I held my breath and wondered if I could follow through my thoughts with actions while simultaneously avoiding any further police presence in the vicinity. I knocked on the wood of the door lightly, but there was no response. I lifted my finger and, after a final panic over whether the consequences could potentially be traced back to me, I pressed the buzzer long and hard.

The hall tutor took so long to answer, I wondered multiple times whether I had lost my chance and should just leave before anyone saw me, but, eventually, he appeared, bedraggled and unkempt, with a scowl on his face which relaxed into a smile once he saw me.

'Hi, Yasmine, how can I help?'

'I'm afraid I shouldn't be doing this,' I started, staring at the floor and trying to appear guilty when all I felt was anger, 'but there is an awful stench of marijuana upstairs coming from one of the rooms and I think Juliette …' I paused there and looked up at him. 'I think Juliette may be smoking it. Please don't tell anyone I said anything. It would be the end of me.'

'Of course. Thank you for reporting it,' he said, sounding genuine.

He walked over to a phone on the table, picked it up and spoke so softly I couldn't make out a single word despite the pricked ears and held breath set to optimise eavesdropping. He popped his head into an inner door and murmured something, put on his shoes, and walked up the stairs, closing his own door behind him before he did so.

I inhaled sharply, then continued out of the building, not wanting to be associated with the events that were about to unfold and yet feeling incredibly smug. Our university was renowned for its tough stance on illegal activities in halls, and I could think of nothing better than our halls of residence without Juliette and her pretentious, bible-thumping hypocrisy.

One down, one to go, I thought, and headed off in the direction of the Union, where I hoped to find Callum.

CALLUM

Thursday 26/10/2000 15:47
Subject: Re: RE:

It really feels like I've been spending my entire time hugging sobbing women.

First Yas, because she'd had some stuff stolen in the break-in.

Then Ruby, who thought there was something going on between me and Yas. (Shut it, you.)

And just now it was Sarah, sobbing over Juan's ejection from our halls.

How do I keep getting myself into these situations?

It's a funny story though. Well not funny funny – just weird.

Some of the guys smoke weed occasionally. I mean, this IS a university. And today the hall tutor apparently went barging into Juan's room. Isn't there some law about privacy? Apparently not on uni property. Well, there you go.

They had no defence, being caught red-handed and all. Campus security were called, their rooms were searched and they were all told that they had to leave halls.

As there were no other drugs except the remains of the joints they were smoking, they weren't charged. They were just told to pack their things and find off-campus accommodation by tomorrow. Ridiculous!

And of course somehow I'm the one left consoling Sarah. Typical.

In need of a pint or ten. Union, here I come …

Don't worry, I'll have a pint for you too.

Cal

JULIETTE

Well, the next part of the story you're going to love. Something about comeuppance and deserved victory for the righteous, I'm sure. But good people were affected. And I, for one, don't think that's right. Hall tutors should keep their noses firmly out of other people's business when people are not hurting anyone other than, perhaps, themselves.

I'm getting ahead of myself again. On the day after the break-in, there were a lot of nerves about. People were understandably upset – tempers were frayed, tears were plentiful, and you could generally feel the elevated stress levels. Most of us hadn't slept either. I mean, you can't sleep after someone's wrecked your room and stolen your property, can you? There's the fear, tension, and a sense of loss. Not so much for the value of things – we all had insurance – it was the loss of items with sentimental value. It was a horrible time. There is a reason 'thou shall not steal' is one of the Ten Commandments.

Anyway, back to the story. We were sat there in the kitchen – talking as usual, although the conversation was understandably more grave than normal – when Simon leaned back on his chair and said that he'd 'kill for a joint'. And yes, he was referring to cannabis. The same herb that – like tobacco – God blessed on the third day of creation. That's Genesis talking, not me, so don't look at me like that.

Where was I? Oh yes – Simon. In response to his throwaway comment, Juan piped up with something along the lines of, 'One of the hockey guys left one in my room the other night. It's pre-rolled and ready to rock.'

And so off we all trooped to Juan's room, cramming ourselves into the tiny space and sparking up. There were people in that room that had probably never smoked anything before, let alone weed. It's them I feel most sorry for. They were simply after a chill-out away from all the drama and – unfortunately – all they got was more drama. Hardly fair, no matter how you look at it.

Anyway, just sitting in the room watching the smoke curl up to the ceiling was enough. You could really feel the relaxation in the atmosphere. The change in stress levels – psychological, obviously, as the drug hadn't had time to act – was instant. So instant, in fact, that my bladder realised it was full, and I forwent my toke in order to pop to the bathroom.

I've often wondered about my timing – if things would have turned out different had I left a minute or two later. And there is some guilt. I mean, it was *my* friend – Turner – the hockey boy who had left the joint in Juan's room. Would they have had to go through all the pain and embarrassment if it hadn't been for me and my in-hall hockey socials? It's no use dwelling on these things now, especially given the more important issues I'm here to discuss today. Ha! OK, so maybe discuss is a bit strong, given this is mainly a one-way conversation. Maybe I'm just here to talk. Lucky for me, you've promised to listen. You've always been good at listening – or at least at pretending you are. You are listening, aren't you?

I'm off course again – sorry. When I left the powder room – or whatever you older folk call it – I bumped into the hall tutor. The man was clearly on a mission – like something had sparked his fury – and if his dishevelled appearance and the lipstick marks on his neck were anything to go by, the man had been interrupted mid erm, yes, well, you get my drift.

He looked at me with a rather confused expression that sent me back into the bathroom to check if I had lipstick smudged all over *my* face. Having made sure I also didn't have burn marks on my shirt or toilet paper stuck to my shoe, I tied to leave the bathroom to head down the corridor, still oblivious to what was happening. But I didn't – leave, that is – as the door was blocked by Matt, apologising 'for following' me but wanting 'to talk about Ruby' and whether she was 'alright'.

It was a bit of a strange conversation, to be honest – especially since Ruby hadn't been involved in the previous night's action. More than strange – a little awkward. So I hurried up and walked purposefully away, although he did keep up.

When we got to Juan's room, the whole scene was already unfolding. You should've seen them – it was horrible. Simon had his arm protectively round Anne, who was sobbing. Juan had a cigarette in his hand, but was pale and shaking. And the evil hypocrite of a hall tutor was shouting at them – actually shouting – and writing notes in his stupid spiral-bound book.

'This is illegal behaviour and the university will not tolerate such behaviour on its premises. Campus security is on its way and you will be dealt with accordingly. The university will also be informed of your actions and may or may not take action with respect to your studies. What is certain is that you will be evicted from these halls of residence for breach of conduct ...' Blah, blah, blah.

He went on and on and ooooon. And we were behind him, in the clear, out of harm's reach. It was one of those moments where you feel lucky and elated and shocked and upset and guilty, all rolled into one. My emotions were in turmoil. Happy that we'd been fortunate to escape. Scared for my friends' futures. Angry at the tutor for his handling of the situation. Guilty for my part in it. Even guiltier for having escaped untouched. The list goes on.

We waited until it was over, despite being told

constantly to mind our own business by the security bullies. We were there for our friends and I'm glad we were, having managed to escape the onslaught ourselves. Although I'm not entirely sure I mean that – it was a very painful victory. The others, unfortunately, had not been so lucky. Even though they were all allowed to continue their studies – they didn't find that out for almost a week, by the way – they were ejected from the corridor and had to find their own accommodation that day or the next. Security and the tutor were not very understanding at all.

When it was all over, we offered to buy everyone drinks and keep them supplied with alcohol all night. It was the least we could do under the circumstances. They met us later, after they'd packed.

As we had nothing better to do after a while – besides standing around useless and guilty, that is – Matt and I figured we'd get a head start and so made our way to the Union ahead of the pack. When we got there, we saw Yasmine and Callum, sitting together at a table by the bar looking very, very cosy indeed while, at the other end of the Union, making her way innocently towards them, was Ruby …

Fractured

The Union's distinct stench of stale smoke and over-aged beer permeated every corner of the premises. After a few laps of the usual haunts within the building, I gave up my search for the elusive Callum. Instead, I sat on a rickety, metallic chair not fit for an NHS waiting room and looked about me at the usual loutish cattle. I could hardly return to halls until the hall tutor was done, just in case he couldn't keep my involvement out of it, and so my pursuit of Callum would have to wait.

The echo of the pool cues scraping the cheap felt and plastic balls made me shiver, like it was a blackboard someone had run their non-manicured nails down. That obviously did not bode well for the concentration levels on the lecture notes I had brought for re-reading. I had just decided to give up on my quest indefinitely and move my belongings along to the library, where I could at least track down some books and journals for my next assignment, when the honey tones of my favourite rich voice gently washed over me.

'Thank God you're here – I was beginning to think I'd have to drink alone.' Callum's eyes bore through mine and, for a second, I got lost in their forest depths.

'Are you OK?' I asked, scared that Callum had been dragged down with Juliette's woes.

'Fine – just too much consoling today!'

'What's wrong?' I asked.

'Haven't you heard?' He tilted his entire frame conspiratorially toward me.

I looked up at him with my most innocent of expressions and mirrored his actions.

'Juan, Tim, Anne, and Simon have been kicked out of halls,' he blurted. 'Got caught smoking weed. You know how stupidly tough the university is on this type of thing. They crack down harder than the law.'

I felt like an industrial strength vacuum-cleaner had sucked all accessible gases from my lungs. It took me over a minute to recover and respond, and even then all I could manage was a bland and plebeian, 'What?'

'Yeah, the hall tutor barged into Juan's room, where they were having a smoke, and busted them all. Matt and Juliette managed to get out of it, but the others were caught red-handed.'

'Juliette got out of it?' I noticed that my voice had risen to the proximity of a shriek and did my best to meditate silently with open eyes in order to control it. 'What happened?'

'Oh, they were just smoking and that wanker of a tutor barged in and caught them red-handed. I think Matt had decided to go find an actual cigarette instead – I know, pretty much the only good smoking story ever?

– and Juliette was in the ladies when the bust went down so … '

I felt my chest tighten as my diaphragm refused to move, denying my lungs access to clean air. There was guilt, too, from the realisation of the effects of my ultimately failed plan on innocent parties. My vision began to spin, as if I had absolutely exceeded the limits of sobriety. I tried to focus and practice Sama Vrtti Pranayama, which, in spite of (or perhaps because of) being the most basic form of breathing, my yoga instructor always swore by for disquieting situations.

'You look like you could use a drink,' Callum said and, before I had time to process the offer, he was already back from the bar with a pint and a glass of the least palate-insulting of available wines.

He pulled up a chair next to mine, brushed my hand with his fingers as he passed me the glass, and flashed me his broad, beautiful, gilded smile. I smiled back, wanting to engage with this gorgeous man, but all I could do was feel as if someone was wringing my stomach and then shaking it out, ready to hang out on a peasant's clothes line.

That Thursday, I broke my cardinal rule and drank heavily. After my third, I started to feel both better and incredibly tipsy. While Callum and I talked endlessly about movies and fashion, we connected on a deeper level so that, by the time he bought me my fourth straight glass of that cheap Chardonnay, we could no longer contain ourselves or resist the chemistry between us. I flicked my hair over my shoulder, and realised he had leant in closer when I felt him touch my arm. His face was barely an inch from mine.

'You smell so good,' he murmured, inhaling the sweet fragrance of Issey Miyake *L'Eau d'Issey*.

'So do you,' I whispered, inaccurately, but with the excuse to glide ever closer to those succulent lips.

I could see his Adam's apple flicker as he gulped gently, making up his mind whether I was worth it. I didn't want to give him too much time to consider so, with all the subtlety that I could muster, I closed the chasm and planted my perfectly lipsticked pout on his soft skin. He responded; his mouth parted ever so slightly and I felt sweet warm breath on my face, his hand gently brushed my hair, and his knees knocked against mine as he adjusted his position. Unfortunately, the moment was all too brief and violently shattered.

RUBY

I could feel the world spinning. My chest was tight. My cheeks were hot with tears. My pride was wounded.

'We have to talk.'

No, Callum, we don't. Go away.

He grabbed my arm, turned me to face him, and pinned me up against the wall.

'Why are you acting like this?'

'Me? You're the one all over Yasmine!'

'Don't be silly. We're just friends.'

Friends?! 'You were just all over each other!'

I stumbled and fell into the brick wall. He picked me

up gently and planted a soft kiss on my lips. While people were watching. *Well, that was definitely unexpected.*

'Don't be silly,' he whispered and kissed me again, harder this time. 'Let's get you to bed, pisshead.'

●

The next morning I woke up in his bed, alone. My head throbbed. My ankle ached. And to say that my stomach was definitely not happy with me was understatement of the month. I just about managed to drag myself to a lecture, then on to my shift. I was glad they liked me there or I'd have been fired for my work ethic. Or lack of.

On my way back to halls, I decided to swing by the Union in case Smithy was there. I'd ended up with her socks the night before (no idea how) and I didn't have her mobile number, assuming she had one. Plus, I needed to catch her up on last night's burglary and other dramas. I figured she'd be drinking. *She's always drinking.*

The Union was surprisingly busy for a Thursday night. *Too many people.* All of them in groups, while I wandered about alone. *They're staring at me. I have every right to be here, don't I? Maybe not. No, definitely not. I'm alone, aren't I?* I was headed for the exit when I bumped into Jules.

'Hi,' she said, coming up to my side at a strange angle so that I had to turn to face her.

'Hi.' *So good to see a familiar face.*

'Hiya,' said Matt, appearing at my other side.

'Do you fancy a drink?' *Why, Ruby, mate, why? You've just recovered from your hangover. It's possible to be friends with people without drinking.*

'Sure. Downstairs?' asked Jules.

But there's no-one ever at the downstairs bar. Don't you want to be seen with me?

'Good idea.' Matt's smile was forced.

Are you ashamed of being seen with me too? I know I'm not dressed for a night out, but neither are you. So then why are you lot even here? And why talk to me in the first place, if I'm not good enough?

Matt's eyes kept flickering between Juliette's face and over my shoulder. *He obviously doesn't want us to be seen together. Have I done something? Or am I that poor company?*

Static X's '*I'm with Stupid*' belted my brain on repeat. *Stop it!*

'It's OK,' I said, hurt. *I don't want to be a charity case. I'll just go back.*

I turned to go and that's when I saw them. Sat together, lips locked. Unmistakeably Callum and Yasmine. I froze. I felt lunch backwash in my mouth. *Run, Ruby, mate, run. Why can't I move?*

Jules put her arm round me. 'Come on,' she said softly, leading me away.

I couldn't see through the tears, but I could hear Matt's shuffle as he walked away from us. In the opposite direction. *He doesn't want to be part of any scene and I can't say I blame him.* Static X started singing at me again.

We walked out of the Union in silence, stopping three times for me to vomit. *By the streetlights, Ruby? Really, mate? Couldn't you puke somewhere less obvious? I swear they're brighter than floodlights. Was that one of my tutors that just walked past? Not cool. As if you ever were, Ruby, mate.*

Finally, we got to my room. Jules offered me a cigarette but I shook my head. My throat was too raw.

'He's not worth it,' she said.

'But he is.'

'He is? You mean to say you're defending him now? Why?'

Because I have to. Because he's the best I can ever have. 'It's OK for you, mate – you can have whoever you want.'

'Wake up, Ruby, so can you.'

She walked out. I was left alone, letting her words sink in. *She's just saying that to make me feel better.*

Isn't she?

JULIETTE

'Thou shalt not covet thy neighbour's wife'. Another one of the Ten Commandments. Yasmine was on a roll.

To tell you the truth, I still feel guilty about it. You see, I intercepted her. Ruby, I mean. All I could think of at the time was that I didn't want her to get hurt. As if that were possible! She was clearly besotted with that poor excuse for a man. He and Yasmine deserve each other.

Matt and I tried to get her away – I'm back to Ruby,

by the way – but, of course, she saw straight through our ploy. Her expression still haunts me. She was terrified and heartbroken and shocked all rolled into one. I just wanted to hug all of it away, you know? But, of course, I couldn't, as Callum and Yasmine were literally next to us, snogging like teenagers. Well, *normal* teenagers, not your kind. I won't elaborate – I'm sure you get my drift.

Anyway, I carried her – Ruby, obviously – carried her back to our corridor, and she unceremoniously threw up *everywhere* along the way. Smithy was walking towards us and started to come help, but I motioned her away with my expression, hoping Ruby hadn't seen. You see, I thought Ruby wouldn't want to face having to tell someone about it, even kind, sweet, witty Smithy. Especially witty Smithy. Don't look at me like that – I know what you're thinking and I don't agree.

Where was I? Oh yes – so I carried Ruby back to her room. I offered her a cigarette but she declined, obviously thinking of Callum's distaste. That got me. What right did he have to complain about Ruby smoking when he was cheating on her? And it *was* cheating. I mean, everyone – including Yasmine – knew they were together even if they didn't refer to each other as boyfriend and girlfriend. It *really* upset me.

I shouted at her that he wasn't worth it.

'Oh, but he is,' she answered, with this expression – argh!

I wanted to throttle her just then, I really did. I wanted to remind her that the man she thought was 'worth it' had had his tongue down Yasmine's throat not ten minutes before. Thankfully, I was a bit more tactful than that. She told me that it was OK for me – that I could have 'whomever I wanted' – don't look at me like that, I'm just repeating what she said. It was the way she said it – in a soft, defeated tone – that sent me into a rage. I was terrified of what I might say next, so I left the room to get her a glass of water.

On my way back from the kitchen, who should I stumble upon but the man of the hour? I have to admit, I lost control and blasphemed.

'Who do you think you are?!' I yelled at him, after a few other, ahem, choice words.

He just asked me where Ruby was and I told the cheating … Yeah, I'm not going to repeat what I said.

Well, anyway, he said he was an idiot and asked after her. He sounded genuinely concerned and – for the first and only time – I, too, was swayed by the Callum charm. He struck me as sincere. I know, that makes me all kinds of gullible. But at the time I thought – it doesn't really matter. I caved. I passed him the glass of water and went off to the kitchen, fully looking forward to a sparring session with my foe. I, too, was on a roll.

CALLUM

Friday 27/10/2000 10:56
Subject: I'm an idiot

This time it's bad. Really bad.

First and foremost: I'm an idiot.

It all started so well. After yesterday's tragicomedy, it was nice to see Yas's familiar face, sitting quietly, alone and just a touch forlorn, in the Union. Not sobbing. Plus I desperately wanted a drinking partner, so I went and joined her. My first mistake.

She was shocked by the news of the evictions – she hadn't heard and she's quite close to Anne, actually. I obviously wasn't in the mood for more consoling so I offered her a drink and talked about films and other rubbish I get enough of at home. Somehow, the drinks kept flowing and I found myself both short of cash and rather slurry. Second mistake.

Suddenly, Yas leaned in and asked me what I thought of her perfume. It was good. But not as good as the view down her top. I could see every pore through that transparent lace bra. If it was a movie, I would have gulped – I probably did anyway. She had that killer smile on and dived in for a kiss. Before I had any comprehension of what was going on, I was snogging her. Third mistake.

I can see you shaking your head as you read this, but I don't know how it happened, I really don't. I can plead ignorance and drunkenness and a million other things but, ultimately, I don't even bloody KNOW how it got to that. I just know that I got caught up in the moment and kissed her back. My biggest mistake.

Just as suddenly as it had happened, it was like I woke up. I realised I had my tongue on someone else's and it wasn't Ruby's. That shook me. I realised what I was doing.

I brought my hands up to Yas's shoulder and gently pushed her away when I heard a very loud thump on the table. We both jumped.

It was a clenched fist that had done it. Matt's. And man was he glaring.

'What the hell are you doing?' he shouted at me.

I told him I didn't know – I didn't – I was so shocked at what I'd done.

He spat at me, telling me to sort myself out. I'd never seen him like that. But fair play. Then he said the words that I still can't get over – will I ever? Three little words: 'She saw you.'

I felt like I'd been slapped very, very hard.

I pushed my chair away and legged it back to halls. What had I done? And – as if my guilt and run-in with Matt wasn't enough – I fell straight into Juliette in the corridor.

She threw words at me with a hatred I never thought her capable of. She even swore – asked me who the fuck I thought I was and called me a cheating scum bastard! Good on her, actually – I deserved it. Still do.

I tried to explain – I wasn't at my most articulate, that's for sure. But I must have got the message across because she stopped screaming and stared at my face intently and, eventually, her expression softened and she passed me a glass of water – presumably for Ruby – and let me pass.

I stood outside Rube's room for what seemed like hours, trying to summon up the strength to face the consequences of my stupidity. I can't lose her – not now, not ever. I realise that now.

'Grow some balls,' I hear you saying. And I did. I knocked and walked in without waiting for an answer.

She was sitting on her desk, staring out the window. Even though she was quiet, you could tell she was crying because her frame was shaking. I had made her cry. I wanted to console her so badly. I wanted to hold her. I wanted to kiss her. I wanted to take it all back.

She didn't look up, she just shook her head and kept her face turned away.

I walked up to her and put my hands on her shoulders as gently as I could. She pulled away – like I repulsed her. I didn't know what to say – I'm such an idiot – so in the end, I told her so. You have no idea how sorry I am about the whole thing. Yas just caught me by surprise, but how do you explain that? It was awful – just awful.

Ruby finally turned to face me and the expression on her face told me all I needed to know – that I was about to lose her.

I tried to sort it out, but she wasn't too keen on hugging or kissing or anything like that – hardly surprising – but it feels like because of drunken stupidity, I'm about to lose the woman I'm falling for. And yes, I'm pretty sure I am falling for her. What's wrong with me?

This is so shit – please tell me your week's been better than this!

Cal

Role Models

He begged and begged and begged. He said things I'd never heard anyone say before. Well, not to me. He wanted me back. He needed me. He was sorry. He …

I bit my lip. I so desperately wanted to believe him. I *needed* to believe him. And it wasn't just the status quo that would be upset if I didn't. It was a lot more than hall dynamics that would sour. *How will I be able to walk down the corridor? Talk to my hall mates? Sit in the kitchen? I won't. I'd miss him, I really would. I need him.*

And I guess I had it coming. I'm an insecure mess and he is … Callum. All sexy abs and god-like stature and gorgeous eyes.

I blinked away the tears and looked up at him.

'Why?'

'I don't know what came over me! Please, Rube, please.'

Don't look at me like that. I don't know whether to slap you or kiss you.

'I just …' *can't get the words out.*

'I know.' He tentatively stretched out his hand.

I didn't have the willpower to recoil this time. His hand touched my face and brought the tears hammering down onto the already waterlogged pitch. He lifted his other hand up to my cheek and roughly pulled my head towards his. Then he kissed me. Hard. *Ouch.* It was so tortured, like he was dispelling demons by bruising my lips. *I guess he is.* I pushed him away.

'I'm sorry. I understand if you don't want to.'

Of course I want to. Just not like this. At least I'm not picturing you kissing her. Fuck! Why the hell did I just think that? Now all I'll be seeing is the two of you together.

'Yeah, well, I umm … Well, I could do with a drink.'

Wow, Ruby, you really sound like a moron.

'Bottle of rum and a movie?'

Sounds awesome. 'Something with loads of mindless violence, please.'

'Done.'

I woke up fully clothed but in his arms. He looked so beautiful lying there, eyes closed, breathing deeply but noiselessly. I still couldn't believe he'd kissed her. Now it just felt hollow, like something that had happened in another life. I guess I had cried out all the pain last night. He was mine. *For now.*

I tiptoed out of the room. I was desperately thirsty and wasn't sure I could brave it, but the kitchen looked empty so I went in. Big mistake. Matt and Paul were sat in the blind corner.

'Ruby?'

Don't sound so concerned, Matt. As if you didn't run away to avoid a scene yesterday. 'Morning.'

'How're you feeling?'

Oh no, I'm not doing this. No way. 'Fine. I missed the game, though. Liverpool? What happened?'

'Oh. 1-0, Heskey. You sure you're OK?'

Obviously not. 'Fine, mate. Fine.' *Run away now, Ruby, mate. This could get even more awkward.*

I forced a smile, walked out, and headed to a lecture. I wasn't going to go, but I had to distract myself: the rawness was back. I had been foolish to think I'd gotten over it that quickly.

It didn't work. I spent the whole two hours, a match with extra time, just replaying the whole lock-lipped moment in my head. It was agony. *Worse than when Rangers beat us in the 1992 European Cup. Yes, I'd been young then, but I'll never forget how much it hurt, especially dad. Poor dad.*

I couldn't go anywhere as I had stupidly sat in the middle of a row. Too many people to move if I left, and there would be a lot of staring that I definitely couldn't handle. So I sat there and thought of them together. It was horrible.

Finally, the torment was over. I walked back, hoping to see no-one. But, of course, life never works like that. I bumped into Jules on the stairs.

'Hey, you OK?'

'No. Not really, mate.' *I'm tired of lying.*

'Understandable. Ciggie?'

'Yes, please!'

'I take it you wouldn't have one in the kitchen?'

I shook my head. She smiled and pulled me along the corridor. It felt like we were moving in a slow motion replay. Past the toilets. Past the kitchen door. Down towards the fire door. We were almost home free, just passing Callum's room, when he opened his door and walked straight into us.

'Hi. Just headed to the kitchen for some food.'

He smiled, grabbed my hand, and dragged me back in the direction we'd come. Just this time it was at full speed. I didn't have time to breathe, let alone explain. And Jules didn't follow.

He pushed open the door to the kitchen and dragged me inside. He stopped. I bumped into his shoulder.

'Mum!' He seemed shocked.

But not as shocked as I was.

The timing couldn't have been more wrong. Unfortunately, there was no doubt about it: it could not have been anyone other than his mother. She had the same green eyes, same cheekbones, same lips. But she was a teetering wreck in shiny, ironed clothing. *Not exactly how I'd envisioned Callum's mother.*

'Darling,' she drawled.

She rushed towards us and hugged him. I could smell the stench of alcohol. *Is this how I smelt last night? Ugh.*

'What are you doing here?' he asked.

He doesn't seem too pleased. Guess he doesn't exactly want to introduce me.

'Well, we still feel guilty for not bringing you up

here at the beginning of term, darling, but you know the London Film Festival was on and I could hardly not make an appearance at my home bash, could I? So we decided to visit and whisk you away for the weekend. Where do you fancy? Paris? Far better than these army barracks you're calling home these days. Although your friends seem lovely. Yasmine and I were discussing my competitors' unfortunate choice of designers at the last awards.'

I just stood there, frozen to the spot. I must have been staring, the way she and Yasmine both stared back. It wasn't friendly. *I don't want to be here. Why am I here?*

'Mum, dad, this is my girlfriend, Ruby.'

I heard the words being spoken. I saw the wreck frown. I saw Yasmine glare. I tried to process it all. At least the gentleman behind them seemed more keen. He was smiling. So I tried to act normal and smiled back.

'Hi, I'm Sam.' He held his hand out.

Everyone's staring. Please stop staring. I shook his hand. It was cold. *Breathe, Ruby, mate. Breathe.*

'Ruby,' I said. *Thank you words for failing me.*

'So I heard.'

Obviously. I'm such an idiot.

Then, suddenly, the penny dropped.

'Sam Hayden-Quinn? As in the author?' *Keep going, Ruby, mate. You're looking more and more like an idiot with every second. His parents love you.*

'I didn't know you read, Ruby,' Yasmine said.

Callum's mum snickered.

'Yes. That's me.' Callum's dad smiled.

Wow. I'm in love. My favourite author in the flesh.

'Charming.' Callum's mum definitely wasn't impressed. She turned back to Callum. 'So, darling, we figured we'd take you to lunch and then we could all head off. Shall we?'

'Sure. Ruby and I were just about to grab a bite anyway.'

We were?

'Oh. Are we lunching with all your friends? Yasmine and I were getting along splendidly.'

Oh no. No way.

I felt Callum's hand on the small of my back. I must have been backing away physically too.

'Just you and me and my girlfriend. The restaurant by the Great Hall does private booths. That alright with you?'

His hand moved up to my arm and he guided me out of the kitchen like he was an official leading me down the tunnel after I'd been red-carded. His parents followed us. I felt awkward under their stares, like Lucas Radebe in a tutu.

We got to the restaurant after what felt like the world's longest and least private walk of shame. Bob was on host duty.

'Hey, Rubes. Private booth?'

'Friend of yours?' Callum's mum sounded amused.

'Co-worker,' Bob said.

'Oh, how wonderful.'

And lunch continued in that same vein. Callum's dad asking questions of me and talking shop with his son while moving the bottle of wine away from his wife. Callum's mum making snide remarks about everything from my interests to my appearance while reaching across the table and topping up her glass. And the more she drank, the more snide the remarks became.

When it was over, I was so glad to see the back of them that I didn't even care that they 'whisked' Callum off to Paris for the weekend. It never occurred to me that the closed invitation was a direct snub against me. It did, however, occur to Yasmine, who made it clear I had an entire weekend of her scornful comments and hints to look forward to. Unprotected.

This is going to be fun.

CALLUM

Friday 27/10/2000 23:07
Subject: Paris

Help!

It's gotten worse. I thought it was bad enough that I had fucked up with the whole Yasmine thing. But no, I had to get my parents in on the fun.

I'm sure I've already said, but I spent last night sweating out nightmare after nightmare. Luckily, every time I woke up she was still there – in my arms – looking sexy and serene. She was – and is – perfect.

But when I woke up from my final nightmare, she was gone. My thoughts smothered me, like big fat props sitting on my head. Maybe I'd been dreaming the reconciliation. Maybe she had realised she couldn't be with me. Well, I couldn't stand for that, actually. I jumped out of bed, threw on some clothes and was about to run to her room when I ran into her, just outside my door. She had been out, clearly, but was coming back to me.

I was so relieved, I took her hand and held it like my life depended on it – sad, I know. I made sure she came with me to the kitchen. Which is when the real nightmare began.

My MOTHER was there, all exaggerated mannerisms and drunken theatrics. You know what she's like. Fabulous. I had gotten away with keeping her from attending the start of term and had stupidly thought that would be it until the end of term at the very least. Oh no.

She was so rude to poor Rube, even though I specifically introduced her as my girlfriend. Mum knew I wouldn't have introduced her if she wasn't important. But did she care? Of course not.

Rube doesn't have the expensive clothes and the highlighted hair and the manicured nails and the posh accent. So of course she is after my money. I mean, why else would anyone want to go out with me? Mum's faith in me is heart-warming, it really is.

The hilarious thing is I'm pretty sure Rube still has no idea who Mum is. It's adorable really – and refreshing. She did very well at lunch too. She held her own through the worst meal I've ever had to endure. She just smiled through Mum's vicious remarks and embarrassing drunken behaviour. It's fine if you're drunk at midday if you're a student – it's certainly not fine if you're a parent.

The worst part of it all is I never got to explain – I didn't get to apologise. I couldn't even manage a text from the car as Mum nattered on while we were driven off by some chauffeur I'd never met before. Which reminds me – I need to find my mobile phone. So, if I'm not answering, I just haven't found it yet.

So now I have a weekend of hell in Paris to look forward to. And then the rumours to contend with when I get back. Maybe uni was a bad idea after all. Maybe I shouldn't go back. Maybe I should just come and join you. Not sure how I'd explain that one to Mum ... Or Rube.

What should I do? Please help?

Cal

YASMINE

The atmosphere in the kitchen was even more toxic than usual, the stench of fresh and stale smoke and long-expired food having been overpowered by the undiluted chlorine with which the cleaner had decided, in her infinite wisdom, to flood the cheap lino. Juliette and I sat at opposite ends of the table, her with putrid grey smoke curling up from her lips and me with proverbial smoke rising up from my ears. Matt and Paul were resting against the window sill, staring at me in a judgemental manner not only unbecoming of them, but also incredibly ironic given the cigarette smouldering between Matt's fingers. Hypocrisy had swiftly instituted itself as the norm in our mismatched clique.

It was bad enough that I'd spent the entire night reciting the previous day's events in my head, wondering where I had gone wrong in my emotional display, pinpointing that exact moment that Callum had decided that an uncouth tomboy was better relationship material than me and why I hadn't noticed the seriousness of the situation. I now had to contend with the vox populi labelling me as a home wrecker (what an archaic, anti-feminist phrase), as if the kiss was solely instigated and executed by me. There were no words to describe the disillusionment I was feeling, and I knew I had to do something to redress the balance soon, or the tide of popularity would turn against me forever.

The impasse was broken by a most unexpected and illustrious arrival: that of my idol, the stylish and incredibly talented actress, Arabella Ellis (trailing her unkempt and unpolished husband). She looked even more magnificent in the flesh, with her high cheekbones and perfectly powdered skin, her exquisitely slim figure dressed in silk and matched with a pair of sculptured couture courts. The resemblance to her son was uncanny, and the only genetic contribution the father seemed to have made was to Callum's hair and to the moderate levels of daytime sobriety.

'Hello.' I smiled and stood up. 'I'm Yasmine. Apologies for the state of our premises. Are you looking for Callum?'

'Hello.' Arabella Ellis' smile was warm and inviting, though they could probably smell the rum back in the Caribbean. 'Yes we are. Is he here?'

'He has yet to join us this morning. I can take you to his room, if you like?'

Callum's father chortled loudly. 'I'm sure he'd appreciate that! No thanks. We'll wait.'

'Please, sit down.'

It was as if the blinds had been raised in the kitchen and sunlight had burnt away the darkness. Everyone suddenly forgot their misgivings and chipped into the conversation, although the spotlight was well and truly where it belonged, on Arabella Ellis. Her magic enchanted us all, until it was shattered by none other than Callum himself.

'Mum!' The surprise on his face brought the facial similarities to the fore.

'Darling.' She smothered him in her arms.

'What are you doing here?' he asked.

He didn't look happy to see his mother, although that was hardly surprising given she then proceeded to talk breathlessly at him for a full five minutes before he finally interrupted her with a line I can never forget.

'Mum, Dad, this is my girlfriend, Ruby.'

Silence ensued as his words echoed. I felt my lungs crying for air but my body refused to respond. Arabella Ellis was also none too pleased with her son's choice and made her feelings abundantly clear through her laser glare. Unfortunately, my pleasure was short-lived as Callum's father stepped forward and gallantly offered his hand to the pale Ruby.

'Hi, I'm Sam.'

'Sam Hayden-Quinn? As in the author?'

It was a wonderful moment, and all the accumulated pain of Callum's betrayal of me shed its agony into a luxurious spa of joy and righteousness. Ruby had destroyed all her chances of ever being accepted as good enough for Arabella Ellis' son by snubbing his mother's fame for that of her lesser known, if not dependably rich, husband. Suddenly everything was right with the world again and my chances of landing the man of my dreams, which had been beyond negligent just a few moments earlier, were now skyrocketing. Even Callum's rude rejection of his mother's kind offer to treat us all to lunch couldn't wipe gratified relish from my face. It would have been impossibly broad had I known then that Callum had opted to spend the weekend in Paris with his parents and without Ruby, who would instead have the immense pleasure of my unforgiving company until his return.

Astray

CALLUM

Sunday 29/10/2000 13:48
Subject: Re: RE: Paris

Paris. The City of Light. Proud owner of the Arc de Triomphe and the Eiffel Tower. Home to the hunchback of Notre Dame and the Mona Lisa. 'Casablanca's 'We'll always have Paris' Paris. Ah, Paris.

So why am I not happy to be here?

Mum would call it ridiculous and selfish. But what does she know? She's holed up in bed with her Dom Perignon and fuck the consequences.

So here I am. No books, no phone – still can't find it so I must have forgotten it in the panic – no Ruby and no more anonymity at uni. Totally screwed. What am I going to do?

Help me!

Cal

Wednesday 08/11/2000 15:26
Subject: More from Paris

Hello? Where are you? You've disappeared just as I need advice.

Days pass and I'm still here. Mum doesn't seem to have noticed and Dad's on one of his writing binges so he definitely hasn't. I'm sure they weren't always like this – or was I too young to realise before?

The real problem is I don't know if I can hack going back. I've spent so long looking forward to uni and now …

CAN I even go back? I was behind enough as it was and now I've missed lectures and seminars and training, it might not be possible.

But I've also missed Rube. A lot.

OK – don't laugh. But it's the way her hair smells. The way she looks down at her hands when she's saying something she thinks she shouldn't be. The way she jumps at her own shadow yet will eat you alive if you dare say anything against her precious Leeds. The way she smiles. The way she looks at me. The way …

I can't not go back, can I? Help me, please.

And stop laughing.

Cal

JULIETTE

Well, the boxing match I was so looking forward

to never materialised. Yasmine and I developed a magnetic repulsion in both corridor and kitchen. That did, unfortunately, mean I missed the crazy arrival of Callum's parents – none other than the immoral, contemporary author, Sam Hayden-Quinn, and his controversial wife, Arabella Ellis. Yes, them. That tells you all you really need to know about Callum.

But that's not really important to my story. Although it's the reason for strengthening Yasmine's resolve, which led to me and Ruby spending more time together, which in turn led to the reason I'm here today, so I guess in that sense it is. The thing is, from that moment on, it was all about Callum – Yasmine the conqueror was born. And boy did poor Ruby bear the brunt of this 'new' phenomenon.

You're confused, aren't you? I'm getting ahead of myself again. These so-called parents turned up and took their son away to Paris, supposedly for the weekend. And, of course, Callum decided his over-privileged existence was more important than actually attending class – he just disappeared. No calls, no texts, and no excuse – I mean almost everyone in our corridor has mobiles, even if he couldn't get through to Ruby. He didn't even send an email. As if whatever lavish hotel he was staying at didn't have computer and internet facilities! Entitled twa– I mean idio– um, man.

Anyway, poor Ruby got goaded and badgered and pushed around by Yasmine like … I don't know. But it was horrible to watch, especially since it was done in such a 'sweet and innocent' manner that nobody could say or do anything – most of the time I was the only witness. I mean, it was so *calculated*, so … *Yasmine* as it turns out. She always knew what she was doing, although I still don't know how she could be stupid enough to think she'd get away with it. 'It is joy to the just to do judgment: but destruction shall be to the workers of iniquity.' Proverbs had it spot on.

Hmm. I guess you can underestimate people. Yasmine definitely did – ha! Ruby's a non-confrontational sort. But when the floodgates broke … well, you had to be there, I guess. Although, unfortunately, none of us actually *were*. Middle of campus and *none* of us from our corridor or hockey or my course were there. But it happened – after a couple of weeks, Yasmine broke Ruby. Just not in the way she – or anybody else for that matter – was anticipating.

RUBY

I had expected a weekend of relentless nastiness from Yasmine. I had. After all, he had chosen me and that was bound to sting. What I hadn't expected was that it would last for more than the weekend. That it would go on forever. That purposeful smearing of ridiculously red lipstick and pursing her lips in my direction. Those allusions to the comfy seats in the Union. The snide references to Adonis abs being oiled. The descriptions of Parisian clubs. On and on and on.

And Callum just disappeared. I tried calling him a few times and got put straight through to answerphone.

I didn't leave any messages. *I hate leaving messages. They always make me sound even more of an idiot than I actually am.*

Emails were out too. I didn't know his personal one and I knew his uni one had been accidently blocked and 'was being sorted' when he left. Besides, I wasn't even sure you could access uni email off-campus. And, even if you could, I'm not sure Callum would know how.

I tried not to enter the kitchen unless there were at least two people in there, preferably three, so that they would be talking among themselves and wouldn't ask me where Callum was. Although they always did.

I started to count the days by major news or conversations that didn't involve Callum or Yasmine. It sort of helped. For a bit.

Monday was first foreign England manager day (some Swedish bloke called Sven-Goran Eriksson that used to manage Lazio).

Tuesday was Halloween.

Wednesday was my first goal of the season (against some poly).

Thursday was … rubbish. I was in a hurry and walked into the kitchen without checking whether the coast was clear. It wasn't.

'Hello, Ruby. Long time.'

Yasmine, I couldn't possibly hate you more, mate, so no need for that over-the-top, sugar-coated tone.

'We were just lunching. Did you know the Union sandwich place has the *best* French baguettes?'

'Hi.' *Matt, Paul, save me. Please?*

'Hiya, Ruby. How're you doing? Heard from Callum?'

'No.' *And that doesn't qualify as saving me.*

'I wonder where he could be?' Yasmine's drama extended to a theatrical search out of the window.

Bitch.

'Paris,' I said. *Have some of that, Yasmine.* And I left the kitchen.

But still no Callum, so the counting continued.

Friday was downpour day (there was widespread flooding round the country, according to the radio).

Saturday was cancelled game day (thanks to waterlogged pitches), but also involved lots of partying for Guy Fawkes' night at the Union. We started drinking at about four. The Social Sec had decided that, since we weren't playing football, we should at least be enjoying some team bonding. At about eight, the Union crowds started swarming but, as we had our tickets, we just stayed and continued our tower game with the bar staff. The aim was to build a pint glass tower with our empties so large that it would topple before they cleared the table. We failed. Repeatedly.

Unsurprisingly, we were all totally plastered by the time Jules and two of her hockey boys walked up to us.

'Juliette!' shouted Smithy, classily spitting out some snakebite as she did so.

'Hey, girls. What's going on?'

'We're drinking.' *That was hard. I'm slurring, aren't I? Ah well, you probably can't tell over the music anyway.*

'We have some catching up to do, it seems.'

Twinkle's eyes are twinkling. Oh dear. So maybe I am a little drunk.

'Indeed we do.' Jules sat between me and Smithy. 'What are we playing?'

❯

The next day was actually Guy Fawkes', although I spent almost all of it in bed. But there was still no sign of Callum, so cue more counting.

Monday was the start of reading week.

Tuesday was some foiled diamond theft at the Millennium Dome that the police were looking at in connection to the Kent Kleptomaniac. (OK, so I'm stretching.)

Wednesday was Leeds against Milan at the San Siro. (One all.)

Thursday was the cracking UEFA Cup Liverpool game. (2-3 away.)

And then came Friday. Friday was where it all went wrong. As if it wasn't already.

I went into the campus bookshop to pick up a new fiction or sport book to while away the long, lonely stretches of time. Staying away from the kitchen had its benefits, but the side-effects were awful.

I had barely set foot inside when I felt Yasmine's breath on the back of my neck like some evil defender haunting me. *I should've remembered she's got the Friday shifts at the bookshop.*

'Ruby, hi! I didn't know you read. The Sam Hayden-

Quinn section is over here.'

'Fuck off.' *Did I just say that out loud? It felt good.*

'Excuuuuse me?'

'You heard me, mate,' I muttered. *Not feeling so brave any more. Please don't push it. People are looking.*

'I'm just trying to be helpful and you *swear* at me?'

Don't react, Ruby, mate. She's not worth it.

'Helpful?' *Shut up, Ruby. Shut up.*

'Yeah, helpful, darling. That's my *job* here in the bookshop.'

Right! 'So I suppose you snogging Callum was you being helpful too?'

'That wasn't in the bookstore and, darling, you really need to get over that.' Her lips stretched into a dirty smile.

Back down, Ruby, people are watching. 'And you really need to get over Callum.'

She laughed. That was the final straw.

'He's awesome in bed, you know. Oh no, wait, you don't.' *OK, she's stopped laughing. You can stop now.* 'You'll never know.' *Stop it, Ruby, mate. Stop!*

I'm normally good at evading. I'm a striker – I have to evade or I get clobbered on the field. But on the pitch, you expect it. You see it coming. I didn't. Until it was too late.

Her hand was already swinging in to slap me and was inches from my face when I moved. The wrong way. My face slammed into a bookshelf and I fell into a display. Smashed sidelong into the table, books, and plastic. I heard a crack.

'Yasmine! What are you doing?' I heard someone yell.

Bile dribbled up from my stomach and assaulted my throat. My wrist was on fire.

YASMINE

The rain was relentless, with droplets as thick as snowflakes, and the mood closely reflected that of the weather, with Callum's so-called disappearance the sole topic of conversation in the dull, now undoubtedly winter, days. The poor man needed to get away from all the fuss and clear his head for a few days and, given the neediness of his girlfriend (I still couldn't believe he had referred to her in such a manner), it was hardly a surprise. Ruby wallowed in a grief so unbearable, it was more contagious than the freshers' flu our halls had mysteriously avoided.

I, for my part, did my best to lighten the mood. I cracked jokes, of varying degrees of wit, at any and all opportunities, and most of my fellow hall residents seemed to approve. Ruby, of course, was so overcome with a sense of bereavement for her short-lived relationship that she failed to see the levity and comedy in my remarks, but I could hardly be held responsible for her distinct lack of a sense of humour.

The days rolled on and it became increasingly obvious that Callum may not be returning. No-one had been able to get in touch with him and Ruby was unwilling to impart any information on the subject, as if we would use said knowledge to our advantage in some corrupt manner. By the time reading week arrived, on Bonfire Night, Ruby looked so much like a recently salvaged sixteenth century shipwreck that even I felt sorry for her.

The boys continued to dote on her, spending evenings in the Union 'watching football' and some other similar euphemisms used to cover the fact that they wanted to get her drunk and make her forget about Callum. Matt, especially, had become very protective, and his ulterior motives were plain for all to see, although Ruby remained staunchly loyal to the memory of what we all assumed to be her ex-lover.

Then, on the Friday of reading week, Ruby decided that I deserved to be punished heavily for my 'crimes' against her, despite the fact that most of the wrongs I had committed were in direct response to the wrongs against me. No matter.

I was working my usual shift at the campus bookshop when Ruby tripped in, saw me, and then proceeded to crudely turn her back on me and pretend to scour the shelves for fiction.

'The Sam Hayden-Quinn section is over here,' I joked.

'Fuck off!' She spat the words at me.

'I'm just trying to be helpful,' I defended myself, in a state of semi-shock.

'Helpful?' She raised her voice to a shriek, and successfully managed to get a number of heads turning. 'And you snogging Callum was being helpful too, I suppose?'

'You really need to get over that,' I said, trying to diffuse the situation.

'And you really need to get over Callum.'

I couldn't help but snicker at the words she should be repeating to herself in front of a full-length mirror.

She whipped me with 'He's awesome in bed, you know. Oh no, wait, you wouldn't. You'll never know.'

I'm very rarely an impulsive person. I've made more than my fair share of mistakes in my life, but they've always been either forced upon me or thought through, if sometimes erroneously, as in the recent case of trying to get Juliette evicted. Unfortunately, Ruby had pushed that hallowed red button that everyone has somewhere, sometime, about something. I slapped her.

The disastrous thing, and I can still see the scene unfold if I close my eyes, was that she moved out of the way with a lot of force, so that she slammed into the bookshelf with what appeared to be her forehead and then proceeded to crash onto the display below it at the wrong angle. The table split in half, like a ravine enveloping Ruby's form, the books took flight, and the plastic display label splintered. All this was accompanied by a stomach-churning crack directly correlated to Ruby's unnaturally contorted arm. I still feel sick at the memory, and no amount of meditation can alleviate that.

'Yasmine! What are you doing?' my supervisor shouted.

I knew from his tone that I was being blamed for the accident and that I was probably going to lose my cosy job but, at that exact moment, I didn't care and quickly dropped to my knees beside the patient.

'Quick! Call an ambulance! I think she's broken her arm.'

Consequences

RUBY

My arm had been sawn off without anaesthetic. That's what it felt like. *But I can handle this. I can handle pain. It's the embarrassment I can't handle.*

I was stuck in the broken display table. Wedged in the hole I'd made with nothing but my weight. Books everywhere. Splinters in my face, my side, my ribs. And people staring. At me.

I tried to detach myself from the wreckage, but just ended up looking like an upside-down dung beetle. My cheeks were burning with shame, and then the tears came. I couldn't help it. But now everyone was staring. *This is the worst day ever.*

Yasmine was shouting for an ambulance, waving her arms theatrically and acting like my best friend. *Like it isn't her fault I'm in this position. Bitch.*

'Oh my god, just look at your arm,' she said.

I looked. Bad idea. The bile that had been burning my throat made its escape. I threw up on myself. *How humiliating. I just want to die.*

St John's Ambulance came and put me out of my misery.

●

The trauma was over but I'd never live it down. I'd forever be the girl that Fosbury Flopped onto the bookshop display table then cried pathetically and vomited green slime all over herself.

So I was definitely *not* looking forward to going back to halls.

I spent most of the bus ride back thinking about what I would do. *Assuming for a moment that I actually show my face in public again, there's still the problem of the cast. No more football till next term. If I'm lucky. Yeah, right. Realistically, my season's over. Which means my time at the football club is up unless I make it to every social and remind them who I am so that if – no, think positively, when – I recover, I can play for them again. I have to make a huge effort to not get sidelined. And even then, what are my chances? Pretty crap.*

What will my life be like without football? Shit is what. Various scenarios pecked at me throughout the very long journey. The bus driver must have taken the trans-continental route.

As soon as we got to campus, I jumped off and ran. *The less time for people to stare at Vomit Girl or Flying, Crying Bird or whatever they're calling me, the better.*

I sped to my room. Then to the showers with a plastic bag to tie over the cast. Then back to my room. I couldn't risk seeing anyone. I had to stay hidden. *No such luck.*

No sooner had I returned to my sanctuary, someone

was knocking on it. *Go away.*

'Ruby?' Juliette's voice was soft. 'I heard what happened. Figured you could do with a ciggie.'

'No thanks, mate.' *I can't think of anything worse than smoke scraping my throat raw right now.*

'Brought you a sandwich and milkshake too.'

Hmmm, maybe.

I unlocked the door then stepped back without opening it. She must have heard me, though, because she pushed it open.

'Is it bad? Twinkle said his friend was there who said it looked bloody awful. His words, obviously.'

Oh god. People who know people who know me were there. Breathe, Ruby, mate. Breathe.

She stared at me. 'She got you gooood. Or bad. Or whatever the phrase is. Eat. Drink. Smoke.'

Sounds good in that order. I obeyed.

Jules just sat on my desk and looked out the window. She kept smoking and, occasionally, glanced across at me.

'Are you OK? Want to talk about it? Or shall I go?'

Don't go. At least not till I've scabbed another fag.

'Please stay.' *Really. I mean it.*

She smiled and tossed the white and gold packet of Davidoff Lights at me. 'Have another. Now, what happened?'

I told her. She nodded, glared, and growled appropriately. When I was done, she stood up.

'Erm, the reason I came here was to tell you that I'm sorry I haven't been more supportive. Callum is a total prick.' She said the last word like she was in pain.

She swore! It would have been hilarious if the circumstances had been different.

'He's not but thanks …'

She interrupted me. 'He's definitely a prick. A massive one. But he is back. In his room, I mean. I don't think he knows about the … the situation.'

He's back? Back?

I jumped off the bed and started for his room.

'Ruby, wait!' yelled Jules. 'You're still in your …'

She stopped yelling. I stopped moving.

Callum was leaning on his doorframe chatting with none other than *her*. I felt my A&E Twix resurface and ran back into my room.

Which, it transpired, was a good thing, as I was still in my towel. *Genius.*

My phone rang as I rushed in, flustering me more. I picked it up without meaning to. It was Smithy, who'd heard about the fall and was making sure I was alive. And that I'd be making it to the social tomorrow night. It was the F-party and we were all to go as fallen angels. *More dressing up. Great. But I have to go now. I have to make sure I keep my place on the team.*

'Hey, gorgeous,' said a voice in my exposed ear.

I jumped. 'Callum!' *Don't sneak up on me.*

'Long time. Sorry I disappeared.'

I hung up on Smithy and turned to look at him. 'Where *were* you? And don't say Paris.' *Tone it down, Ruby, mate. You sound like a damsel in distress. It's not cool.*

'Are you OK? Your face! And what the hell happened to your arm?'

I looked down and anger I didn't know I had jumped out my mouth. 'Yasmine broke it for me. Didn't she enlighten you in your cosy chat just now?'

'What? What happened?'

Don't come so close. I can't think. I can't be angry. I can't …

He kissed me. Gently. His lips were cracked and flaky but warm. *So warm.* I kissed him back and let his hands run down my back. My towel dropped and the moment was gone: I felt very exposed. *What do I really know about this bloke?*

He pulled back. 'You OK?'

I nodded and dressed hastily, pulling on whatever was nearest. Fast. Once again I failed, as my cast wouldn't fit through my blue top's sleeve. *Baggy T-shirt it is.*

Callum sat on my bed and patted the space next to him. I obeyed. It felt like I'd been doing that a lot lately.

'I'd really like us to go out to dinner together. You know, talk.'

I'm confused.

'Dinner or talk?'

He smiled, I melted.

'Both. Just spend some time together. I've missed you.'

Really? 'I've missed you too.' *A lot.*

'Tomorrow then? It's a date.'

Nooooo. 'I can't tomorrow. I've got a football social.'

'Well, blow them off.'

I wish I could, I really do. 'I can't.'

'Ruby, I haven't seen you in ages. Please? You see those girls all the time.' His eyes creased at the corners and his mouth was so straight it was parallel to the floor.

'I can't.' I felt the Twix again. 'Lunch?'

'Tomorrow's really important to me.'

'Tomorrow lunch?' *This is torture.*

He shook his head. 'Dinner.'

He leaned forward and kissed me again. His decision was final, it seemed. I, on the other hand, was both undecided and fucked either way. The bleakness that hadn't visited since I'd left school was back.

JULIETTE

I heard it from Twinkle who'd heard it from some guy on his course who had remembered seeing them together at the Union so, well, word gets around pretty quickly on campus and – before I knew it – there were rumours that some blonde librarian had bludgeoned a fresher to death. Funny how there's rarely ever smoke without fire though, don't you think?

Well, anyway, Ruby survived – although scarred forever, as all of Yasmine's victims seem to be. She looked terrible, with her arm in a cast and her face and body all scratched up like she'd been glassed. I got to speak to her just as she got back, standing there shivering in her towel as she struggled to get her clothes out of the drawers one-handed. No, don't look at me like that – you've got it all wrong. Ruby's the facilitator, not the object. She was the reason I found … I'm getting ahead of myself again. I want to tell you the story in order – so that maybe, just maybe, you'll understand.

So, Callum returned. Ha! All pomp and grandeur and indecisiveness. And, once again, it all went wrong for Ruby.

Which is unfortunate, of course – and I shouldn't revel in other people's misfortunes – but this is the part of the story where it all started to go right for me. Yeah, fine, not in your opinion. But 'judge not, that ye be not judged' – Matthew 7:1. You taught me that much and you taught it well.

Now let me explain.

YASMINE

Callum couldn't keep away, drawn to our own private version of Astavakrasana, knotted and entangled, whether we knew it or not. I'd assumed he knew all about the whole Ruby melodrama, so when he waved me over to his room with smiles and welcoming embrace, I took it as a sign that all had been forgiven. He did callously brush me aside to follow and no doubt sweep little miss righteous off her feet, but I was content in the knowledge that sexual relations would be minimal with Ruby's battered body, cast arm, and cheap purse full of potent painkillers. A small consolation, but a consolation nonetheless.

I'd played my role as Ruby's carer admirably, exceeding any possible expectations of duty to a girl whose actions had, ultimately, cost me my job. In fact, her performance had had far more pervasive and damaging implications for my cash-flow and, consequently, my lifestyle. Not only was I fired from the bookstore over the (admittedly show-stopping) accident, but, as a result of the stifling closeness of the community, nobody else was willing to hire me. It appeared that I had been blacklisted from any and all service jobs available within a commutable radius of campus and there was absolutely nothing I could do to reverse my fortunes.

Thankfully, my fellow hall residents were gracious and understanding of both my predicament and my lack of blame for the horrific bookshop incident. This was especially true of Sarah, whose strategic position as unofficial 'head' of our congregation was invaluable for tipping the balance of hall sentiment in my favour.

The problem of bankruptcy remained, however, as the funds supplied by my parents were minimal and simply enough to cover basic essentials, and so I decided to embark on a journey of reduced food intake while I continued my search for jobs. This plan had the benefit of both reducing my monetary outflow and ensuring that I dropped the extra pounds that the excessive, yet unavoidable, university drinking culture had bestowed on me.

Given the circumstances of my plight, I thought it fair to continue my pursuit of Callum, my knight in rich, sparkling armour, who would soon be rid of his snivelling, pretentious vagrant of a girlfriend if I got my way. And, back then, I always got my way.

CALLUM

Saturday 11/11/2000 11:13
Subject: Happy Birthday

Happy Birthday! Wish I could be there, celebrating with you, but stuck in rainy England instead.

Yes – I'm back! Thanks for the advice – of course you were right. Everyone's happy I've returned and it all seems so stupid now.

I got back yesterday – back to the drinking, back to the studying and back to Ruby.

I was – and still am – happy to be back. But it's odd.

I'd just dumped my stuff and was about to go find Ruby when Yasmine cornered me. She was making small-talk, I wasn't listening.

That's when I saw Ruby. She ran out of her room in a black towel with her hair dripping down her chest. I wanted to rip that towel off then and there so I ran off after her, but she turned and fled back into her room. I just re-read that and thought I'd point out that I didn't mean to sound like a sexual predator, obviously. I know you know what I mean. I just followed her – Ruby, obviously – pushing past a glaring Juliette. What is that girl's problem anyway?

Ruby was on the phone, her back to me. I did what boyfriends are supposed to do. I put my arms round her waist and whispered in her ear. She jumped.

The reception wasn't as warm as I'd imagined, actually. She asked me where I'd been with some spirited fire – never seen THAT side of her – and, apparently, Paris was not a good enough answer.

I wasn't up for an argument, even less so when I noticed the marks on her body. You should've seen her! Her arm was in a cast, the one side of her face was bruised, she had scratches on her shoulder and she looked a right mess.

I asked her what the hell had happened and she just said 'Yasmine', but didn't elaborate. I still don't know what it was about – I'm very embarrassed, don't worry, and I will find out – but my body just took over – I wanted her so badly. She kissed me back – it was amazing, actually.

Afterwards, in her bed, I realised I cared more for her than I'd thought. I know, I know – you told me and I didn't listen. But you're right and I do. So I've decided to celebrate your birthday with her this year, since I can't spend it with you. Rube and I will go out to dinner and I'm going to tell her all about you – I can trust her.

I'll let you know how it goes. It's going to be amazing, it really is.

Cal

Sobriety

RUBY

It was all so bleak and getting worse. I'm sure Soul Asylum playing in the background didn't help. *I'm slowly but surely losing it all and I don't know how to get it back. Callum, football, friends. I'm pretty sure I had them, once. But now …*

Breathe, Ruby, mate. Breathe.

I sat on my bed, my options laid out on my duvet. *Callum or football? Football or Callum?* I shouldn't have had to choose. But, in the end, Callum had cheated on me and run off. Football meant a lot to me and I didn't want to get sidelined.

He didn't take it well. 'But Ruby pleeeeease.'

'I can't, I'm sorry.'

He shook his head and pursed his lips. He was silent after that. It was as if I'd stabbed him in the back. And as if he hadn't done that to me. *Twice.*

But, since I'd made my decision, he'd been different. Less caring, more distant. I felt like a fan sat in the gods more than a member of his team.

›

I had thought making weekly socials was enough. I was wrong. There was the issue of unplanned socials, and the football girls kept forgetting about me.

I bumped into them at the Union. 'Hey, Ruby, we just came down for a drink after the match.'

But you didn't invite me to join you or anything.

The next time it was 'Hi, Ruby, didn't someone tell you about the social? We're watching the Italy game. Want to join?'

Yes, please. That's why I'm here, mate. But why didn't you invite me earlier? Did you forget? Or are you just being polite now?

Then 'We didn't see you at the house party yesterday. Where were you?'

Not invited. Unsurprising really. But at least I get to watch the Leeds game with you all tonight. We can beat Real, I know we can.

And so on.

To top it all off, halls weren't that fun anymore. Even though Christmas was around the corner. There were events and a hall Christmas feast and all that. But there was no help or sympathy. People kept forgetting I was disabled.

'Sorry, mate, I thought you had it,' said Paul as the kitchen door closed on me.

Sorry? My hand's got a beer bottle in it. I can't hold the door with it too! Are you taking the piss? Did you do it on purpose? Or am I just being seriously paranoid?

'Oops,' said Matt as the tray he passed me tipped and crashed to the floor.

Cheers, mate. I may have been a waitress but I'm obviously not anymore. I'm one-handed. And a tray that big needs two hands. You're so bloody useless, Ruby, mate. And they all hate you.

'Why did you leave that there?' asked Yasmine, pointing to the wall of empty Becks bottles shielding my plate.

Because I've got a fork in my hand and am trying to eat. Do you remember how to do that?

But I couldn't say what I wanted to say to her face. Everyone was concerned about Yasmine's turn at anorexia. She'd lost half a stone in a month. She looked thin, but it was self-inflicted. Unfortunately, everything was always about *her*.

Even Juliette disappeared. Earlier in the term, she had turned up to a few football socials with her hockey mates, where she'd been the life and soul. But lately I hadn't seen her at all. Except for at the Christmas feast. She was probably avoiding me.

At least term was almost over. Then there would only be Callum to worry about. *Will we see each other over the break? Will we still be together next year? Or are we just waiting for the final whistle at the end of term?*

It was all so bleak and getting worse. And then that awful thing with Matt happened.

YASMINE

As Christmas break loomed, life was as agreeable as ever, with no sign of the fatal events still to unfold.

The diet was paying off in that my bank balance was healthier, I had reverted to pre-university weight, felt fresh and potent, and was receiving more compliments than ever. Callum and I had eased into spending some quality time together between lectures, in defiance of his continuing infatuation with Ruby. Upsettingly, he still referred to her as his girlfriend, despite the increasing void between them. Ruby had become introverted and withdrawn, spending very little time outside of lectures in our company or anyone else's.

I stood by Callum throughout this period, providing the support that Ruby should have been, and knowing that, at length, he would recognise the ideal relationship we shared. Theirs seemed to centre around two rather tenuous and unimportant things: their mutual love of sport in general and football in particular, and Ruby's status as Callum's personal tutor in all things academic (and, unfortunately, boudoir). His lack of recognition of the fact that on all other grounds, be it background, schooling, finance, film, books, or academic interests (no matter how much she pretended), their passions were as divergent as the spectrum allowed, was infuriating.

In the wider context of our university existence, external events were building and soon to concuss our party. Catherine Zeta-Jones' marriage to Michael Douglas and Judith Keppel's conquering of the top prize on *Who Wants to be a Millionaire* were trumped in newspaper articles by coverage of the scandal which suddenly embroiled the little town adjacent to our campus. The town's oversaturation with police and reporters, when items linked to the Kent Kleptomaniac were discovered, proved disastrous on multiple fronts.

However, always oblivious to the real issues at stake, it was the indirect effect that had the general student population sweating and exploring darker and far more expensive avenues than ever before. In short, there was an illegal drugs drought, brought about by the increased police and investigative presence in the greater campus area. That, it appears, was what was on everyone's mind as the term bumped unhappily toward its unsavoury conclusion with an unfortunate incident involving our very own Matt and Juliette.

CALLUM

Sunday 12/11/2000 02:33
Subject: Happy birthday again

Yeah, so that was an anti-climax of the worst type, actually. Hope your birthday panned out better than my attempt to celebrate it.

Rube's decided to blow me off for some football social. That's right – here I was ready to spill all and she makes a choice like that – I'm gutted.

So, instead, I celebrated drinking in the kitchen with Yasmine and the boys. Which wasn't much of a celebration because I couldn't tell them what I was celebrating – not without raising questions about you. And I don't think now's the right time – they're still digesting the parents' behaviour from earlier this term. Argh!

Am I even making sense?

Anyway, happy birthday again – I've had a few Stellas for you.

Cal

Thursday 16/11/2000 11:42
Subject: Re: RE: Happy birthday again

Hello!

Thanks for the email. Glad you're having an awesome time out there – don't think I'm not jealous.

I'm OK, although Rube blew me off again yesterday. She chose to watch the Italy game with the football girls. (See? I've been getting into football – you're right, it's infectious.) She said it was important. I watched her from our table in the Union – all she did was drink and watch the screen. She didn't speak to them once! How can snubbing us to watch a game with people you don't interact with be important?

Maybe I'm reading a little too much into this? She's definitely not happy – she's taken her arm break as a sign of eternal doom and damnation and is acting accordingly. Maybe her and Mum have more in common than they like to think.

Girls, eh? Hope you're having better luck where you are.

Cal

Thursday 30/11/2000 11:29
Subject: Re: RE: Re: RE: Happy birthday again

Hello.

Not forgotten about you – just nothing's been happening. Same old assignment woes, same old Rube issues.

She's still lovely, don't get me wrong. It's just that she's so UNHAPPY all the time. Take last week. Leeds lost 2-0 to Real Madrid and she acted like it was the end of the world. Come on! I get fandom, I do. Even when it comes to football. But realism never hurt anyone. Having said that, I hope they win away at Lazio next week, I really do.

Then there's Yasmine – that girl is EVERYWHERE. It almost feels like I can't even go to the gents without having her pop along. It's disconcerting. And it's really not helping matters with Rube.

On a happier note, my academic – life? sphere? what's the word I'm looking for? – is improving. Rube's help's been invaluable and even the sarkiest of my tutors has sat up and taken notice.

Then there's the Christmas meal to look forward to next week, although I'm not as excited as I was. And then it's the holidays. Off to some chalet in Switzerland this year. In the meantime, I guess I'm going to have to get Rube a Christmas present. Any ideas?

Thanks,

Cal

Friday 08/12/2000 10:48
Subject: Crazy stuff

Hello.

It's utterly crazy here, actually. Matt's in hospital and Juliette's blaming herself. It's pretty awful.

It all happened yesterday. Apparently the mass expulsion was not a good enough excuse to quit smoking. Who knew? They're all such idiots. Juliette and Matt sourced some marijuana from somewhere or someone. I'm quite sketchy on the details.

First I knew about it was Juliette running into the kitchen with ruby-red eyes – yes, yes, I know, one track mind! – and all teary. Matt had been rushed to hospital – apparently the marijuana they smoked was too strong or laced with something – I didn't quite understand through the hysteria. All I got was that Matt passed out, Juliette freaked, called the first aiders and Matt was rushed to hospital.

We still don't know if he's going to be OK – and we all leave for home tomorrow.

Really puts things into perspective. Be careful out there. Please.

Cal

JULIETTE

It's not actually that simple, of course. This is real life – there's no obvious magical pivot point where it all goes right. But it started to. How? Well, Ruby and Callum's relationship started to go from rocky to shipwrecked. I never got what she saw in him anyway – he's as bad as his parents. That whole family is overcrowded with dirty little secrets.

Sorry, I'm getting ahead of myself again. Ruby was getting more and more depressed. I obviously hadn't realised because if I had, I would have done something about it sooner. The whole broken arm thing had really gotten to her. She felt lost, alone, drifting – I don't know, something like that – and I was too focused on my own problems to see it. Some friend!

It's funny, looking back. Gives you perspective. Like how she did her best to stay in the loop with the football girls. She made it to their socials and even blew Callum off a couple of times. Ha! It was her way of getting away from her problems for a while, I suppose. And it was my path to discovery. The more she hurt, the more she forced herself to make the effort. The more she made the effort, the more time I got to spend with her, which in turn laid the foundations for life as I'm living it now. I really can't thank her enough.

But, as always, there were bumps along the way. For me, I mean. I, ahem, was smoking something heavier than tobacco every so often, although it was harder and harder to come by. You see, the whole Kent Kleptomaniac fiasco had blown up again – this time in our back garden – and local weed prices had skyrocketed as a result.

The worst issue – the classic issue – was that any

reputable dealers – and by that I mean students doing it on the side – stopped dealing. So I had to source my weed from some individual of questionable conduct. It was that or none at all and, well, pleasure trumped sensibility.

Yes, I know. 'Know ye not that your body is the temple of the Holy Ghost which is in you, which ye have of God, and ye are not your own?' Ha! Corinthians said it first. But they were right, if for the wrong reasons. Please don't look at me like that – the point of the story is it ended badly.

Anyway, I met Matt on his way back from lectures and asked him if he fancied a smoke. I remember how he hugged me – he put his arm around my shoulders and steered me in the direction of the lake. It's a perfect smoking corner – there's a bench under a tree surrounded by bushes, the spot is sheltered from both wind and rain, and it's secluded so it's fairly well-hidden from prying eyes. Well, at least it used to be before *this* happened.

Anyway, we sparked up and smoked and talked. He became more and more quiet which – let's be honest – is not unusual under the circumstances. Contemplation and inner peace. Not a surprise it's such a staple with pseudo-intellectuals. And actual intellectuals, of course.

But, well, he suddenly passed out on me – pulled a proper whitey. It was scary – he just slumped sideways onto the grass and I couldn't hear him breathing. I checked for a pulse and felt nothing – nothing at all. I ran to the Union, grabbed a first aider and got them to check him. Thankfully he was alive – I'm obviously useless at taking pulses – but the prognosis was unknown.

I cried and yelled and howled and even gave the ambulance people my remaining weed. I was *so* out of it. And so *scared*. The first-aider checked me as well, of course, but I'd smoked less and I clearly have good, strong smoker's lungs. That's a joke – you're supposed to laugh. Never mind.

I just ran back to our corridor and into the first pair of arms that would take me. That's how I ended up being consoled by the poster-boy, Callum. The shame! But I would have taken Yasmine at that point, I really would've.

It was the worst possible ending to term – Matt was in hospital, we had no idea if he was OK, and it was all my fault. Would he make it? And what would happen if he didn't?

Term 2:

JANUARY TO MARCH 2001

Revelations

YASMINE

Christmas break had been and gone, thankfully without the heavily feared tragic climax, and we had returned to the hallowed rooms ready to start the year afresh. The germs and fungi had been busy reproducing in our absence, and the carpet had acquired a different tinge of grey, more mossy in texture, and with a chlorine-and-vomit-infused aroma. My homecoming was, inevitably, a both nervous and unhappy affair, but the sight of my emerald-eyed Callum did wonders to lift the spirits. His skiers' tan, which makes most individuals look like stuffed badgers, gave his face a deeper symmetry and refinement that any designer seeking a model would be in awe of.

'Hi,' he whispered, smiling.

I returned the favour with my most engaging and approving version. 'Good Christmas? Skiing clearly suits you. Where did you go again?'

He didn't respond initially, as we caught each other's eye in a manner not conducive to conversation. But, in line with the convention to date, we were rudely interrupted by Ruby, who walked out of the bathrooms and began her slow, kyphotic trawl in our direction.

'They're still together,' said a phantom in my ear, sending a shockwave of chilled breath down each vertebra of my back. 'Tighter than ever. Rumour has it they've been sharing secrets. They've certainly been holding hands and snogging constantly. Love is definitely back in the air.'

Sensing the start of a battle, I turned with what I was confident was an apathetic but measured demeanour, and faced my adversary.

JULIETTE

We already knew what had happened when we got back. It's hardly difficult these days is it? It's the era of mobile phones and email after all. I mean, you can reach someone, anyone, so easily – same day more often than not. Life is no longer static. How the world has changed since the New Testament was first scribed!

Where was I? Oh yes, we all knew by then. Well, those of us that cared I suppose – and I'm not including Yasmine in that particular subset. Her first thoughts and actions on her return revolved around throwing herself at Callum. She didn't even ask about Matt. So – and I admit it was totally un-Christian of me – I was unnecessarily straight about her chances with her prey at the time. She deserved it.

Yes, Matt. It was all my fault, of course, and I had spent a few days after the end of term ringing him and – yes – praying. It had taken a while, but my phone had finally rung from his number. I remember staring at it, flashing on the cover of '*The Maltese Falcon*' as that stupid Nokia ringtone played and played. I was terrified of answering. What if it was his parents? What if he hadn't made it? I finally muttered a prayer and answered.

'Hiya,' was all he said.

I practically screamed into my mobile, asking him if he was alright, asking him where he was.

He was fine he said. Embarrassed about the whole thing but, hey, who can predict dodgy reactions? He seemed calmer than I would've been.

At least he was home. In a bit of trouble with his parents – but that's to be expected, right? I was so relieved I could have kissed Yasmine. No, please don't look at me like that. It was a figure of speech. I – never mind. I wouldn't worry yourself too much, though, because by the time we had returned to our corridor for the start of the second term, the urge to make up with Yasmine had well and truly gone.

Maybe things would've turned out differently if I had actually made up with her then? Maybe if I had never ... Unfortunately, it's too late now. Or fortunately? It's all a matter of perspective, isn't it? That was definitely the case back in our corridor.

Callum and Ruby had evidently not seen each other over the holidays which I saw ... I saw it as a sign of things to come. Yes, even then. But they – they saw it differently. It was like it had galvanised them in some strange way. Suddenly they were co-conspirators – you know, hushed tones and knowing looks. They'd clearly confided in each other and somehow it had brought them closer together. At the time, it was lovely to see. In retrospect, it could've been the spanner in the story. Really mixing my metaphors – sorry. The point is it was a passing moment of weakness – for all of us.

But luckily – I can say that now! – one could always count on Yasmine to interfere. And interfere she did.

CALLUM

Sunday 09/01/2001 14:31
Subject: Re: Bikinis beat all-in-ones any day

Hello.

I'm back! I have to admit it feels pretty good being here. It's nice to see everyone again. And the girls seem to have got fitter over Christmas. I wish I could send you photos – remind me to show you some next time I see you.

Or if you visit (I'm dreaming now) you can meet them. That'll have the added bonus of you giving me your opinion on the Yasmine versus Juliette thing. There's something odd going on. I don't understand. Maybe they're repressing their love for each other or something. Mmm, now there's a thought. Wow – definitely a thought!

But one story at a time. First – Matt. He's looking like he never died and he's up for it more than ever. Although I did notice there was no crate of beer on arrival this term – maybe his parents focused on the negatives. He's fine –that's the important thing.

And then there's Rube. Ah, Rube! She's better than ever. I was scared – I admit it. We had been drifting in the run-up to Christmas, and I didn't know what to expect this term. But fear not – all is well in Cal's love-life once more. You're not the only one getting lucky!

It was so easy, even though we'd hardly spoken at all over the hols. As soon as I got back, I just strode into her room and kissed her. She made some totally adorable comment about my tan – she didn't realise you could get one skiing! – and then she kissed me back. Score! What had I been worrying about?

I realised how much I'd missed her. And sex. I'd definitely missed sex. Chalet girls aren't all they're cracked up to be as you know. Especially the ones Mum hires. (Looking not touching – obviously – in case you get the wrong idea.)

Later, when we were lying in bed, we had a rather intense conversation. It's scary opening up to people, isn't it?

It didn't start that way. We were talking about football, actually. Not your usual pillow talk, but she is my number one for a reason, right? But the conversation turned a little more personal. Did you know she'd once been to trials for a 'top league club' – she didn't use the word Premiership or give me a name – when she was little? She'd made it through until they'd realised she was a girl. Said being outed was the most embarrassing thing that had ever happened to her – she'd almost written off football for life. But her dad and brother had been very supportive so …

I kinda felt it was the right time. I told her the whole story. You know I'd been thinking about it over Christmas. I felt that something had been getting between us by the end of last term. And I knew it was us. You and me. I HAD to tell her. For my sake, for her sake, even for yours in a way.

I know I can trust her. She's not like the others. She's quiet and doesn't really care about tabloids and such.

So I did it. I just looked directly at her and said, 'I need to tell you something.' And I did. I told her everything: about you, about school, about Mum.

God help us all if any of it gets out.

On that note, hope you're having a great time and don't worry about anything.

Cal

RUBY

I was scared. I was on my own. I was unsure of what to do.

I was back.

Dad had helped me unload my stuff quickly and then left. I didn't want to go to the kitchen, so I just sat on the bed and stared at the duvet while '*Dookie*' played in the background. *What am I going to do?*

There was a knock on the door and it swung open. A

figure danced in and the door shut behind them.

'Hi. How was your Christmas break?' asked Jules. She continued her little Brazilian goal-scoring celebration dance thing in the centre of the room. 'Good?'

'Fine, yeah,' I said. 'Yours, mate?'

'"Let us now go even unto Bethlehem, and see this thing which is come to pass …"'

'Huh?' *Is she singing the bible at me?*

'Mummy being her usual stifling self.'

'Ah.'

'How are you? How's Callum, dare I ask?'

Oh god. 'Fine, fine.'

'Fine?' She lifted her eyebrow cheekily. Then she took out her pack of Davidoff Lights and shook it at me. 'Fine enough to refuse one of these?'

I sniggered. I leant over to take one when there was a knock on the door. I stopped.

'Come in?'

It was him. *He's got an amazing tan. Really brings out the colour of his eyes. But I thought he'd been in Switzerland? What else has he missed out his emails?*

'Helloooo. Oh hi, Juliette. How was your holiday?'

'Lovely.' She smiled, winked at me, and ran out. 'I'll see you both later.'

'Hi.' *Been a while.*

He sat down next to me. Kissed me. I inhaled, remembering his smell. I'd missed him. I had received a few emails over Christmas and they had been, scarily enough, signed 'love and stuff, Cal'. But there was nothing of note in them (heh!). And no calls.

'How are you? I've missed you so much.' He put his lips to mine again.

It felt good. I'd *really* missed him. He ran his hands through my hair and we took off our clothes. It was like we'd never left.

❯

We lay in bed, awake.

'I've really needed to tell you something for a while. I just … haven't been able to.'

He's cheated on me again. I knew it. Or he wants to break up?

'Yeah?'

'It's hard for me to discuss it.'

Fuck. He has *cheated on me.* 'Mmm?' *Don't cry, Ruby, mate. Don't you dare let him see you cry.*

'I can trust you. Right?'

Not to cry? Or not to kill you and whichever whore you've pulled this time? I nodded.

'It's about my brother.'

Definitely not what I was expecting. 'What?' *What do you mean, your brother? I thought you were an only child.*

'My half-brother, technically.'

Definitely confused now. 'OK.' *Really, Ruby, mate? You're a conversational genius.*

He shifted onto one elbow and looked at me, first concentrating on my left eye then on my right. He inhaled deeply, like he was taking a drag, then exhaled loudly. I was almost surprised not to see smoke. I felt nervous. *This is ridiculous.*

'It's complicated. I don't really like to talk about it.'

Just tell me! 'OK.' *What encouragement! You're on fire, Ruby, mate. Really going to get him to tell you now.*

'He's my dad's, actually. Dad was in a … threesome? Polygamous relationship? They weren't married or anything. Not until Mum served him an ultimatum after she got pregnant. Then he and Mum made it official in the mid-80s – but, by then, David and I were already three – he's a few months younger. The fly in the ointment. My brother from the third wheel. And Mum never knew – still doesn't know.'

He grabbed my wrist and I bit my lip so I wouldn't yelp. He had a manic look in his eye.

'She *can't* know, actually. Do you understand? She can't.'

Ouch. I nodded and tried not to wince as his nails clawed my skin.

He continued, seeming not to notice my pain. 'David and I would only see each other when she wasn't around. And at school. But …'

'At school? You were at *school* together too?'

'Yes. Dad engineered it that way. He wanted us to be close. The whole thing is weird, right?'

Oh, Ruby, mate, you're so slow. 'The bullying?'

'Yes. We were in the same year at school.'

You were bullied by your own brother? I can't imagine Josh bullying me. Ever.

'Yeah, Dad's threesome was never a secret, so I was

ripe for the picking. David was the only one that ever stood up for me, even before we knew.'

Oh right. Slow and stupid. Not even extra time would help me now. 'But then how did it never get out? I mean, if people knew about the threesome, then they must have known about the other woman's pregnancy?'

'We have different surnames and Dad was the celebrity, not Mary, so ... Dad was very careful, obviously. And tabloids weren't as erm thorough back then. It's not as if there were photos of Dad with women draped on each arm. But what it means is now we're at this point in our lives and it's still buried alive. I ... I don't know what I'd do without him – David, I mean.'

'So you're close?'

'Very. Solidarity and all that. We've spent our lives growing up together. At school, at parties, and sometimes at home – when Mum was away. Sometimes it's very, very difficult, actually.' He stopped looking at the sheets and stared at me again.

I put my arm across his chest. 'With your mum? And what about the press? Isn't this the kind of shit they plaster all over girlie magazines?'

'Mum wasn't famous then and tabloids didn't care about authors as celebrities in the same way. Nobody asked, nobody dug into it, people forgot. But now – that's why I don't really talk about it.'

I laughed. It sounded awkward and fake, and was followed by a lot of ceiling-gazing.

I eventually broke the weighty silence. 'Well, I'm glad you told me. I won't tell anyone, obviously. But a secret brother? What does he look like?'

'Like me.'

But you look like your mum.

As if he'd read my thoughts, Callum said, 'You'll be shocked at the resemblance when you meet him.'

'Oooh, so he might visit?'

'Maybe next year. He's on his gap year.'

'Oh, cool. Come on, what's he like?'

Callum pulled my arm so hard, I had no choice but to follow it. I lay on top of him and stared into his face. He kissed me. He'd gotten his story off his chest and replaced it with me. Fair enough. I kissed him back.

There'll be plenty of time for me to find out more about this David later. Won't there?

Faith

CALLUM

Friday 12/01/2001 10:49
Subject: Boring work moan

Hello.

What a week! I'm fucked. Not the drunk kind, unfortunately. Nor the fun type. The shit type.

The studying over the holidays was supposed to have paid off, yet somehow I'm back to arsey seminar tutors and ridiculously hard assignments and argh!

At least Rube's here – she helps me through my stuff. She's great. Beyond helpful, actually. Although she's often wanting to go out. She's already been out twice without me. Says she 'doesn't want to sink back into depression', whatever that means. What is it with girls and feelings?

Hope you're having better luck.

Cal

Thursday 18/01/2001 11:35
Subject: Re: RE: Boring work moan

Hello

Glad it's all going well in paradise – not so for me. Bad to worse is my motto these days.

Rube – ah, Rube. I've got this song called 'Ruby Soho' stuck in my head. She's been making me listen to all sorts of weird music. But she's fine – thanks for asking – and no, she hasn't mentioned anything since that conversation at the start of term. But things aren't quite perfect, so maybe that's why. She keeps getting annoyed about me spending time with Yas – who is still popping up in the library and the kitchen ALL the time – but then Rube's actively avoiding spending time with me. So what's a man to do?

And I'm continuing to struggle with my bloody course too – although, in fairness to Rube, things would be a lot worse without her.

But at least the Aussie Open's on. Will you be in Melbourne in time to see any of the matches?

Cal

Thursday 25/01/2001 15:46
Subject: Women!

Hello.

I've had it with women – they're all SO annoying.

Rube's been moaning constantly about Yasmine and

become obsessed with the whole cheating incident again. It was last term for goodness' sake! And Yas has been pouring bucketfuls of bloody ether on the flames to add to the party. But the final straw was yesterday. Rube went to a football social and never came back! I was in the kitchen until 2am – the Union shuts at midnight when their stupid sports night finishes.

I finally saw her this morning and man was she in a foul mood, actually. She said she'd spent all night chatting with Juliette by the lake. As if anyone would spend the whole night outside in this cold. And she reeks of second-hand smoke – I really don't like it. Something's going on.

This whole situation isn't helping my concentration, actually. How am I supposed to work?

Going for a run now to calm down. But thanks for letting me vent!

Cal

RUBY

Callum just sat there and stared. The papers in front of him weren't the ones for the assignment he was supposed to be doing. But I didn't say anything. I just squeezed his shoulder. And tried very hard not to make it obvious as I checked my watch.

'You OK, mate?'
'Help me, pleeeease?'
'OK.'

I perched on the side of his desk and started to explain GCSE level maths. Again.

❯

I was getting ready for a standard Wednesday social when he pushed the door and walked in. I jumped into the cupboard.

'What are you doing?' he asked.

'Getting dressed?'

'In your wardrobe?'

'No I ...' *I'd prefer it if the whole of the corridor didn't see me naked, thanks. Especially not skinny Yasmine.*

'Well, sorry for interrupting, but I'm really stuck on this assignment. Same stupid module. Who made it a core requirement? Idiots! Can you help me please?'

No. 'Of course.' *Rancid's '... And Out Come The Wolves' should get you out pretty quickly. One of the few benefits of you liking crap like Robbie Williams and S Club 7.*

I changed the tape and pointed to the chair. He sat and passed me the assignment. I showed him what he was supposed to do, then continued to get myself dressed and ready. He just sat there and scratched his head.

'It's just this bloody module,' he moaned. 'I've managed to get everything else sorted.'

True. But I have stuff I need to do too, mate. Everyone's got problems, yeah? 'I know, I know. It's OK. You'll be fine. Do you get it now?'

'Mmhm. Thanks gorgeous.' He pulled a face. 'What are we listening to?'

I laughed and ran out the door.

I was getting ready for a 'convicts and policewomen' dress-up social, sticking on fake tattoos, when Jules knocked and walked in.

'Where're you going, dressed like that? And where's the green-eyed monster?'

'Sitting crying about his course to the skinny one?'

'Ouch! I didn't think you had it in you.'

I smiled. *I can pretend it doesn't bother me, but what good would that do?* 'You coming?'

'Can I?'

'Why not? They love you. Plus, if they're not happy about it, I'm the one that'll get the drinking penalty. So why not?'

I stuck a tat on her arm and she danced around the centre of the floor while I searched for my coat. We then walked out the door and headed to the Union.

'Eighteen, nineteen, twenty.' I laughed and looked to my left at Jules.

'Not again! Twenty-one.' She downed her pint then shook her head. 'Mummy would definitely disapprove.'

'What else would she disapprove of?' asked Smithy

suggestively. She was leaning into Jules.

I grinned. 'Don't even think about it, mate.'

'Why not? Aren't you tempted? She's fucking brilliant.'

Jules clapped her hands. She was properly pissed. 'I am, aren't I? Anyone want another?'

Nine girls raised their hands. Jules pretended to count then gave up with a shrug.

'Don't worry, I'll help,' said Smithy, rising.

We all watched them walk to the bar and then The Captain yelled, 'To my riiiight – one' and we were off again.

❯

Four(ish) pints later, we were on the dance floor, grinding down to the likes of *Wake Me Up Before You Go-Go*, *Eye of the Tiger*, and *Ghostbusters*. The soundtrack blurred into one long 80s mix.

The Captain had climbed onto the stage to be groped by some rugby boy. The rest of the first team used my left leg as a limbo stick, while I drunkenly hopped on the other leg to keep my balance. And Jules danced by the pile of coats in the corner while she lit a fag off her previous butt.

That's when it happened.

Billie Jean mixed (inexplicably) into *Summer of '69*. The dance changed from the limbo to praying air guitars. And Smithy pulled Juliette.

'Fuck me,' I muttered.

'Oh my gawd,' screamed Laura in my ear as she pointed.

Someone pulled out a camera and took a photo. The flash was masked by the strobe lights, and they didn't stop. We all looked on at the snogging couple, fascinated.

'*Living On A Prayer*' came on and we were suddenly back in a circle. We sang our lungs out. A few songs later, I got bored and patted my pockets. I felt the packet and looked around. No Callum.

'Can I have one? I'll stoop to Mayfair Lights tonight,' said a voice in my neck.

'Jules, mate. Having a good time?' I laughed, turned, and looked at her.

I stopped laughing. She wasn't looking too good. 'You OK, mate?' I shouted over '*Material Girl*'.

She pointed to the door, passed me my coat, and led the way. *The night's over, is it?*

Once outside, she kept walking towards the lake. I pulled my coat tighter and fished my beanie out the pocket. Then I followed.

'You OK?' I asked.

She shook her head and I realised she was crying. I continued to walk beside her. *This is very awkward.*

She sat on the bench and I sat too. It was wet. *Hopefully the alcohol will keep us warm. For a while.* I tossed Jules the packet and patted my pockets for a lighter. I found a blue Clipper that definitely wasn't mine. *Must've nicked it off Smithy earlier. She'll live.*

'You OK, mate?' I asked. Again.

'What am I doing?'

'What d'you mean?' *It's freezing out here.*

'You saw. Everyone saw. What was I thinking?'

'You're ... drunk and you ... pulled someone?'

Jules pulled out another fag and lit it.

She's a quick smoker. I leant over and took out one for myself.

'I kissed a girl.'

I know. I was there. 'So?'

'Don't you get it? It's a sin!'

'What?'

'"If a man also lie with mankind, as he lieth with a woman, both of them have committed an abomination".'

Please don't quote that shit at me. 'Are you really quoting the bible, mate? Isn't it like a few thousand years old?'

'Leviticus. Mummy and the Vicar are always going on about it.'

I see. So you totally missed my point then. 'It's not a sin. It's a drunken kiss, mate. Or just a kiss. Whatever.'

'You can say that. You're going out with a man!'

'Are you ... are you saying you like her?' *Dangerous play.*

She lit another fag. 'I don't know. What am I doing? She's a girl. I can't like girls! What am I thinking?'

I'm thinking this is going to be a long night.

❯

Two hours later, we climbed the steps to our halls. Another pack later (thank god for vending machines), I finally left her room and headed to the toilet. As I came out and started back to my room, I saw him. He was leaning against the wall by my door. All green eyes and testosterone.

'Where have you been?'

Really? Not now, mate. I'm knackered. I unlocked and pushed my door open. He followed me in.

'Where have you been?' he repeated, this time very loudly.

'Out.' *I'm not in the mood for this.*

I went to my sink and picked up the glass with my toothbrush in it. I held it to my forehead.

'Yeah, I can see that. But where? With whom?'

'For fuck's sake, Callum! Do I ask you where you've been when you're out?'

'You always know where I am.'

'Oh yeah, that's right. With Yasmine.' *Easy, Ruby, mate.* 'I was sorting out Jules's problems, OK?'

'Till eight in the morning?'

What the hell are you doing up at this time anyway?

'I was worried about you,' he said. 'I called you a few times.'

'Oh. Sorry.' *You know I never take my mobile out when I go on the piss. It'll only end up in a pint glass or toilet bowl.*

'You look terrible.'

'Thanks.'

I kicked off my shoes and clothes and got into bed. I had more important things to worry about. I thought.

JULIETTE

And now we have a problem. We both know you don't want to hear this part of the story, but I can't resolve anything if I don't tell you. Please keep listening – I really need you to. It is, after all, why I'm here.

So Yasmine was stalking Callum. And – worse still – she was making cutting remarks and blowing kisses at Ruby and constantly reminding her of the cheating incident – when she thought no-one was looking, of course. And – in his typically stupid way – Callum was oblivious to it all. All *he* cared about was the module he was failing, so he kept harassing poor Ruby into helping him. He should've depended less on other people doing the work for him and more on himself. Selfish gi– person.

Anyway, Ruby wanted to get away from it all, so she kept meeting up with the football girls. This particular time, I went with her. Now, you know Smithy and I, we knew each other – we'd met before. But this time ... this time she bounced and bounded and exuded this amazing energy and positivity. I realised then that she wasn't just all verve and vigour – she was interesting and intelligent and ...

And it was a *social*. So we got drunk. Inebriation is common in my house, as you know – no, don't look at me like that. I read somewhere that the word for wine in Hebrew and Greek can mean fermented grape juice as well as the alcoholic kind. But we only have the latter variety in our house. And don't trust everything you read, huh?

Sorry – where was I? That's right. So, I did it. I got drunk and Smithy kissed me and I didn't resist. There – I've said it. What will it be now? Genesis, Leviticus, or Romans? My personal favourite is Genesis, although it is about men. 'Come, let us make our father drink wine, and we will lie with him, that we may preserve seed of our father.' Oh, is that not the verse you were thinking of? Sorry – I don't mean to mock. Well, not really. I'm just saying that maybe we shouldn't trust everything we read because we're either interpreting it wrong or we're interpreting it right and it's so dated that it's now in direct conflict with the base principles of our religion, you know? And yes, I do mean *our* religion.

Back to the story. When I realised what I was doing – by that I mean when I'd mentally processed the act – I pulled away and ran to Ruby. She's always there for me – then, later, and now. She's a saint masquerading as the devil. She pulls you to drink, to smoke more, to socialise with the gayest sports club at uni, and yet … she's always *there*, you know? She spent that entire January night sitting and listening to me.

She was amazing. But – unfortunately for her – before long, it was me who would be returning the favour. Trouble was heading Ruby's way a long, long time before it headed mine.

Shattered

RUBY

I woke up in a hot sweat. It was dark and I desperately wanted a fag. I was tired, still pissed, and without Callum. My hair stank of stale beer and fag ash. My throat felt like it'd been studded repeatedly. And my brain was all over the pitch. *Ugh.*

I got up and dressed myself. Then I dragged myself to the kitchen.

'Hiya,' said Matt. 'You look rough. What happened?'

'Can't you see she's been in a fight?'

Paul, mate, you're so funny. Really. 'You should see the other girl,' I said. *Why am I fuelling this?*

'Did she drown in the barrel of decomposed bodies and excrement you seem to have fallen into?'

Yasmine, the bitch. How nice of you to join us. I leant over and sniffed my arm. It hurt my head but was worth it. 'You're right. I do smell a bit like you.'

Matt and Paul howled.

Definitely worth it.

'Hardly,' was Yasmine's only response.

Callum walked in. 'Afternoon.'

'Hi.'

'You look awful.'

What a lovely boyfriend. 'Thanks, mate.' I felt last night's tequila swimming up my throat, so I sat down and put my head on the table. Not the best start to the day.

'No more witty yet inaccurate statements to entertain us with?'

Shut the fuck up already, Yasmine. Nobody likes you. Just fuck off.

'Have I interrupted something?' Callum looked first at Yasmine then at me.

'No,' we replied at the same time.

He sat down next to Yasmine.

Red card, mate. Red card. I got up, slower than I would have liked, and headed for the showers.

○

There was a knock on my door. The aggressive kind.

'Come in?'

The door was shoved open. It was Smithy.

'Hey.'

'Mate! Glad it's you.' *I was expecting some arsehole.*

'Like your room.'

'Cheers, mate.'

'Can I err talk?'

Oh, here we go. 'Jules?'

Smithy giggled and sat on my bed. 'This is nuts.'

I shrugged my shoulders. It made my whole neck ache. 'So's tequila.'

'Whose idea was that shit?'

'Funnily enough, I don't remember.'

She looked up at the pin board over my bed. There was only one photo there. 'Who's that? He's hot.'

'My brother, Josh. Thought you were into women?'

'Does that mean I can't find men attractive?'

I shrugged again, like the genius I am. The movement hurt my neck.

She giggled a nervous high-pitch sort of thing.

'Take your time, mate,' I said, gently. 'And you're welcome to smoke.'

'Thank fuck for that.' She took out her pack of fags and offered me one. 'The thing is, I like her. It wasn't a random pull. Well, it was, but it wasn't. Am I making any sense?'

Of course not. 'Sure.'

'What do you think?'

I think I have no idea how I ended up as everyone's agony aunt. I think I'm not cut out for this. 'I think you probably swear too much for our mate.' I laughed, just to make sure Smithy knew I was joking.

She joined in, properly this time. 'Shut the fuck up!'

'Something like that. Nah, mate. I think she *likes you* likes you too. She's just all confused. Don't think she realised this was an option sort of thing.'

'Did any of us?'

'Huh?' *What's she talking about now? My head hurts too much for this.*

'Yeah, sorry, what would you know about it?' she asked.

'About lesbians or relationships? I think I'm a bit shit on both fronts.'

'Boy trouble?'

'Always, mate. Always. But we're talking about you.'

'Fine. The thing is, I like her. What the hell am I going to do? Is there anything I *can* do?'

'Maybe give her some time to get her head round things?'

'You think?'

The door swung open. Callum strode in, stopped, and glared at Smithy.

'Are you smoking in here? Rube's obviously too polite to say anything so I will. It's disgusting. Just because there's an ashtray doesn't mean you can smoke. They come with the room. We have no choice in the matter.' He stood and glared at Smithy.

She continued to smoke, looking happy for the first time since she'd walked through my door. I tucked my unlit fag under my leg, cringing.

'Callum,' I said, 'we're … we're having a discussion here. Can I please come see you in a bit?'

He turned to me. 'What's wrong with you? Are you so spineless?'

'We're in the middle of …'

'I'm amazed, actually. Simply amazed.' He stood in the doorway and shook his head.

Smithy stubbed out her fag end and got up. 'We'll speak later, yeah?'

'Sure, mate.' *Just leave me here with him. Great.*

She walked up to Callum and held out her hand.

'Smithy. Pleased to meet you. You're Callum, yeah?'

He just glared at her and kept his arms crossed. *How rude.* She turned, winked at me, and left. Callum took two steps into the room and let the door close behind him. He looked at me.

'What is wrong with you? You're acting insane. You disappear all night, without telling me where you've been or what you've been doing. You refuse to tell me who you've been with. You're so rude to Yasmine. And you let people smoke in your room. Your *room.* I mean, I know the football girls mean a lot to you but this is …'

'Rude to Yasmine?' *That's rich, mate. Join the bitch's team, why don't you?*

'I heard your comment in the kitchen.'

Of course you did.

'Did you hear hers?' *Don't rise to it, Ruby, mate. Don't do it.*

'Rube, this is about you …'

So that would be a no then. And I hate it when you call me Rube.

'… and your erratic behaviour.'

My what? 'What are you on about?'

'Have you not been listening to a word I've said?'

'Obviously. I just don't see your point.' *Stay calm, mate. Stay calm.*

'My point, as you put it, is you're not behaving like yourself. You're acting like this weird person. Even by women standards.'

You what? You sexist wanker. 'You seem to bring

out the best in me,' I said. *Less of that, Ruby, mate. Tone it down.*

'Charming.' He stopped for a minute. 'Why are we always fighting nowadays?'

I shrugged. 'It always seems to be like this, doesn't it? When we're together, I mean.' *Good girl. Keep it all nice and calm.*

'Well then, maybe we shouldn't be together.'

I stopped talking, breathing, hating. I looked at him. He was serious. I tried to breathe but couldn't.

Breathe, Ruby, mate. Breathe. You always knew this was going to happen.

I felt my eyes twitch. I turned and walked past him and out of the door. He had effectively run me out of my own room. But he would not see me cry. He was the last person in the world I'd want to see me cry.

Wrong as usual.

CALLUM

Thursday 25/01/2001 19:19
Subject: Balls

I think we've broken up. Me and Rube. Actually broken up. It's over. Things are shit.

I just don't know how this happened, I really don't. I mean, I know things have been a bit shit lately, but this? Fuck!

I bumped into her in the kitchen a few hours ago and she was incredibly hung-over. She was bitching at Yas so I tried to crack some joke to diffuse the situation and she just rolled her eyes and left. I figured she was just going for a shower – she stank of hardcore partying – so I just sat down with the boys and Yas. But then she never returned, so I went in search of her.

Guess what I found? She was just sitting there in her room chatting to that football girl – the one with the strange eyes. And Rube was letting her smoke! In her room! I don't know what's going on with her, actually. She's suddenly been hanging out with idiots and smokers and swearing and bitching and generally losing that lovely sheen of innocence she used to have.

So I said something – I told that girl that just because Rube's very polite, people shouldn't take advantage. The ashtrays come standard with the bloody room – it's not like we have a choice – we were allocated smoking halls; we didn't CHOOSE them.

That girl just sat there – calm as anything – and continued to smoke. Ruby just kept her head down – embarrassed, no doubt – and fiddled nervously with her trousers.

Then she looked up at me and glared – actually glared. What's happened to her? She used to be a lovely, non-confrontational sort.

'Callum,' she said to me, 'we're having a discussion and it doesn't concern you.'

I was shocked and amazed, actually – completely amazed. I just stood there rigid, trying to process it all.

The girl just stubbed out her cigarette – didn't clean

the ashtray out, why would she? – and made a little pretence of introducing herself while blowing smoke in my face – disgusting.

She sneered at me when she left. I tried to straighten things out with Ruby. I tried to make her see sense – that her behaviour was erratic, that she was behaving like an immature schoolgirl, that she was spending inordinate amounts of time with the football girls and that she'd been incredibly rude to her friends recently and that it was all very unbecoming.

She just stood there, seething.

'I just don't see your point. You seem to bring out the best in me,' she said in a sarky tone I'd never thought her capable of. 'It always seems to be like this when we're together.'

I admit I lost it a bit there. It was the way she was squaring up to me – there was something so ugly about the situation that I lost my mind and told her that maybe we shouldn't be together.

I know, I know – I'm an idiot. I'm making her sound terrible – making me sound terrible. But things haven't been THAT BAD. And after I'd said it, I so wanted to take it back.

But she closed her eyes in relief – RELIEF! – like I'd voiced exactly what she'd had in mind all along. Then she grinned at me, patted me on the shoulder like I was some lapdog, and left me there. And didn't come back.

The situation is fucked. Please call when you get this? I could do with your advice right now.

In the meantime, crate of beer in the kitchen: here I come.

Cal

YASMINE

Juliette had spent the first few weeks of term rubbing salt into that notorious and well-analysed wound of mine. I subsequently realised that her adversarial stance was nothing more than a misguided attempt to protect Ruby, the increasingly antisocial element in our halls.

Fortunately, the heavens, for all their religious tampering and self-worship, were finally on my side. Callum began to show inevitable frustration at Ruby's belligerent and inconsiderate behaviour and I ensured that I was always there to lend a sympathetic ear and arm. It took an inordinately long time, almost three entire weeks from our return after the Christmas break, but eventually he capitulated under the pressure of their forged 'relationship'.

It began, as these things often do, with a seemingly innocent scene in our kitchen. Ruby entered, looking like a bedraggled stray that had been dragged through thorn bushes, bird droppings, and a sewer, and smelling like someone that had miraculously evaded drowning in a swamp, and sat down to infect our table with microbes of unknown origin.

'You look rough,' said Matt, in his heavy but vivacious accent. 'What happened?'

'Can't you see she's been in a fight?' Paul attempted to be polite and brush off the seriousness of her condition, but I could see him wrinkling his nose.

'You should see the other girl,' Ruby said, no doubt considering herself amusing.

'Is she as in dire need of a shower as you are?' I joked.

She brought her unfashionably clothed and accessories-free arm up to her pug nose and inhaled noisily, just as Callum pushed the kitchen door ajar. Her actions were so base and disgusting that even the boys flinched. 'You're right. I do smell a bit like you,' she said, wholly inaccurately and incredibly rudely.

Callum cleared his throat and murmured, 'Afternoon.'

'Hi.' She batted her eyelids at him in an attempt to recover from being caught in the act of extreme boorishness.

Callum was, finally, not fooled by the temptress's actions and spoke accordingly. 'You look awful.'

'Thanks,' she replied.

'No further witty yet inaccurate statements to entertain us with?' I ventured, uncharacteristically openly but, given that Callum now appeared to be on my side, worth the risk.

'Have I interrupted something?' Callum looked at me enquiringly.

'No,' Ruby and I responded in atypical unison.

Callum slowly crossed the floor and pulled a seat next to mine, while Ruby turned deeper shades of bloodshot cherry and I poured all my strength into preventing the corners of my mouth from hitting the ceiling.

●

A short while later, Callum rose and headed for the door. I made my excuses to the others and followed but, by the time I had exited, it was too late, for he had already reached Ruby's door and was holding it open. Any misgivings that I may have had about my sluggishness in catching him instantly evaporated when I heard his seething tirade.

'Are you smoking in here? Rube's obviously too polite to say anything, so I will. It's disgusting. Just because there's an ashtray doesn't mean you can smoke. They come with the room. We have no choice in the matter.'

I froze, aware that any movements on my part, however small, may have alerted the corner of Callum's eye, and therefore Callum himself, to my presence.

'Callum, we're having a discussion here.' Ruby sounded decidedly sheepish.

'What is wrong with you? Are you so spineless?' he asked.

'We're in the middle of …'

'I'm amazed, actually. Simply amazed.'

I heard a third voice, one I didn't recognise, say in distinctly Northern tones, 'We'll speak later, yeah?'

'Sure, mate,' came Ruby's uneducated response.

A petite, pretty, and incredibly bouncy girl walked out of Ruby's door, smiled politely when she saw me, and headed down the stairs. The door crept shut behind her but, before it did, I heard Callum raising his voice.

Things were finally looking up, but it was then, more than ever, that I knew I had to be careful.

Healing

CALLUM

Friday 26/01/2001 15:51
Subject: More moaning – sorry

Hello.

I'm such a fool. The more I think about it, the more I realise that it's probably all my fault. Maybe if I hadn't said what I said then maybe …

My head hurts. The boys helped me with that crate of Stella, but I couldn't sleep so I took a bottle of vodka to bed with me. Rube had left it in my room one night so I thought – well, fuck her, actually, she doubtless did it on purpose – probably thought I'd need it sooner or later.

I need sleep! And my bloody assignment is due in an hour and it's crap because I never got Rube to look over it and now … You get the picture.

Ring me, man – it'd be good to talk.

Cal

Wednesday 31/01/2001 19:03
Subject: Re: RE: More moaning – sorry

Hello.

Andre Agassi is my hero! I know he's American, but still – can't believe you were there to watch him win! Lucky sod.

I – as per usual – am less lucky. Yes, we're still broken up and Rube couldn't care less. I bumped into her in the toilets this afternoon, finally – I hadn't really seen her in the last week – she hasn't been about – out on the piss all the time according to the others.

I thought she was a bit weird with me really – unnecessary, given everything. I said hi and she didn't even look at me. She just grunted and slammed the toilet door behind her.

It's totally over then. Shame, she was looking good in her football kit. I think it's the socks. There's just something very kinky about football socks on girls, don't you think?

Enjoy Fiji – don't believe you that they have a rainy season there – jealous!

Cal

Sunday 04/02/2001 12:11
Subject: Rugby season whoo!

Hello.

Did you watch the game? We bloody thumped

them! And in Cardiff too! Always a pleasure beating the Welsh.

The only downside to the whole thing was bumping into Rube. She was there with her football friends – totally ignoring us, actually, and acting like she owned the Union. She didn't even come and say hi when we waved and shouted happy birthday to her – Matt and Paul noticed it too. She spent the whole time giggling with that girl with the odd eyes.

I got a text message from her later – all it said was 'Thanx 4 ur wishes. Sorry cudnt come over' – as if that explained her rudeness. I've kept it anyway – the text – what an idiot.

Anyway, I'm so over her, actually. Matt always says, 'all women are crazy', and he's so right.

Heading down to watch the France-Scotland game now. I don't get people who don't get rugby – do you?

Send some sun this way.

Cal

Friday 08/02/2001 15:39
Subject: Why do people smoke?

Hello.

I just caught Ruby SMOKING in the kitchen. Yes, smoking.

She was just sat there chatting with Juliette when Matt, Yas and I walked in and she just turned and nodded at us – like nothing had happened! And her and

Juliette burst out laughing and just kept going. I have no idea what was so funny. Not sure I care.

Yas asked them to stop but they ignored her – Juliette always ignores her, and she and Rube are now inseparable apparently, so ...

I don't know why I should care. But Yas is right – it's just such a SHAME, you know? Rube's a great girl underneath it all – she's just being dragged into a life of drugs and smoking and nastiness and bullshit.

Even Matt is being odd about it all. He just keeps changing the subject when the talk in the kitchen is about Rube – and it always seems to be about Rube these days. She's not spending any time with anyone from halls anymore, you see. Well, other than Juliette – and she's the same, you know.

Shame, shame, shame ...

But I'm good, actually. Things are looking up and everyone here's been great about everything.

Keep having fun out there!

Cal

Wednesday 14/02/2001 16:25
Subject: Bloody Valentine's Day

Hello

Happy Valentine's Day! Yes, of course I'm being sarcastic. Seriously, though, why do people care about today? Isn't the day supposed to be all about some man that died? Whatever – it's a crap day – if you're in a relationship, you have to buy cards and presents and other stuff and if you're not, you're just supposed to feel shit. Either way, a waste of a 'celebration'.

And yes, I am feeling particularly shit today. I was just heading out to the library when who did I see creeping up the stairs in smudged makeup, tight trousers and an incredibly low-cut top? Ruby. Definitely walk of shame. Why does it bloody hurt so much?

Hate Valentine's Day.

Cal

YASMINE

My financial woes were deepening and, if I wasn't careful and economical on a number of fronts, I'd have to resort to something risky soon. Added to that, winter was showing no signs of abating and Callum's desire for Ruby was following a very similar and unwelcome trajectory. The inevitable breakup had, for a far-from-brief interlude, sharpened his desire, and he could often be found in the kitchen staring at the door like a loyal pet. I took this as a sign that endurance was required to mend his broken heart by nurturing our growing attraction and, luckily for me, patience had always been my strong suit.

Also working in my favour was, as always unseen by her short-sighted but naturally glass-free eyes, the fact that Ruby herself was ensuring total isolation from the group. She took up smoking with Juliette, stopped joining the weekly group homework sessions we held in the kitchen, spent all her time with those unpolished sports types, ignored the boys (who, for reasons far beyond my understanding, still idolised her), and flaunted her myriad of new male friends.

It was, indecently enough, on Valentine's Day that the uncouth, charity-shop dresser finally nailed the coffin lid shut on their toxic relationship. I had walked into the kitchen on my return from my silversmithing course and there Callum sat, in his usual haunt, staring at the beer bottle in front of him.

'Everything OK?' I asked. 'You're not looking particularly happy this morning.'

He grunted a non-committal response, so I tried again.

'It's Valentine's Day. Love is in the air and all that.'

'Hate Valentine's Day.'

'Don't be such a grump,' I said.

'She's right, stop moping,' chuckled Paul, joining in the fun.

'I just caught Ruby on a walk of shame.'

The room fell silent. We all knew it to be true, the way her actions had been post-breakup, but the effect on Callum was so profound that we all sat silent, chewing on the bitter cud of sympathy.

RUBY

I ran straight for Jules's room after an hour of crying quietly in the toilets. I couldn't be seen, what with my red eyes and bloated face. But Yasmine was waiting for me, man-marking me all the way to Juliette's. She gave me her evil smile as I finally brushed past her in my race for the door. I will never forget that smile of hers. Ever.

Having reached what I thought was safety, I pushed Jules's door. Nothing. I knocked. Nothing. I shouted her name. Nothing. And still Yasmine stared and sneered. I ran back to my room to hunt for some contraband fags.

○

The next four days I spent in my room, with only Smithy and Jules to keep me company. Separately, of course, as they were avoiding each other. Everyone still had their own problems to worry about.

But they both brought vodka and fags and I didn't need anything else. I just cried and smoked and drank and talked shit at them. *Not proud.*

On Tuesday, I made it to my two lectures. Then to Costcutter's as my stocks were low. I picked up some Mayfair Lights, a lighter, and a bottle of Smirnoff, then went back to my room.

Jules came in. 'What *are* you listening to?' she asked.

'Mix tape. Josh gave it to me.'

'I always wanted an older brother. But this is pretty depressing stuff.'

'Really? It's '*Higher*' by Creed. They're a Christian rock band. And the previous one was '*The Distance*' by Live. I think they're a Christian rock band too. Well, they seem to talk a lot about pews and other churchy stuff.'

Jules laughed. 'Maybe Mummy would approve – I should get her to give them a whirl.'

I laughed too. It felt good.

'You look better,' she said.

You mean my face is not all swollen up? And I'm not crying into your neck? 'Thanks.'

'Do you feel better?'

Nothing more fags and alcohol can't cure. 'Yeah. Plus, I need to sober up. Town tomorrow.'

'Ah yes, the tattoo. Want me to join?'

'If you want to. Smithy's coming with me as she's getting another one. Somewhere naughty, apparently. But you can come too?' *Don't bait her, mate. She's being helpful.*

'I have lectures anyway.'

On a Wednesday? And since when do you go to lectures? 'Cool.'

❯

They gave me my leg back. It was a combination of painful and numb. But I'd finally done it – I never thought I'd have the guts to follow through.

'Look at you.' Smithy grinned at me.

'I have a tat!' I did a slow, hopping version of an aeroplane goal-scoring celebration round her.

'I know! So do I! Not sure I'll be able to sit for a while but, hey, let's go party.'

We headed back to campus and down to the Union to play pool and drink pints while smoking and doing all the other things you can do with a leg wrapped in cling film.

A couple of pints later, I saw Jules walk past with some shopping, and skipped down to get her to join us.

'Look!'

'Brilliant – that cling film looks great.'

'Oh yeah, I'd forgotten about that. We're drinking. Join us?' *Am I slurring?*

'Who's us?'

'Footie girls.' I winked at her. 'Come on, you know you want to.'

'Sorry, I've got to take these back. Maybe later?'

'Stop making excuses.' I grabbed her arm.

'No, no, no, no, no.'

She's quite strong. I'm losing this tug-of-war to a hockey girl. That's embarrassing. And a first. 'Come ooooon.'

'No. I'm not going into the Union with a see-through bag of sanitary towels.'

I stopped. My last pint swam up my throat. The alcohol hit my temples. 'Shit.' I ran.

'Ruby?' Jules sounded out of breath.

How am I back in my room? I don't remember getting here.

'Fuck I …' *I can't be. It can't be. No.*

'What *is* it?' Smithy asked.

What are you doing here?

'I forgot.'

'Forgot what? Please, you're scaring me.'

'Me too. What's up?'

I started to cry. Then I looked up at them. 'My period. Yesterday was the 30th. Right?'

'Oh.'

Don't look at me like that. Please, you're supposed to be on my side. 'I'm fucking late.'

They looked at each other. 'Well, maybe …'

'I'm never late. Ever. I'm on the pill. Oh fuck.'

'But err didn't you erm use …'

Condoms, Jules. They're called condoms. 'I'm on the pill and we've been together so long. Were together so long …' *Fuck.* 'What do I do?'

'Pregnancy test?'

Thanks, Smithy. 'Sure, I'll just go up to the counter at Costcutter and ask for one, shall I?' *This can't be happening.*

'I'll do it.' Smithy jumped up and skipped off.

She's got no shame, clearly. Thank fuck for that.

I lifted the bottle of vodka to my lips, then put it down again. *What am I doing? What do I do if I'm pregnant? Oh god.*

Jules came and silently sat next to me. She put her arm gently round my shoulders. I cried into her neck. We stayed like that until Smithy's return, which felt like a full ninety minutes against a much fitter side. 'These things are fucking expensive.'

'Thanks, mate. I owe you.' I took it from her and ran to the toilet.

Callum was there. *The universe hates me.* I died of

shame and jumped into the cubicle without speaking to him. I hoped he hadn't seen what was in my plastic bag. I couldn't handle that.

Three minutes is a very, very, very long time. But there was no blue cross. I was sure. I even took it back to my room to show the others, just in case I was dreaming.

'Ewww. Did you just piss on that?'

'Shut up and tell me what you see.'

But it was fine. And Smithy and Juliette had forgotten they were ignoring each other. So we went back to the Union to celebrate once more.

Suddenly, it was Friday night, and I was winding my way back from the Union. Not sure what had happened in between, only that it had. Jules had disappeared earlier. I was pretty sure it was earlier today. But I couldn't be sure. Not really.

I tried to unlock my door and dropped my key. I bent to pick it up and clashed heads with Matt.

'Easy,' he said, and straightened up.

'Sorry, mate.'

'You OK? Been worried about you. You know, with the whole Callum thing.'

I shrugged. 'I'm fine.'

'Sure? 'Cause you're constantly pissed and you smell of smoke.'

I looked up at him. He looked hot. 'Want a fag?'

Ruby, mate, what are you doing?

'Sure.'

Shit. This is a bad idea.

He followed me into my room. I shook my last two Mayfairs at him. He took one and sat next to me on the bed. *Double shit.*

'So?'

Yes? What do you want?

'Do you have a lighter?' He smiled.

'Oh, sorry. Of course.' *You're being paranoid, Ruby, mate.* I passed him my lighter. 'So Roma away next week, eh?'

We talked about football until we'd finished, and then he said goodnight.

I thought the whole thing was a little weird.

The next day, Smithy dragged me to the Union to watch England play rugby.

I tried to protest. 'I don't really watch rugby.'

'Who cares? It's your birthday, right? We're drinking.'

'But I don't know the rules!' *How can you watch a sport without knowing the rules?*

'I'll explain as we go along.'

We sat and drank and cheered and smoked. At one point, I caught sight of the boys from my halls. They waved and shouted happy birthday. But I had a fag in my hand and knew they'd disapprove, so I just nodded. Plus, I wasn't going to go over with both Matt and

Callum there. *What is going on with my life?*

Two pints and some shots later, I texted Callum sorry.

Never text people when you're drunk, Ruby, mate. It's a bad, bad idea. Well, at least I didn't tell him I loved him. Shit. Did I?

The drinking continued into Sunday (more rugby), Monday (The Captain's birthday) and Tuesday (£1 WKD and Smirnoff Ices at the misleadingly named Campus Bar, located just off campus).

After the bar closed, I carried Smithy, who I thought was more drunk than me, back to hers. Then I threw up in her sink and passed out on her floor.

JULIETTE

It was when I got back to my room and had time to think – really think, rather than just talk, you know? – that's when it all got unbearable.

Leviticus 18:22 and 20:13. Genesis 19. Romans 1:26-27 – although there's also 24: 'Wherefore God also gave them up to uncleanness through the lusts of their own hearts, to dishonour their own bodies between themselves.' 1 Timothy 1: 9-10. Jude 1:7.

I can go on, and I know I've missed some, but these are the main ones, right? I read and reread and reread them. I sat with The Bible in my hand and thumbed and thumbed. I called Night Line and The Samaritans. I even emailed the Christian Society – I couldn't face speaking to them directly.

Anyway, you get the idea – I was tormented. I haven't

always been good, but there are certain sins that are less open to interpretation then others. Well, that's what I thought at the time anyway. Now …

Don't look at me like that – please keep listening. I'm – well, I'm finding it hard too, and you did promise to hear me out. I need to tell my story. To *explain*. To try to get you and Mummy to understand. The same way I tried and finally understood.

I felt really alone and needed someone who could help me. So I tried Ruby again – only when I got there, I found her in tears. He'd dumped her. It was like our worlds were both falling apart simultaneously, only she was far more fragile than I was.

And – as the days went on – it got worse for her. They were deliberately alienating her. You could depend on Yasmine for that, of course. And Callum had dumped her so that was inevitable. But Matt? He was being so awkward – boys' solidarity, I guess.

It was all a bit much. But it was the pregnancy scare – *her* pregnancy scare, so please don't look at me like that – that got my hockey ball rolling again, as it were. It was a terrifying moment when she realised she might be – pregnant, I mean – but Smithy stepped up and helped out. Smithy always knows what to do in a crisis – it's a rare gift. I mean, there's *no way* I would have been able to go to Costcutter *on campus* and get a pregnancy test. I mean, can you imagine?

It was all fine in the end – Ruby wasn't pregnant – but it meant that Smithy and I got thrown together again – alone in Ruby's room waiting for her to return – and we spoke. About nothing important – don't get me wrong – but it was then that I truly appreciated how special this girl was. Nobody this sweet, kind, and thoughtful could possibly be the embodiment of sin, you know? Looking into her eyes, I was thrown off balance – no, I don't mean to be cheesy – she's got odd eyes – one blue and one green. Anyway, I realised I had to act.

Rituals

It was the Sunday after Valentine's Day that convinced me. I had precisely one month left on current estimates, assuming I continued to stay within my budget. Time was running out for me in an unanticipated way and, although I knew the importance of waiting, my circumstances were pushing heavily on risk's door.

Callum sat at the table, drinking vodka straight out of the bottle like every film's stereotype tramp on a park bench. His eyes, normally vivid with their gem-like sheen, were staring, unblinking, searching for answers he already had in the depths of the distilled, clear liquid.

I sat down next to him and placed my sympathetic hand on his. He continued to stare at his bottle, oblivious to both his surroundings and his resemblance to his mother, both in terms of looks and behaviour. Matt and Paul sat quietly sipping beer, occasionally stealing furtive looks at us, but I noticed with dejection that neither of them were trying to help their friend.

'Are you going to the Union for the quiz tonight?' I tried, looking directly at Callum so that Matt and Paul would understand I was addressing only him.

'No,' he replied, his eyes not having diverted an inch from their fixed position on the label.

'Can I help?' I asked.

He shook his head, but my intervention clearly affected him because he got up, picked up his bottle, and made his way out of the kitchen in an inebriated manner better suited to the early hours. I turned to Matt and Paul.

'Aren't you worried? Can't you do something?'

They just shrugged indifferently and continued to sip their beer, ignoring their power to aid their friend in his dark hour.

'Really?' I snapped at them. 'How immature can you be? Your friend needs you.'

'What do you want us to do?' asked Paul.

'It's about Ruby,' added Matt.

There is nothing in the world I despise more than losing, but, at that moment, it became clear to me that I had, in fact, lost, and that there was but a single, and unfortunately, incredibly dicey, option open to me. And so it was that I went back to my room to practice the Primary Series and formulate my plan in serenity. Thinking is a dangerous act: I was plagued by my actions, preyed upon by my knowledge, and anguished by my ambitions for the future. I knew what I had to do, how to do it, and why it had to be done; but the question of when, the answer to which may or may not have had repercussions on the rest of my life, still remained.

CALLUM

Sunday 18/02/2001 11:44
Subject: More moaning

Hello.

This hangover is killing me. I drank so much yesterday – the drinking to forget kind – and I can't really understand why. Is it so hard to get over one girl? Come on!

I mean, the Valentine's Day thing killed me – what the fuck does she want rubbing it in my face like that? But then today – well, she did something really fucking weird. Something that shouldn't have got to me, actually. But it did. I mean, I caught her and Juliette on their way out looking rather well-dressed so I had to comment, right? And she – Ruby – said they were going TO CHURCH. I mean, yeah right.

But that got me thinking – I mean, either way it's weird, right? Ruby going to church – weird. Saying she's going to church when she's not – weird. So what is going on? And why does it bother me so much? Why, why, why? Help me!

On a brighter note – did you watch the Six Nations? Thumped Italy – you owe me a tenner. (No, I haven't forgotten!)

I need to come join you! Bloody university will be the death of me. Wish I was joking.

Cal

JULIETTE

It's hard explaining this to you – really hard. But as a result of my, erm, insecurities, I hadn't gone to Church for a while. I couldn't face it. I felt damned, impure, lost, a hypocrite, all of the above. And it hurt me. Church was where I'd always found solace and peace and now – well, now I had nothing.

I had broken the ice – speaking to Smithy again on the day of Ruby's pregnancy scare – but it wasn't enough. I couldn't *speak* to her. Not really. It was so awkward. And – ultimately – it was about her. You can't turn to someone and go, 'my world as I know it is completely fu– lost'. So … what? Help me? Save me? Ha! Easiest way to ensure you never see them again.

So it had to be Ruby, you know? And, actually – you may not see it this way – it was her that pulled me together. She made me see that there was another way. That reconciliation could be made. I know the bishops at the 13th Lambeth Conference said that homosexual acts are 'incompatible with Scripture' – I read up on stuff. But I disagree. Yeah, and you disagree with me, but hear me out, OK? Please? You did promise.

It started when Ruby came into my room on Saint Valentine's Day looking pale and sick. She'd passed out in Smithy's room after a particularly crazy night out, but as Smithy had been talking about me – Ruby's words – she thought she'd pop by and check up on me. That was her story, anyway.

So she walked in and looked at my notice board. We

have this cork board that's the only place we're allowed to put stuff up in our rooms, supposedly – though people blu-tack posters and stuff up all the time – blatant disregard for the rules. Anyway, mine only had a note – the one that I'd recently put up and stared at all the time – the one that said 'Go to Church?'

And Ruby looked at it, laughed and said, 'I didn't know Church had a capital C.'

I explained to her that it was one of the few things I still held onto from Daddy. She looked confused for a second and then asked if sermon had a capital S in my world. I asked her if she'd ever been to Church. Amazingly, she hadn't – at least not for a service. But she said she would do if I wanted someone to go with.

And so we decided to go to Evensong.

It was very strange for me. The music brought me calm, but the lessons brought me more conflict – it's silly, but it felt like the words were aimed at me. The first lesson was Proverbs 31 – 'In Praise of a Good Wife' – and the end haunted me. 'Favour is deceitful, and beauty is vain: but a woman that feareth the Lord, she shall be praised.'

That pounded my brain.

Then there was the second lesson – Luke 8:1-3. 'and certain women, which had been healed of evil spirits and infirmities, Mary called Magdalene, out of whom went seven devils.'

Oh, the whole thing was a *disaster*. I felt like I was being reprimanded and I couldn't wait to leave. You think I was being justly punished, don't you? That's horrible and it *was* horrible.

But Ruby stayed with me throughout, nudging me every now and again. I had no idea what she was thinking, so there was no way I could have anticipated how this little adventure would have affected her. And – of course – how that would, in turn, affect me.

RUBY

My head felt like the keeper's hands probably do during penalty shoot-out training. My ears whistled. And my body was sore and refusing to move.

Smithy was still asleep, snoring, on the bed. She had spent the night talking about Jules, which was probably why we'd both got beyond hammered on a non-night.

I picked up my clothes and headed back to halls. I walked up the stairs and had just crossed into the hallway when I saw Callum. I felt Smirnoff Ice in my lungs.

He just gave me a fucked off look and brushed right past me. I had no choice but to head in the opposite direction, which was away from my room. I kept walking and got to Jules's door. Matt and Yasmine were chatting by his door and stopped to stare. I had to knock.

She was in, but looked miserable. *It's so easy to forget that everyone has problems these days.*

I stood around as she hunted for her fags. Her room always looked unlived in. She didn't have a single poster or photo up in her room. But there was a new Post-It on her board. It just said, 'Go to Church?'

'I didn't know church has a capital C,' I said, trying to make conversation.

'Some people do. Some churches more than others. But it's an Americanism, really. Not very C of E. Daddy used to write it like that so I guess that's why I do it.'

I didn't really expect a sermon, but OK. 'Does sermon have a capital S?' *Shit, Ruby, mate, are you thinking out loud?*

She laughed loudly. 'You ever been to church?'

I went to my cousin's christening once. But that's not what you're getting at, is it? 'Nope. Were you looking for company?' *Why, Ruby, mate? Why?*

'Would you mind?'

Oh god. No pun intended.

She looked so thankful that I decided to follow through, even though the service was definitely not where I wanted to be on a Sunday. Or on any day of the week. *I'm missing £1 happy-hour pints at the Union for this. But at least the place didn't burst into flames as I walked in.*

'Glory be to the Father, and to the Son, and to the Holy Ghost,' chanted the priest.

'As it was in the beginning, is now, and ever shall be, world without end. Amen,' the congregation responded.

What are they talking about? Would it be rude to ask? Probably.

The music bits were OK. Some of the students had really good voices, and the songs themselves weren't as bad as I'd expected. *Or as bad as S Club 7, who are probably playing in the Union right about now.*

The priest read 'the first lesson'. He started with 'Who can find a virtuous woman? for her price is far above rubies. The heart of her husband doth safely trust in her, so that he shall have no need of spoil.'

Wow, this is the most sexist thing I've heard in years – and I play women's football! There's me thinking I'd heard it all. Don't be so disrespectful, Ruby, mate.

I looked over at Jules, but she was listening so intently, I couldn't ask whether it was supposed to be interpreted differently or whether these people were stuck in the dark ages. *Don't be rude, mate.*

'She riseth also while it is yet night, and giveth meat to her household, and a portion to her maidens.'

I know I've never had maids, but am I missing something? I thought they were supposed to do the housework?

I turned to Jules again, but she had her eyes closed and was grasping her hands so tightly her fingers had gone white.

After that, there was some other stuff, a 'second lesson' about healing or something, then some chanting about believing in god and Jesus and hell. I tried to look interested. Juliette looked ill.

Then the priest gave a speech about nature and religion. It was pretty interesting, although I disagreed with most of what was said. *Inevitable really.*

Jules looked like she was about to cry.

The service finished and we got up. I had to support Jules, who was shaking. We walked past the priest who said, 'Welcome back, Juliette,' in a tone that didn't sound very welcoming or Christian to me. Jules' face turned even more white. She looked like she was about to pass out.

We headed straight for the Union. *I need a drink. And Jules definitely does.* I knew where she was headed. I'd been there many times and it wasn't pretty. *Fuck Yasmine, fuck Callum, fuck Matt, fuck all of them.* Jules needed me and I would be there for her.

I made her sit while I headed to the bar. I turned to look at her, but she had her head down, staring at her hands. I was safe.

I picked up my phone and dialled Smithy's number.

Liaison

YASMINE

The importance of dishonesty in any operation cannot be overestimated. Not only would my experience have been different had I not been honest, but my life could have been considerably longer. Unfortunately, conscience tugged at my subconscious and shaped my actions, with fatal consequences for both my truest and most serious relationship and for myself. Ethically, of course, I was right. However, had I a better grasp of the situation both within halls and beyond the safe haven of the campus boundary, I may have acted differently.

I sat at my desk, with the door locked and the curtains drawn, and stared at the string of pearls in front of me. They were cream and dull, cultured and of a low quality, and try as I might to rearrange them into an interesting fashion accessory, failure ensued. The initial plan had been to combine them into my latest silversmithing project and then sell my creations, but inspiration failed me. Sitting there, drowning in an ocean of delinquency, I swept the guilt-inducing items to one side and replaced them with a notepad, on which I drew a vertical line and headed up each column. I stared at the paper, then propelled myself toward it and began to write.

On completion, I stared at the two columns, whose contents I can no longer accurately recall, but whose outline on the page I can never forget. The left-hand column, headed 'confess', was far shorter than the right-hand column, 'don't', and yet the guilt weighed heavily and would continue to do so until, a few months later, I would come up with the third solution.

Theft at my hand had never, in all my years of indulgence, planning, and execution, been a crime that I believed could affect people's lives. I always ensured I took only from people who could afford it, to make up for what I couldn't have, but, had I envisioned the pain a simple break-in could effect (which I experienced first-hand in October), I would have foregone necessities rather than inflict that type of hurt.

A knock on the door dragged me screaming from my reverie, shredding the page with my bare hands and, throwing the necklace in the false lining of my suitcase, I opened the door while pretending to fix my bra strap. The charade was wasted on the recipient, Sarah, who looked past me toward the drawn curtains and spoke, as usual, without once initiating, let alone maintaining, eye contact.

'Me and the boys are off to the Union quiz, yeah?' she said out of the side of her mouth. 'You coming or what?'

I locked the door behind me and followed her white miniskirt and silver stilettos to the end of the corridor, where Callum and the boys stood, waiting. Callum was stealing furtive looks at Ruby's firmly closed door, while Matt appeared to be monitoring this progress with a keen eye. A poisonous, cold mist infiltrated my brain and dripped slowly down my body, but I pushed through it, smiled, and threaded an arm each through Callum's and Matt's.

The Union was astir with inebriated students and quiz bravado, which was thankfully balanced by '80s power ballads. Callum was, unbelievably, given the quantity of alcohol already consumed, still comprehensible, and we talked over Sarah's screeches, Simon's snorts, and Paul's guffaws, ignoring a portion of the quiz itself to discuss things of interest. When the picture round was distributed, however, we all gathered in for a focused look, except for Matt, who was staring into the crowd behind me.

'That's definitely 'NSync,' said Sarah, squashing the second answer sheet with her ample bosom as she pointed.

'And that's New Kids On The Block,' offered Callum.

We all looked up him and roared.

'Busted!' I said.

He looked up at me then, and placed his hand on top of mine. I fanned out my fingers and let his fall naturally into the spaces between, then squeezed. He squeezed back, with a drunken gentleness only Callum could muster. I looked up and saw his caring face, slightly distorted by the drink-induced sagging mouth and eyelids, but still gorgeous. I smiled warmly at him.

'It's happening', my mind sang chirpily at me.

He moved our hands closer to his groin and I obliged to a degree, giving him enough leeway to keep responding to me, but not enough to end this silent flirtation. At some point during this game of sexual chess, the quiz ended and he pulled me up, fingers still intertwined, and hauled me off to his room with an urgency I couldn't help but respond to.

CALLUM

Monday 19/02/2001 11:44
Subject: Girls

Hello.

I know I only wrote yesterday but my life is getting very complicated, actually. I pulled Yas – get in! Yes, I know what you're thinking and no, I don't disagree. But she's so sexy, she's worth the potential crap. I mean, fuck it. I'm single, aren't I? So why shouldn't I sleep with her? Rube? She's made her position clear – it's over and I'm never going there again. Others in halls? They all WISH they were in my position.

So how did it happen? Well, I got drunk, as you do. I was just sitting there, drinking my way through another one of Rube's bottles of vodka – if she's going to leave it in the kitchen, she should learn to deal with the consequences. Yas started pestering me before speaking to the others about me as if I wasn't there, then – just in time to avoid me having a go – she ran off. I remember thinking how good her ass looked – how can you be a tit man? I mean, I get the attraction, obviously. But asses are, well, so much more defined and – wow.

So, Yas. Half a bottle later, Sarah dragged us out to the Union for the quiz – the five of us – me, her, Matt, Paul and Yas. Juan, Simon and Anne joined us there. No Rube or Juliette – probably somewhere praying – but it was fun even though Yas kept ignoring everyone else to talk to me. Still, she's hot so I had to oblige, right? Then she put her hand on my leg. Just like that. And I had to move it up – didn't I? – and one thing led to another and … you get the idea. A lot of heavy petting under the table followed by a hot, naked girl riding me in my room. Sex wasn't brilliant – I was wasted and you know how that goes – but it was sex. With a hot girl. Riding me. No complaints.

Right – now that I've got that out of my system – how are you doing?

Cal

RUBY

Roxette's '*It Must Have Been Love*' played threateningly in the background. Smithy's line was busy. I pushed into the crowd at the bar and tried again. It rang and rang. *Come on, come on.*

'Hello?'

'How do you feel about the bible?' *Easy there, Ruby, mate. Don't frighten her. You want her to come down, remember?*

'Huh?'

What the hell am I doing? Maybe this isn't a good idea.

'I need to see you. I think this religious crap is really fucking with Jules's head.' *'Come to the quiz' would probably have worked better, you twat.*

'Umm, OK. You at the Union? I fancied the quiz anyway.'

Brilliant. 'Thanks, mate.'

She appeared at our table about five minutes later, along with The Captain and her latest squeeze. I couldn't tell if it was a boy or a girl and he/she was very unhelpfully called Ashley. I just smiled at them and turned to Jules. She looked like she would faint. And just stared at Smithy like she was a big, scary monster.

Twinkle saved us. 'Hey, girls, are you quizzing? Mind if we join? This is Toby and Monty. They play rugby, but please don't hold it against them.'

Wow. They're hot.

'Hey,' said Smithy. 'Sit next to Ruby – she's the straight one.'

Oh god. Don't blush, Ruby, mate. Just don't.

They sat. I blushed.

'Team name?'

Thank you, Jules. You're a saviour.

The boys made various suggestions. We laughed at them and eventually went with 'Football versus hockey – it's all balls' (we decided the rugby boys didn't count).

The pints seemed to help Juliette, whose face was now a healthier shade of pale.

On my second bar run, I spotted Juan and was about to say hi when I saw who he was with. *Callum. Yasmine. Matt. Fuck.* I turned away and took the long way round back to our table.

'You took your time,' said Toby.

You can take me anytime, mate. Oh fuck. I didn't say that out loud, did I? I looked away. 'The others are over there,' I said to Jules.

We lit up. Took a drag. Knocked back the tequila shots. *Better. Much better.* Next round: sports. *We've got this.*

We were in second place at half-time. With two rounds left, we were still there. I had broken the golden seal so had to run off at the end of each round. I sneaked a peak at the other table on my way back from the toilet. *Bad idea.*

I felt as if my stomach was being studded repeatedly with a very heavy boot. Callum was sat back in his chair and Yasmine, sitting very close, was giving him a hand-job under the table. I ran.

JULIETTE

And it gets worse – but please hear me out. We went

straight to the Union for a drink. We'd both had enough, you see. Ruby because she had to sit through what must have felt like a lecture on cr– boring stuff she wasn't interested in, and me because I was scared, damned, in pain – the list goes on.

She just dumped me at a table while she went to the bar. I just wanted to cry but held myself together long enough for her to bring me my drink. She turned up with a shot of tequila and a pint of snakebite and black – horrible stuff, don't know why we drink it.

Then – most unexpectedly – I saw her in front of me. Smithy, I mean. She and two of the football girls came up to us. They just sat at our table – like nothing was wrong – like they'd been invited. I couldn't believe it. There was nowhere to hide – nowhere to run. I was terrified, shocked – and yet also conflicted. It's hard to explain.

Then – thankfully – I heard Twinkle's familiar and soothing voice asking to join us. He introduced two friends from his corridor – Toby and Monty. They were rugby boys, which struck me as a little odd with Toby. We all have our prejudices, don't we? After all, that's why I'm here.

But, anyway, it was all looking less awkward until Smithy came out with 'Sit next to Ruby – she's the straight one.'

Twinkle's eyes flicked to mine, but I looked down. I was going red, I knew it. It was terrible. But Psalms got me through. 'Yea, though I walk through the valley of the shadow of death, I will fear no evil.'

I asked the group to quickly come up with a team name.

We settled on one, then hit the pints and shots. Toby was flirting incessantly with Ruby, who – in her typically Ruby way – hadn't really noticed. She just kept smoking and laughing along – she really gelled this random group together.

But then she returned from a bar run looking a little off colour. She'd apparently seen the others at another table. She was very shaken, judging from the pace she downed her pints. Poor Ruby. It was a bad night for her all round. But then she made it worse for me by disappearing.

She'd been gone a while by the time the quiz ended, so I tried calling her, but there was no answer. I was confused – it was very unlike her.

Anyway – that's when Smithy insisted on walking me home.

Disassociation

I had finally got what I had been coveting all year and now, I knew, I had to be cautious. Callum had, as expected, begun to spend a moderate amount of time in my quarters, so I had to ensure that the proceeds of crime in my possession were intricately concealed at all times. I did, on occasion, have to delve into my supplies to extract an item or two for use in my silversmithing projects, but this was always conducted at times when Callum was securely in lecture theatres or in his room typing away on his computer. The latter was mildly curious to me, but, whenever I enquired, he would cut me off with a simple 'it's course stuff', while the screen of his computer would flicker as he minimised his Homemail so I couldn't read what he was writing.

It was not always plain sailing, this dreamt of and highly anticipated relationship with my kind, thoughtful, and gorgeous beau. He dragged me to a couple of football games, as if sport and the inevitable presence of Ruby would be on my list of top entertainment. She was always smiling her crooked, ironic smile and, despite her self-control and extensively visible best efforts, her jealousy was evident for all to see. I stayed close to Callum on these occasions for fear of being waylaid by her and her steroid-ingesting, short-haired friends.

It wasn't until an event I witnessed, between Juliette and her odd-eyed pixie sidekick, that I began to realise the extent of Ruby's influence and corruption on Juliette, and vice versa. The bond between those two grew stronger daily, and I knew then that they could create unimaginable trouble for me. I therefore decided to take action, to rid myself of a dangerous enemy and fray to breaking point the invisible rope that united them.

CALLUM

Thursday 22/02/2001 11:45
Subject: Re: RE: Girls

Hello.

Thanks for your email – and yeah, I did sleep with her again – sometimes it's scary how well you know me. But what you said did get me thinking. Do you really think I'm one of those serial relationship guys or were you just taking the piss? I get your point about having fun at uni, but it's not like we're going out or anything – just having a good time. Mostly between the sheets. Yas is really hot.

It happened yesterday, actually. Everyone had gone to watch the Champion's League game in the Union but I didn't want to bump into Rube – I still haven't seen her since pulling Yas. It was just the girls in the kitchen and, well, you know how it goes. Less drunk this time too – much better.

Of course, the only problem is what she thinks. A shag is just a shag, right?

Cal

Thursday 01/03/2001 11:39
Subject: Re: RE: Re: RE: Girls

Hello.

South America sounds amazing – maybe I can make some excuse to Mum and come out during the Easter holidays – I'll keep you posted on that one.

We had all gone down early for some event and the only free table – there was a game on – was next to the football girls, so – I saw Rube. It was the first time I'd seen her since this thing with Yas started – I'd just caught the occasional hi, etc, when she was running out the door – nothing personal. Yas was very prickly, Rube ignored me and it was all very awkward. Why do I always have trouble with women in my life?

On the upside – Six Nations on Saturday – come on!

Cal

Sunday 04/03/2001 15:22
Subject: Re: RE: Re: RE: Re: RE: Girls

Hello.

Plans are afoot for South America – Mum's buying the 'I'd like to do a language course in Argentina to complement my studies' bullshit so I think we're good to go. I'm just going to pop into STA Travel later and get my flights booked – come on!

As for Yas – you're right as always – how do you do it? I got introduced to one of her course friends as her boyfriend yesterday. It was soooo awkward. I mean, RUBE WAS THERE. Yas was complaining about having to go see the rugby in the Union so we were late, and when we got there we found the others were sat with a bunch of girls including – typical! – Ruby, Juliette, the football girl with the odd eyes – her name is Smithy, apparently – who is called Smithy? – and some randoms. Yas sat next to me and held my hand – what are we, like, twelve? And she pointedly smiled at Rube who politely smiled back – it was like she didn't care. No, seriously – I looked into her eyes looking for disappointment, anger, pain, anything – there was nothing. She's so over me. Rubbish. But then Yas spotted this girl in the football circle that she knew from class and she just jumped in with 'and this is my boyfriend, Callum.' I wanted to die.

But I lived. And you've been vindicated again – I hate you!

Cal

Friday 09/03/2001 15:47
Subject: Countdown to Argentina begins...

Hello.

Flights booked – yeah! Can't wait.

Nothing much happening here – I missed the game on Tuesday because I didn't think Yas would approve. And I didn't think I could face Rube. She's done something to her hair, I think. It looks really good – she looks really good. I missed the Liverpool game too – Matt didn't really want to talk about it today – in fact he hasn't wanted to hang around the kitchen much these days. It's quite unlike Matt, but other people's problems are not really my concern right now.

I'm coming to Argentina! Can't wait!

Cal

JULIETTE

So Smithy walked me home. And we talked and ... Don't look at me like that – nothing *happened*. We just talked.

I was torn – very torn. Here was the perfect embodiment of what I always wanted – someone sweet, fun, interesting – and they were female. It was taunting me, haunting me. It was a tough time – Ruby was turning into this social butterfly and I, I just kept churning verses in my head, hoping for a different interpretation, an *answer*.

But I kept going to events that I knew she'd be at

– Smithy, I mean. It was like a – like an addiction, an obsession. I wanted to see her, sit with her, breathe in her goodness and, well, you get the idea even if you don't want to.

But I kept away too. I made sure we didn't touch, didn't look into each other's eyes, didn't share certain things … I tried to balance the obsession with purity. I was winning, I was. Life started to be about things other than Smithy versus Church.

And that's when it happened.

RUBY

I sat, uncomfortably, while Queens of the Stone Age did their thing loudly in the background, and stared at the glowing lighter in my hand. I didn't want the flame to stop as looking at it made me feel warm. But I wasn't. I was cold.

The inevitable had happened. The truth slapped me in the face. No matter how much I pretended, acted, or ignored it, I still loved him. It hurt to even think it.

I lit up. Inhaled. I swear I had been in that position for hours, maybe even days.

There was a knock on the door.

'Hiya,' said Matt. He pushed his way in without waiting for me to say anything.

I ignored him. He pulled the chair out from under the desk I was sitting on and sat facing me. He took one of my fags out their packet and leant across to take the Clipper out my hand. I realised he was going to touch me and I threw it up for him to catch.

'Thanks.'

So what are you doing here, mate? Come to share gossip of how your mate is shagging that blonde whore? I stayed silent, smoking. He had been looking at the desk, but he looked up.

'You OK?' he asked.

Sure, sure, couldn't be better. 'Fine.' *Why wouldn't I be? My ex is shagging my best mate's torturer, and you're here to gloat.*

''Cause you look like you haven't slept.'

That's because I haven't. No idea what day it is. 'What day is it?' *Shit, did I just say that out loud?*

'Tuesday.'

'What? Are you serious?' *No, he's laughing. He's not serious.*

'Yes, it is. So you haven't slept?'

'Shit.'

He looked at the fag as if it had magically appeared in his hand. I looked at him.

'I think I'm going to go to bed,' I said, and nodded towards the door.

He took the hint.

●

I woke the next afternoon to loud knocking on my door.

'Where the fuck've you been?' asked Smithy.

'Bed?' I sat up and reached over for my pack of fags. It was empty.

'Here,' she said, as she held her pack of Marlboros in front of my nose. 'You can have one if you get up.'

I groaned and let her pull me up. I lit up.

'Chain-smoking's bad for you.'

Really, Smithy? Pot calling kettle black, mate. 'Smoking's bad for you,' I said.

She laughed and lit up. 'You do have a point. But we're all going to die sometime. Right? Coming to the Union to watch the game? You're not answering your phone.'

I jumped up, suddenly energetic. Put some jeans on, kept my Leeds shirt on. I followed her out of the door to the Union, which was packed. I saw the hall gang, including Callum and Yasmine, at the table next to the footie girls. I knew I couldn't hack it, so I turned to leave, but The Captain saw us and waved us over to the table.

'You missed training on Monday.'

'Sorry, mate.' *I don't want to talk about that just now.*

She shoved a pint of snakebite at me. I downed it. Smithy passed me another one and I sat down. *Time for the game.*

Jules appeared at half time. 'Mind if I join?'

Smithy pretty much sat on The Captain to make space. She patted the couch next to her. Jules sat. I realised I'd missed something.

'What's going on?' I asked.

'Nothing.'

Come on, mate, I know that look. And it doesn't say nothing. Maybe give her a minute. I'll ask again straight after the game.

But, after the game, we headed straight into the club bit of the Union and bumped into the rugby boys. Toby grabbed my arm and twirled me round and, before I knew what was happening, he had his lips on mine. I felt my heart beating to the rhythm of '*Mr Vain*'. He pulled away to grab his pint. Smiled at me. *Fuck it.*

I put my arms round his neck and pulled him to me. He opened his mouth slightly and let me in. His hands dropped to my waist. His grip hardened and so did my need. I tugged his hair gently. He let go of my body, then pulled at my arm, and dragged me back to his. It was a good night.

❯

'So?' Smithy looked at me through the smoke in the Union.

'I'll tell you if you tell me?' I looked back to the screen.

'There's nothing to tell,' she said.

Is she being serious? I think she's being serious. But … 'But yesterday you two looked so cosy.'

'And you looked like you were eating a rugby boy's face. A rugby boy! Don't you know what they get up to?'

Ugh, yeah, don't remind me. I've heard stories and I'm pretty sure they're all true. 'OK, OK. I slept with him. It was fun. No dirty pints, puking, or drinking from bums or shoes. Just a shag. OK? Now tell me!'

'Nothing happened,' she said sadly, looking up at the

screen as Guigou scored.

○

The next two days were chaos, with a few assignments due, so I didn't have time to see Jules for a proper chat until the weekend.

It was a no-game day. When I popped back to halls after training, I didn't want to head down to the end of the corridor where Callum, Yasmine, and Matt all lived, so I rang her. Two minutes later, she was at my door.

'Smithy says we have to go watch the rugby.'

Smithy does, huh? 'So, mate, you and Smithy?'

Jules blushed. 'Oh no. We're just good friends. I explained it all to her and she gets it. So friends it is.'

She gets it? Don't laugh, Ruby, mate. Don't.

'So what you're saying is you're interested, but you're back to hiding behind your religion?' *Whoa – that came out harsher than I meant. Ruby, mate, watch what you say.*

I looked up at her and saw the hurt in her eyes before she looked down.

Shit. 'I'm sorry, I …'

'No, you're right. I do like her. But I can't *like* her like her. I can't. You don't understand. You can't.'

You're right. I don't and can't. 'Try me.'

She just shook her head and walked me to the Union, where we sat with the mostly unchanged footie girls. Smithy was clearly uncomfortable.

And then I saw them. Our hall gang. The boys waved

and then they all came and sat next to us. Matt smiled at me. I felt guilty. *Why?* I smiled back. Callum ignored me.

Then Yasmine came to join the fun. *She knows even less about rugby than I do and she genuinely hates sport, so why is she here?* She sat next to Callum and took his hand. I had a flashback from the quiz night. I felt my last pint rising.

'Dana!' Yasmine said. 'I didn't know you played football!'

No, she just dresses like this for fun. Sweaty shirts and padded shins are all the rage. Haven't you read the latest issue of 'Cosmo' or whatever it is you read?

She smiled at me. I smiled back, focusing on keeping my pint down.

'Have you met my boyfriend, Callum?'

Great. So it's official now, is it?

I raised the pint glass to my lips and looked over at Matt. He was watching me. I looked down.

The rest of the day was better. Lots of alcohol and little else. Twinkle came by at one point and nudged me knowingly. I blushed and stupidly looked to Matt who, thankfully, wasn't looking at me.

Sunday was spent in bed. And not in the fun way. Jules had gone to church and Smithy didn't answer her phone. I went out for a run by myself.

Monday was crammed with lectures and seminars,

a forced hair appointment (Juliette's idea), and then training. On my way back, I heard a yell.

'Hey, Ruby!'

Oh my god, Toby, mate, you scared me. Wow, you are hot, aren't you? I'm sober and you still look amazing. Focus, Ruby, mate. 'Hey.'

'You been to training?'

Shit, I look terrible. 'Nah, mate, I always smell this good.'

He laughed. 'So, how're you doing?'

Better now. 'Sweaty.' *Yeah, keep drawing attention to that, Ruby, mate. Great.*

'Ha ha. Well, see you around.'

Absolutely. 'Yeah, see ya.'

I had almost reached the front door when Matt jumped out at me.

'Who was that?'

Oh no, I'm not doing this. 'Who?'

'The guy you were talking to. You know, six foot two-ish, about yay wide, milk-chocolate skin.'

'Toby.' *I can't do this. Keep looking down, Ruby, mate. You'll be fine.*

'And who is Toby?'

Oh god! 'A mate.' *Why did you just glare at him? Wouldn't you be asking if it was you?*

'Oh. You watching the game tomorrow?'

'Of course, mate. We'll be at the Union about six-ish if you wanna join?' *Why tell him that? Now he'll come.*

'Cool, I'll see you there.'

What are you so afraid of, Ruby? He's a mate. 'Cool.'

●

The Union was in full party mode, and the Real Madrid fans were outnumbered about ten to one. The footie girls, Jules, and most of the boys from our halls were sat together.

The Union erupted when Smith hit the back of the net, but before we could celebrate properly, Raul had evened the score. By half-time, we were 2-1 down. *Story of my life.*

Smithy was doing her best not to look obvious, but she was sat next to Jules and kept brushing her hand against Juliette's arm or leg. It made half-time amusing. Until The Captain moved from her seat next to me to talk to someone and Matt took her place.

'Predictions?'

'Arse.' *Yup, you're still hot, mate. I don't think everyone's hot these days, do I?*

'I didn't want to say but …'

'So then don't.' I smiled, he smiled back. 'Want a fag?'

He looked around. 'Sure.'

Hilarious, mate. So you're the new Ruby. I was hiding from an anti-smoking boyfriend. Who the hell are you hiding from?

I lit his cigarette. He inhaled smoke, I inhaled him.

The second half kicked off. By the time Viduka equalised, we had smoked our way through the entire packet.

'Since when do you smoke so much?' I asked, looking at the empty packet.

He shrugged. 'I'll pay for it in the morning.'

'We all will at some point, mate.'

Raul scored, I cried. Matt put his arm round me and I closed my eyes. *You smell so good, mate.* I sighed. Too loudly.

'You OK?'

I nodded, got up, and headed to the bar. Two pints later, the six of us, Matt, Smithy, Jules, Paul, John, and I, walked back to our halls.

Matt walked next to me but kept daylight between us and avoided touching me.

Typical. I guess the others are watching, are they? Why am I so angry?

I said goodnight at the top of the stairs and went to my room. I wanted to scream.

○

We had an away game Wednesday so, by the time we got back at six-ish, I had about half an hour to get ready for the social. Smithy and I drank heavily. I kept asking her about Jules. She kept telling me nothing had happened.

Thursday came around. I was wired. *Something's going to happen today, I can feel it.* After my final lecture, I went straight to the Union.

Matt, Paul, and Juan already had a table near the screen.

'Game's not on for hours! Everyone OK for a drink?'

They all signalled more was welcome, so I came back from the bar with a trayful of lager.

I sat next to Matt. Took out my pack of fags and offered him one. He shook his head.

'How do you rate your chances tonight, then?' I asked the two Liverpool fans.

'In the bag,' said Matt.

Confidence is attractive in a man. What am I saying? Stop it, Ruby, mate. Dangerous play.

'Porto won't know what hit 'em,' said Paul.

We stared at our pints. Paul analysed the state of play. Matt shared his usual, wild optimism. The night was heating up.

Kick-off. The drinks kept coming. By the end of the match, we were merry. As we walked home, Matt slipped his arm around my waist, Paul around my neck. They both let go when we got to the stairs.

Matt made a show of heading towards his room, but, as soon as Paul walked into the toilets, he turned back and followed me to my room.

'Ruby,' he started, drunkenly.

Don't, mate. I'm too drunk for this. And I might take advantage.

He stood in front of me and placed his hands on my shoulders. *Shit.* I held my breath. He leaned in. I inhaled, gently.

'Ruby! You in?' Smithy's voice clanged and the door banged.

Matt and I jumped apart and turned to look. She had opened the door and just stood there, crying.

Dislocation

The source of inspiration was the enemy itself. I witnessed their brazen behaviour in the putrid hallway of the northern wing, concealed by the solid part of the fire door. The plan was, as ever, brilliant in its simplicity. I had learned at a young age that complexity may make something theoretically better, but it is simplicity that is the key to success, as precision is the key to execution. It may, in retrospect, have been a desperate move on my part, but I believed in myself then, in a ruthlessly naïve fashion. I was, unfortunately, unaware of the elasticity of some bonds where, the further apart you hold them, the closer they eventually end up.

I told Sarah what I'd witnessed and elicited from her a promise not to pass on said information or its source. As expected, Sarah went and communicated everything to the boys (with the exception of who had told her), and the rumour spread in the way these things do. Before long, Juliette and Ruby were heard arguing. The seeds had been sown, and I withdrew my interest in their problems, steering conversation away from the blighted pair whenever my fellow residents ignited the topic. I had my own concerns.

Callum and I had settled, as the Easter term rolled toward its conclusion, into a wonderful routine of mutual appreciation of both physical and intellectual capabilities, but it was duly shattered by an event that led me to doubt his total immersion and trustworthiness. It began, as these things inevitably do, with something as guiltless as a conversation about the impending break.

'Will you come and visit over Easter?' I asked him.

'Sorry, I can't. I'm not going to be in the country. I thought I'd told you?'

'Well, maybe I can come and visit you?'

'I'm doing a course. I won't have time for socialising,' he said, with an abruptness that tugged at ulterior motives.

'Not even with me, darling?' I asked, wrapping my arms around his neck and ensuring his eyes held mine.

'Not even with you.'

He leant forward to kiss me, but I recognised the evasion tactics and wasn't keen to indulge.

'Where is it that you are going again?'

'Argentina. To learn some Spanish.' He sighed and stepped back to avoid my eye line, but I stepped into the space to maintain it.

'You've never shown an interest in Spanish before, darling.'

He tried to look at his feet, but ended up staring at my breasts instead. 'Well …'

'What aren't you telling me?'

'Nothing.' He shrugged, but the intonation signalled finality.

This little exchange weighed heavily, leading me to make yet another mistake, one that would seriously jeopardise my situation if discovered and, as I feared, lead to a permanent change in our dynamics.

CALLUM

Monday 12/03/2001 11:38
Subject: Bring on Argentina!

Hello.

I really can't wait for the end of the week – it's so TANGIBLE now – yeeeeeah! Just two assignments to do and I'm on a plane.

Things are a bit weird around here at the moment. There's been a stupid rumour flying around that Rube's been kissing girls which – although an incredible turn on – is obviously a pile of crap. Paul agrees that it's bullshit but Matt says it explains a few things. Not a chance, I say.

Anyway, Rube's disappeared completely since the rumour started, while Juliette's started hanging around the kitchen. Not a good thing really – she seems so MISERABLE all the time. And devout – not the crazy party girl I knew. She's reminding me of that religious nut in that cult movie you made me watch last year – 'Static', I think it was called? – you know, the one with the crucifix factory guy that hijacked that bus.

Girls are so unpredictable, actually. Don't you think?

Cal

Friday 16/03/2001 10:03
Subject: Re: RE: Bring on Argentina!

Hello.

What a week! I'm drowning in crap here.

First there was the bloody assignment – I really HATE the course. Everyone had gone out to the Union, even the girls – there was some event on – you know how these things are. So I sat in the kitchen to do work – closer access to the fridge and all that. And then Rube walked in.

She looked AMAZING – tight top, hair down – but then she saw me, mumbled 'hi' and took some food out the cupboard and put her hand on the door as if to leave. Then – she obviously had second thoughts – she turned back and asked me if I was OK, as if it wasn't obvious that I was most certainly not.

You'll be proud of me. I was not going to stoop to being pitied by my ex so I told her I was fine, actually.

She persisted, asking again if I needed help, knowing that I did and knowing that I knew she knew – which of course made it harder, right?

I politely refused and watched her cute little ass walk

away in a tight pair of jeans I hadn't seen her in before. It was TORTURE.

Then this thing with Yas yesterday – ugh! We're still together – thanks for asking – but sometimes she's so FULL ON. Anyway, she started harassing me about where I'm going for Easter and with who and why can't she come and – argh!

Ah well, problems to deal with next term, eh? I'm off for a run now. See you in two days!

Cal

JULIETTE

It just *happened*. It was so unexpected, so …

OK, I'm not making sense now, am I? Basically, what happened was … Smithy called me on the Thursday of the second-to-last week of term. She sounded a little upset and she'd been so good to me with everything, so I told her I was there if she needed to talk to me.

Well … well, she took that literally. So the next thing I know, Smithy's knocking on my door, holding a bottle of vodka and a pack of ciggies and shaking them in my face. I remember the urgency – of the shaking, I mean. It was like she was a percussionist abusing maracas. Passionate, you know?

Anyway, as I stepped out into the corridor – I didn't want her to see my room – it was covered in books and photocopies for my assignment. She asked if I had any mixers with so much bounce that I knew it couldn't be good.

I asked her if she was OK. I can still remember how she shook her head slowly, against the rhythm. And I'll never forget that phrase – 'it's no good' – and how she looked when she said it. It was like someone looks when they've lost a battle – a really important battle – like for their life or their soul or something.

'What's no good?' I had to ask – and I hoped it had nothing to do with me.

'Life,' she answered – very seriously – and passed me the bottle, brushing her soft fingers against mine as she did so and – and then …

And then she put one palm on each cheek and pulled my face towards hers. 'Why are you resisting?' was the last thing I remember her saying. Her lips touched mine. It felt so right that I forgot it was wrong. Don't look at me like that. How do you reconcile feeling so right with what you've known all your life as wrong? How? I don't know. Well, I didn't know. I do now – obviously – which is why I'm here. But I didn't then – I just freaked.

It was awful – I'm so ashamed of my behaviour now but it – well, it all came flooding out. Forget the Ark, this was – I can't put it into words – it's embarrassing to remember. I just turned and walked into my room and slammed the door. Then I felt bad and opened it again – but she was gone – just an empty corridor.

I closed the door again and started to cry. After a few hours of wallowing in my misery, I got up to go to the toilet. That's when I saw them – Smithy and Ruby – hugging, in front of Ruby's room. It's so stupid to think of it now but … but I didn't want to see anyone so I closed the door again.

The next day, there were rumours everywhere – well, everywhere in our corridor – that Ruby had been spotted snogging a girl. Obviously, they meant Smithy. And obviously – given what I'd seen the previous night – it was true.

I acted *appallingly* towards poor Ruby – I refused to listen to her, avoided her, ignored her – the usual. She tried to reason with me, denying everything, but I knew what I'd seen and I couldn't get it out of my head. Little things, like their ritual of getting the other in a headlock and ruffling their hair – things that used to seem innocent but now all I could see was flirtation – things like that really *haunted* me. I couldn't stand to see her. I couldn't. It was terrible. It was … a truly awful way to end the term. But obviously not as awful as how the next one started.

RUBY

Smithy just stood there, crying. We sat her down on my bed and Matt excused himself.

'What's wrong?'

'Juliette,' she said, and raised a shaky hand to light her fag.

'What?' *Is she hurt? Is she ill?*

'I … I pulled her.'

Oh. 'OK?' *So why are you crying? Was it that bad? Don't laugh, Ruby, mate. Don't. There's obviously something wrong here.*

'She hates me. I shouldn't have kissed her. But I swear she kissed me back. But then she pushed me away. She hates me.'

Easy there, mate. Slow down. 'She doesn't hate you, mate. She's just got religious crap issues.' *Keep your voice down. Jules had better never catch you talking about her like that.*

'You think?'

I saw hope in her face. The tears stopped. *Thank god.*

We sat. And smoked. And drank our way through a bottle of rum that had mysteriously appeared in my room sometime.

'Thanks,' she said when we'd polished off the bottle. 'I needed that.'

'No worries.'

She was out of the door when I saw her pack of fags on the bed. I ran out and gave them to her, she hugged me thanks, and I went back to my room. To think about Matt. *Did I really almost kiss him? What the hell is going on?*

The next day, I ran into the kitchen to grab some chocolate to eat on my way to my shift, when Paul punched me lightly on the shoulder.

'I heard you've been kissing girls. Was Callum that

bad that now none of us boys are good enough for you?'

What? What the fuck are you on about?

I laughed. 'Definitely not good enough for me,' I said, and ran off to the restaurant.

When I got back, I went to Jules's door and knocked. I could hear some monotonous dance beat, so I knew she was in. I pushed the door. It was locked. Maybe she'd left her music on.

I walked into the kitchen to grab a beer out the fridge. Matt and Callum were there but stopped talking. They looked first at each other then at the table.

Fine. So it's going to be like this, is it? I left.

It was Saturday before I realised what had happened. Smithy rang me up.

'Umm, so you know your mate, Juan? He just came up to me and congratulated me on pulling you. No, not Juliette. You. I told him he didn't know what he was talking about, but he said something about how someone'd seen us and you'd confirmed it. What the hell's going on?'

Oh, fuck. I rang off and jogged to Jules's room. Her door was open, so I walked in. She glared at me and walked out.

'Hey! Wait! I …' She jogged to the toilets and slammed the door.

I waited for her. She came out, shouted 'How could you?', jogged to her room, and slammed the door.

I knocked on her door. No response. I shouted. No response. I rang her. No response. *Fuck this.*

I gave up, texted her, and went to drink with Smithy.

›

We kept drinking till Wednesday's social, where we watched Lazio equalise in extra time. *This term's getting better and better. I can't wait for it to end.*

On Thursday morning, I heard the others discussing going to the Union for the Liverpool game and some stupid event after. My hall (ex?) mates hadn't invited me, Matt had been ignoring me, and I was shattered. I texted Smithy to let her know I wouldn't be down that night.

At about half-time, when I could be sure no-one was about, I went to the kitchen to grab some dinner.

Callum was there, books spread across the table. He looked tired. He glanced up.

'Hi,' I said, not wanting to be rude.

I grabbed some food and made to leave, then thought better of it. He really did look miserable.

'You OK?' I asked. *You look ill.*

'I am, actually.'

Right. So Yasmine's keeping you satisfied then? Shut up, Ruby, mate. What do you care? Because I care … Stop it. Leave. Now. 'Sure you don't need any help, mate?' I said. *I'm asking him about work. There's nothing sexual about it. Why am I thinking about sex?*

'No thanks,' he said.

Good. I left.

My phone beeped in the corridor. I put the pack of crisps under my armpit in a rugby hold and looked at the screen. I read the message, looked around to make sure no-one could see me, then deleted it. I wasn't in the mood for that sort of thing tonight. Maybe tomorrow. If not, next term …

Term 3:

APRIL
TO
JUNE
2001

... to Ashes

JULIETTE

Well, it didn't *start* terribly – not really – although, obviously, by the Monday of week two it all went to – it all fell apart.

Ruby and I had started talking again over the break – she'd sent me an email and I realised that, apart from being wrong, I'd been unforgiving and un-Christian, stooping to lows that were way beneath me. 'Take ye heed every one of his neighbour, and trust ye not in any brother: for every brother will utterly supplant, and every neighbour will walk with slanders.' I didn't know how the false – I now know it's false – rumour had started – although, of course, I did suspect – but I forgave and moved forward.

The issue – of course – was that somebody had *seen* me. This was definitely a case of no smoke without fire and the knowledge scared me. So – in the same way Ruby and I had gotten closer again over the break – I hadn't found the strength to speak to Smithy. She texted a couple of times but then stopped – I suspect because I didn't respond. So I wasn't looking forward to going back.

But it started well – the first weekend back was great. It all seemed to have subsided – the drama, I mean. I managed to avoid Smithy – I have to admit I made some excuses – I didn't lie – I just concentrated on my workload far more than I needed to, really. I actually ended up getting hooked on research for my discourse on crime in 20th century literature – deciding to focus on burglary – contrasted with depictions of crime in modern media. Sorry – I'm not here to talk about uni papers – not even interesting ones.

So, anyway, before it all happened, I decided to go ask Callum for his copy – it's his favourite novel, apparently – for his copy of '*The Return of Sherlock Holmes*' – you see, I just wanted to look something up and I couldn't be bothered to go all the way to the library – so I went to Callum's room. I was engrossed – you know how I can be, sometimes – so I didn't knock – I just walked in. And Yasmine was there, unmistakeably reading his emails – it was homemail, you see, and I knew Yas only had her uni one as we'd had that discussion in the kitchen recently. Confused? Basically, different colour backgrounds for online mail providers. Never mind. Anyway, she closed the laptop immediately, of course, but I'm not a particularly good actress, so it was obvious I'd already seen. Of course, I still pretended I hadn't – I just asked for the book, then went back to continue on my essay.

And, before I knew it, it was the second week of term. I got up very late that day – no lectures on Mondays, lucky me! I was alone in the tight corridor, groggy from sleep. I remember walking slowly to the toilets

– they're by the doorway to the stairs you see – very slowly, dragging my feet, looking down, rubbing my eyes. My mind was slowly waking up. I wish it hadn't, because then – maybe – I wouldn't have reacted like I did. Who knows? Maybe He does, though I doubt our little worries are of any consequence to Him.

Anyway – that Monday morning on my way to the toilets – that's when it happened.

CALLUM

Sunday 22/04/2001 19:18
Subject: Back in the UK

Hello.

I'm back at uni. Missing Argentina – it was awesome. Ah well, summer before I know it, right?

It's weird being back. Yas keeps harassing me about where I've been, who with, etc, etc – I swear I never had to put up with crap like that from Rube. I've been doing my best to fob off the questions, but she's very persistent. But I can't tell her. After the debacle with Rube last term, I'm not telling anyone.

Speaking of Rube – the awkwardness persists. In fact, it's probably worse. Maybe those rumours last term were true? Although you're probably right in your assessment – highly unlikely.

Let's sort out summer, yeah? Enjoy Brazil.

Cal

Monday 30/04/2001 22:46
Subject:

Something crazy's happened – Juliette's fallen down the stairs and was rushed off in an ambulance this afternoon. No idea what's happening or if she's OK. Everyone's distraught here. I'll let you know more when I know.

Keep safe.

Cal

RUBY

I stared at the pint glass in front of me with horror. It was almost empty and I knew the next round was mine. Not that I minded, but we were already so *drunk*.

'Wow – you girls look … interesting,' came a familiar voice behind my neck.

My hairs stood on end, but I smiled and turned to face Toby.

'No talking to anyone outside the circle – three fingers!' yelled The Captain.

I finished off my pint and nodded to Toby to follow me to the bar.

'How've you been?' *Shit, Ruby, mate, you're slurring.*
'Good. You look good.'
You offering, mate?
I smiled. 'Thanks. You into high-powered women then?' *Wow. Definitely slurring. And don't act like that, mate. You're not desperate. Well, not that desperate.*

Although he's hot so, technically, it's not desperation, is it?

'Never thought it possible, but you pull off that suit so well.'

I twirled for his benefit. 'Well, you know, us investment bankers ...'

'Ruby!' Twinkle appeared on my left. 'You look great. Where's Jules? She's not answering her phone and it's not like her to miss the first social of term.'

Stop staring at my tits, mate! 'She's got work, unfortunately.'

We got to the bar. I sidestepped through a gap and hooked my elbows under my breasts, letting my jacket open slightly. I wasn't wearing a shirt. I smiled at the barman.

'Four pints of Carlsberg, three snakebites, two Strongbows and ... what are you boys having?'

'Such a cheat. It's outrageous how women always get served first.'

Not my fault I was born with assets, mate. Even if they are small. As you know. 'So you don't want a drink, mate?' I raised my eyebrows at Toby.

'Four Carlsbergs and two pints of Stella, please.'
Better.

'Two Stellas and a Smirnoff Ice,' said Twinkle.

We looked at him and laughed.

He joined in. 'It's obviously not for me.'

The week continued.

Thursday was some drum and bass night at the Union, which Smithy dragged me to.

Friday was an Eighties' themed extravaganza.

Saturday was quiet drinks in the pub with the footie girls after our firsts versus seconds game.

Sunday was the Union quiz with Smithy and some of her hall mates, followed by a quick smoke in Jules's room (I didn't mention Smithy).

Monday was … bad.

My afternoon lecture finished and I walked back to halls. I turned the key in the front door lock and then I saw her. *Fuck.* Contorted, immobile. Blood everywhere. *So much blood.* I screamed and ran for the tutor.

Things happened. I don't know what. There seemed to be a lot of people running around, asking me questions. I had no idea what was going on or what was happening.

I can't believe it's Juliette.

The crumpled form at the bottom of the stairs. The body lifted onto the stretcher. The blood.

Why won't they tell me if she's OK?

'… drugs …' I heard the ambulance people say.

Seriously? It's just weed. She wasn't taking anything else. I'll vouch for that. Even if it lands me in a world of trouble.

I rested my head on the wall. It was cool, made my cheeks burn less. This was not how term was supposed to go. First year of uni was meant to end on a high. Just not the drugs' variety.

The police walked past, continuing their conversation

about 'pills, some coke and a rolled up note'.

Juliette's? But surely the only thing she had in her room was leftovers of an eighth?

I patted my pockets as our hall tutor brushed past me. *Nothing. Where are my fags?*

Breathe, Ruby, mate. Breathe. She'll be OK. Matt was. But then he collapsed on the spot, not at the top of the stairs.

They shut the ambulance doors and the sirens wailed.

What's happening? Where are they taking her? Can someone tell me please? Does anyone care?

I felt the brick against my face. It wasn't helping any more. I needed to cool down. *I need a drink. And a smoke. I need to move. Why can't I move? Help, someone. Help!*

But no one was interested. *All wrapped up in their own worlds. Making up stories. Oh yes, the rumours will be even wilder after this one.*

I caught a movement and looked over at the huddle by the grass. He grabbed hold of her hand. And then looked over at me. *Am I supposed to care?*

I sniggered, possibly out loud. *It's pathetic of him.*

But at least it shook me out of my trance. I felt my leg muscles twitch and was able to move again. I turned and headed up the hill to clear my head and start my hunt.

Once I was armed with fags, I picked up my phone and rang Smithy.

'Mate,' I began.

YASMINE

I didn't mean to kill her. It was never my intention and I have spent many a sleepless night since relaying the whole event in my head. It was all a misunderstanding, a terrible accident, something for which I am sincerely and unreservedly apologetic.

My subsequent actions, however, were a result of necessity. I had to ensure that no undue questions were asked so that neither my relationship with Callum nor, indeed, my education were jeopardised.

Term had started uneventfully, despite Callum's reluctance to tell me where he'd been. I questioned him to no avail, and his secret burned through me until it was stronger than my love for him. I began to watch him, quietly, piecing together his passwords and waiting for my chance for access. I needed to be party to this secret that had built a seemingly indestructible wall between us.

Eventually, I cracked the laptop and email passwords (they were different) and, while he was at a lecture, I sat down to read. I'm not proud of my actions, but I was angered, shocked, and puzzled by his emails to 'David'. Callum had not, I saw, painted a particularly flattering nor honest picture of me to his friend and, added to that, his lust for Ruby appeared not to have abated. I began to conduct a detailed search of his room and found hidden, behind the books on his shelf, an intricately boxed pair of small diamond studs and a sealed card addressed to Ruby. This find both angered and focused my search on the shelf and I discovered, tucked between the pages of one of his books, some photos. The resemblance was there, and the final confirmation came in the shape of an old journal, hidden rather inexpertly under his bed. A secret brother! The magnitude of this discovery overwhelmed me and, after replacing the journal, I sat at his desk to re-read the emails.

It was then that Juliette walked in, breathless and wild. I closed the top of the laptop as innocently as I could and helped her locate some book of Callum's that she was after. I was acutely aware of the fact that she'd seen what I was doing, but rationality told me that she was highly unlikely to have recognized that they were not my emails I had been immersed in.

I observed her closely over the next few days, but she never gave an indication of any untoward thoughts and, besides, she was deeply absorbed in penning an assignment for her 'stimulating' course. But the issue was never far from my mind, especially as the need to confront Callum about his feelings for Ruby almost overwhelmed me on a number of occasions. Thankfully, I held my poise and simply ensured that any social commitments we had were geographically removed from her potential location, until I could be certain that he had removed her permanently from his desires and that he wasn't simply leading me on when it came to our relationship.

When the incident with Juliette occurred, I was shaken to action. I had thoughtfully relieved one of my school 'friends' of their cocaine sachet and some pills at a nineteenth birthday party in a manor house that I had attended over Easter, as I had, correctly, assumed that they may be of use. I wiped them down and placed them into Juliette's pocket along with a pre-rolled joint that was already there. I then went out for a walk, ringing an old acquaintance of my father's that I knew could help me.

Upon my return, I joined the others, and we all stood there, in a tableau of conflicting thoughts and shock. It was one of us in that ambulance, and the tension reverberated across the grass verge outside our halls of residence. We stood in a circle, roughly grouped into the cliques that had grown out of a single hall cluster over the last two terms, with only Ruby standing apart from the rest of the crowd, leaning casually by the building opposite and staring at the ambulance that held Juliette's comatose form.

The hall tutor indicated strongly that the authorities believed drugs were involved. The drug paraphernalia found in her room had clearly helped form this impression, along with the fact that Juliette was lying unconscious at the foot of the stairs with nothing but a joint, a lighter, some pills, and a plastic bag with half a gram of coke in her pocket. None of the 'responsible' adults were forthcoming with any enlightening information.

I stood on the wet grass in the comfort of the main group. I felt his hand squeeze mine, and warmth filled what just a second before had been a void of feelings and thoughts. I smiled and looked up at him, expecting to see his caring, rich face peering down at me in concern. I couldn't have been more wrong; his gaze was firmly set on *her*, standing in solitude and guiltily patting her pockets every time a policeman walked past, wondering, paranoid, if she had any drugs on her person. It was truly worrying how close Ruby and Juliette had become, and I couldn't help but wonder how much Juliette had confided in Ruby prior to that ill-advised plunge down the stairs.

'Darling, this is horrible. Could we please go get a drink?' I said, pulling on his arm and steering him away from halls and *her,* toward the safety of the Students' Union. I never realised how extensive the repercussions of my actions would be, especially the effects on Callum; I never imagined the possibility of the ensuing fallout, or the pain I would put him through.

Tales

CALLUM

Wednesday 02/05/2001 14:52
Subject: HIDE

Where are you? All hell's broken loose here. Dad's
called me like 500 times and we've both been trying to
reach you at the hostel. It's a shitstorm. Someone leaked
shit about you to the press. Hide. And CALL US.

Cal

Thursday 03/05/2001 00:27
Subject: CALL US

Sooo … we still haven't gotten hold of you. WHERE
ARE YOU? It's bad – really bad, actually. Mum's holed
up at home, Dad's in some hotel and you are nowhere to
be found. This isn't funny.

Just so you know – when you do get this – I've had
it out with Rube. She was acting all innocent and – argh,
I hate that bitch! I can't believe I ever dated her. What's
wrong with me?

CALL US!

Cal

RUBY

I held my breath. I closed my eyes. I crushed the pack of fags in my hand. *I can't go on.*

The silence at my end was clearly unbearable to Smithy, who screamed 'What? Tell me!' down the phone.

I held the mobile away from my ear then brought it to my lips. 'I'm coming over,' I whispered. 'Then we're going to drink.'

'But training ...'

Fuck training.

'Fuck training,' I said.

❯

Smithy cried loudly. I'd never known her to cry like this before. Not over the Juliette thing last term (she'd sobbed). Not when she called me to tell me her dog had died over Easter. Not even when the fat keeper from that aggressive, red team from up North had studded her in the Achilles. This time the tears were packed and real.

I shook my fags at her.

'But how? And what's happening? Is she OK?' she asked for the twentieth time.

'No idea, mate. Our hall tutor called her mum and she promised to notify him but ...' *You know how these things go, mate. People say they'll do something, some even mean it. But what's the use?*

I shrugged. She took me by the hand and led me to the Union.

What do we look like? Two zombie lesbians making our way through the crowd? Two friends drowning in their pain? And how can I help her? What can I do?

A voice broke through my thoughts.

'You OK?'

If I got a beer for every time I'd heard that at uni, I'd be happily comatose by now. No such luck, though.

'Hi, Toby. Shit day. Jules ...'

He put his arm gently across my shoulders. I snuggled, unwanted, into his chest. Under his armpit, I saw Matt and Callum staring at me. I closed my eyes.

'Is it true?' Twinkle's voice somehow made it even more real. I took the pint from his hand and held it to my head.

'Get a pitcher for us, will you, mate?' I let Toby go and sat with my back to the others' table.

Monty arrived with the drinks right then. *They must have been waiting for us, must have found out somehow.*

They asked me to tell them what had happened. I lit up, found my voice, and began to talk.

❯

I don't know what happened that night, or the next day. I just know that I woke up on Wednesday in Toby's bed. *What happened?*

My head hurt. My biceps were sore. My throat stung. *Inevitable, really.*

'Lunch?' he asked.

'Ugh. What time is it?' *I've missed the morning lecture for sure, but I've also got another at one.*

He looked at his watch. 'Quarter past two.'

Fuck. 'Lunch.'

Lunch lasted a couple of hours and pints. I tried Jules four times. No answer.

Toby left to go to a four o'clock, and I walked back to halls. I stared at my feet and for the first time noticed the way I dragged them when I walked. Dad was always going on about that. *Hmmm, maybe he has a point.*

'Hey! Watch where you're going.' I looked up to see Matt's face. 'Oh, Ruby, sorry I didn't realise it was you. I …' He looked down at his feet.

'You OK, mate?' I asked. *Why does it all have to be so difficult these days?* 'Been a while.'

'Yeah it has.' His tone was soft this time.

'Want a fag?' I shook my pack at him. He looked around, then nodded. He took two out, passed me one. We both lent into my lighter simultaneously. Our eyes met.

'So. You and the black rugby boy, eh?'

Of course. Why was I so slow? He just wanted the gossip.

'Over your theory that I'm a lesbian, then, mate?' *Want to play games? I can play games.*

'Heh. Yeah, sorry. I just thought – you know – you never seem interested in guys, you know?'

'So Callum and Toby are?' *Female, obviously.*

He stopped, swallowed, looked at me.

'Callum is my friend.'

Of course. We're having that *conversation now. OK, mate. Bring them all on.*

We'd reached the entrance to our halls, so I stubbed out my fag and raced up the stairs. *Boys are ridiculous sometimes.*

I needed to cheer up. Less Than Jake it was. I'd just turned up the volume when there was a knock on my door.

'Look, Matt, I know …'

I stopped as the door I'd just unlocked stood open to reveal Callum. He was angry. Very, very angry. I'd never imagined he could look like this and it sure as hell didn't suit him.

'Can I help you?' I asked, in my best waitress voice.

'How could you?' He gritted his teeth, clenched his fists.

I stepped back. 'How could I …?'

'We've been *fucked* thanks to you. I can't get hold of him. Mum's in a state and Dad's – argh! How could you?'

What the …? 'I'm sorry, I'm not sure what you're

talking about.' I rubbed my temples. I had a hangover. *How can I possibly have a hangover? It's afternoon and I haven't stopped drinking. Have I? Ugh.*

'Nobody else *knew*.'

'Knew what, mate?'

'I *confided* in you. I *trusted* you. I *defended* you when people were talking shit about you. Shit, I *loved* you.'

That got me. I didn't care what this argument was about, I just wanted in. 'You also dumped me, you dick. For *her*.'

'Oh, so *that's* what it's about, is it? The break-up? You're so delusional.'

'Fuck the break-up. Fuck you, mate. And fuck Yasmine.' *Wow. That felt good. Still don't know what you're on about, though. Why are we fighting?*

'So, you did this to me – to *us* – you fuck my whole family because of Yasmine?'

What? 'What's your family got to do with it? We're talking about *you*.' *Aren't we?*

'What's my family got to do with it? What's my family got to do with it? What's my …?'

'I got it the first time.' *Good use of tone, though, mate. Ever considered being in a band?*

'How *could* you?'

It was getting boring now. I'd enjoyed shouting at him, but now I just wanted to smoke. Plus, I was very confused. And my head hurt.

'I really don't know what you're talking about, mate. I'm sorry,' I said, lowering my voice.

He raised his. 'You're *sorry*? That's what you have to say? You're *sorry*?'

About the fact I don't know what you're talking about. Not about whatever it is you are talking about, mate. What are you talking about? I need a fag. Where are my fags?

I looked longingly at the packet on my bedside table. 'Please leave,' I said quietly.

'Fuck you!' he spat at me, and left the room.

I stared after him, in shock. His words hurt me, especially now that I had time to think them through. *I wonder what's bothering him? Did I do something when I was drunk?*

I sat on my desk and opened the window. *The days are getting longer.* I took a fag from the pack, lit it. Inhaled, exhaled. Watched the smoke curl upwards.

Fuck this. I'd had enough. I picked up my phone and dialled Jules's number. It rang and rang. No answer.

I lit another, smoked it, then rang her number again. On the third ring, someone picked up. The person on the end of the line was definitely not Jules. And they were definitely crying.

YASMINE

It had played out very differently in my mind. No-one was supposed to suffer the consequences apart from Ruby. I had never anticipated that the effects of a simple conversation, conducted over the static of my mobile to an individual I'd known all my life could be cataclysmically destructive. My motivation had been selfish, albeit sincere. I needed to divert the media's attention so that they would not, as I knew that they were accustomed to doing (and doing it well), investigate further into the unfortunate Juliette affair.

In the Union, sitting next to my darling Callum, I wondered if I could ever explain my actions to him, if he'd ever knowingly forgive me for what I had done to Juliette but, more importantly, to him. I traced the sadness in his eyes as he stared at the back of Ruby's head, willing my jealousy to subside.

I slept very badly that night, despite being wrapped tightly in his soothing embrace. Thoughts flew through my dreams and pecked at my nightmares. What if she woke up? What if she told them? I'd removed the evidence on my walk, but no crime can stand up to complete and thorough examination. No matter what the press may portray in their pages or screens, the truth is, evidence is always there to be found, if people know exactly what it is they're looking for.

And so it was that, the next day, I sat at my computer to write. It was an old, heavy, cumbersome PC that my father had insisted I carry to university. He couldn't afford, he told me solemnly one night, to buy me a laptop, as he had retired and, besides, school fees had been replaced by uni contributions. Although he did have a point about housing costs, university fees were, as everyone knew, a pittance, and his argument was even more insulting given he was holding a pair of round-the-world tickets for himself and my mother as he made it. You can't pretend you're sacrificing everything financially for your daughter while planning a year of travel.

I spent the whole day writing, pausing only for food and even declining Callum's proposals that evening. I continued the next day, knowing that my time may be limited, that I may suffer unduly if she didn't die peacefully in her hospital bed but came to life, fighting and demanding justice.

That afternoon, Callum walked into my room, shaking, and I had to control myself from throwing my guilt at his feet and begging for clemency.

Instead, I wrapped the blanket of my love around him.

'Darling, what's wrong?' I asked.

'It's all … it's all so terrible. I just can't believe this is happening.'

'I'm sorry, darling,' I said to him. 'I don't think I understand.'

He looked at me with his once emerald eyes, now merely fake glass replacements.

'We had … a family secret. And now it's all over the tabloids.'

'Oh, darling, I'm so sorry. What happened?'

He sat down on my bed and put his soft, warm hands over the back of his head, pressing his forehead down into his knee in some perverse, and undoubtedly painful, sit-up.

'I don't know,' he whispered, and I bent to him, holding his head between my palms and attempting to kiss all my errors away.

Even then, I didn't understand the pain that Callum would be subjected to, the fear, the inquiry, the mass hysteria.

'I'm so sorry,' I whispered back.

He looked at me, into my eyes, and I witnessed moisture filming over the glass.

'I don't understand,' he said. 'We've kept this out of the press for years. For years.'

'Oh, darling. Then how did this happen?' I croaked, the guilt crushing my windpipe.

'I don't know. Nobody knew. Nobody.' His eyes suddenly re-acquired the fire I so admired in them. 'Ruby!'

He stood up and strode to the door.

'What?' I asked.

'Rube knew,' he said, anger filling his muscles, broadening his shoulders, elongating his frame.

I watched him go, dejected at my part in the matter but also pleased that I had managed to re-ignite the spark that had simmered under the flood of upcoming exams. I was in the unenviable position of initiating an explosion of passion in my lover, while intensely aware that it was a reaction to an agony I'd caused.

I can only hope my subsequent actions and reassurances went some way toward alleviating the torture I unthinkingly put him through.

Betrayal

RUBY

I tried to speak but nothing came out. I stared down at the fag simmering between my fingers. Still, the sobbing continued.

'Hello?' I tried. 'It's Ruby. I'm a friend of ... a friend of Juliette's.'

The sobbing stretched on. Then the person at the end of the line blew their nose. 'Hello? I apologise for my outburst there. I'm sorry, who did you say you were?'

'Ruby. I'm ...'

'Oh, are you that friend from the Christian Society? She's spoken very highly of you.'

Shit. What do I say to that? 'I was wondering how, umm, if she's OK?' *Breathe, Ruby, mate. Breathe. You've got to ask. You need to know.*

'We'll be taking her home. My baby.' The sobbing returned.

What does that mean? You're taking her home how? Normally? Or in a coffin? Fucking tell me!

'Umm. Mrs ...' *Shit, what's her surname? It's not like Jules ever receives mail or anything.*

'One moment please.' There was more nose-blowing.

Then some white noise at the end of the phone. Then it went dead. *Shit.*

I took out another fag, lit it from my old one and stubbed the previous one out. I took a drag. *Better.* I looked at the phone in my hand. *Worse.*

I jumped. The ring had reached me before my eyes registered that the screen was flashing. *It's her again.* I lifted it up to my ear.

'Hello. Mrs …'

'Ruby! I'm so glad to hear your voice. They've been keeping me in solitary here. Well, that's what it feels like.'

'Fuck, mate. I was *so* worried. You OK? What *happened*?'

'Don't know. Police have been asking me, Mummy's been asking me, Edward's been asking …'

'Edward?' *Who is Edward?*

'The Vicar. He's – well, he's been there for us since Daddy died. I …'

Oh god, more religious people hounding the poor girl. Just what she needs. More Christian guilt. Great for recovery and all.

'So what happened, mate?'

'I don't remember. It's all very fuzzy. Doctors say it's normal with head trauma, but it does feel very strange.'

'But you're OK?'

'Fuzzy. But OK. I'll be going home soon.'

'*Home* home?' *Please no.*

'Mummy's spoken to the university. I'm going home for the rest of term. What happens next year, well, that's up for discussion. Mummy wants me to quit and go to a local uni. I obviously would rather not but …'

No, no, no. Please don't quit, mate. Please no. Hold on …

'Is she listening?'

'Yes.'

'Ah OK, mate. Speak later then, yeah?'

'Yeah.' There was a pause. 'Err, I think Mummy would like a word, if that's alright?'

With me? What the fuck for? 'Of course.'

More white noise.

'Hello, Ruby. As Juliette just told you, she'll be heading home with us. Would you be able to notify the hall tutor that we will be coming by your residence to pick up her things?'

'Of course. Now?'

'No, no. Not in the middle of the night! We still have a few things to discuss with the doctors tomorrow. Friday morning. We'll be there after Matins.'

Which means …? Probably best not to tell her I've no idea what she's on about. For Jules's sake. 'I'll let him know.'

'Thank you, my dear.' The phone went dead. I took another drag, then went to the Union to watch the Leeds game. *I'll tell the tutor in the morning.*

'So, do you think I should ring her?' Smithy looked into her pint like she was trying to find something she'd lost in it. There was definitely no penny there.

'I don't know, mate.' I shrugged. 'She seems to be seriously under the influence of her obviously *very* crazy mother.'

'So I shouldn't ring her?'

'Why don't you give her a ring tomorrow, 'after Matins', when her mother's here? Probably easier to talk then?'

'What time does Matins finish?'

Seriously, mate? You're asking me?

She lifted her eyes to mine and we burst out laughing.

'Something funny?' Yasmine's evil take on sarcasm smashed through the hilarity to the back of our home net. She stood over us and smiled through gritted teeth.

Standing behind her were Matt and Paul. I took out a fag from the packet, even though I wasn't in the mood to smoke. I lit it, inhaled shallowly, and blew smoke in their direction.

'We're celebrating Jules being alive.'

'She OK?' Yasmine gasped, so emotionally she almost made me believe she cared.

'She's alive. Not really OK. Her mother's here. She's one creepy lady.'

'Did she tell you what happened?'

Oh, so now you're interested, are you, mate? 'She doesn't remember anything.'

'Nothing?'

I shook my head.

'We might never know what happened,' said Smithy.

'Some trauma victims never get that bit of their memory back.'

We all looked at her.

'That's what mum said. She's a doctor. Not here, unfortunately.'

'How lovely. We're off. Need to furnish Callum with supplies before he starves. He's hiding from the press who are after him, thanks to you.'

'I would probably eat some of that food too, if I were you,' I shouted after her. Then I took another shallow drag and emptied my lungs in her direction.

○

The next morning, I felt the effects of our late-night drinking session throughout the lecture, but at least the anger following the run-in with Yasmine had gone.

I came back and ran into a short lady dressed in a dark blue, flowery, knee-length dress. She was carrying a box and looked like a Fifties' housewife. It had to be Jules's mother.

'Hello. I'm Ruby. We spoke yesterday?'

She looked up at me with hatred. I stepped back. *What have I done now?*

'You! You're the girl that's been filling my poor Juliette's head with all this homosexual nonsense? She's a good, clean, Christian girl. A good, clean, Christian girl.'

This woman is definitely crazy. How the hell did Jules turn out so normal?

'Umm, I'm not Smithy. I'm, I'm Ruby,' I stuttered. *What had Jules told her? And why, Jules? Why?*

'You and your debauchery. Sport and feminism. Girls don't know how to be women these days.' She shook her head with a sadness that almost made me feel sorry for her. Almost.

'I'm not gay. I'm her friend,' I tried again, but the old lady didn't hear me. Or didn't care.

'The lord works in mysterious ways indeed. I am glad for this accident. I had not realised how far she had strayed. But I am thankful to him for I can now save her.'

Thankful to who? And who speaks like this? Seriously crazy, mate.

'Juliette *is* a good girl. A good friend.'

The old lady stopped and glared at me again. 'She has friends. Friends who care about her. Friends who want to save her from this. You are not one of those people.' And with that, she turned and walked towards the car park.

I took out my phone and rang Jules. No answer. I rang Smithy. No answer. I checked my texts. The first was the weekly cheeky text from Twinkle. I'd been getting them since last term. I always replied with something witty, but not today.

'Not funny. Jules in trubl' I typed and sent.

Then I looked at the other one. It was from Smithy, a single word. It wasn't good.

'Vodka', it read.

CALLUM

Thursday 03/05/2001 11:01
Subject: Shitstorm

Hello.

So glad Dad got hold of you but do ring me – need to talk. Dad's in bad shape, obviously. Mum's not been very understanding which is understandable but ... Anyway, at least the university banished the press from campus – postgrads have already started exams apparently, so they used that as an excuse.

I've managed to avoid Rube this morning but I still want to kill her. How can someone ACT like that? I never thought she'd stoop that low. To fuck us all like that because she's harbouring some twisted hatred over our break-up? Which she wanted! Fuck off, actually. Bitch!

Call me when you can. And keep a low profile for a while yet. The shitstorm's not over.

Cal

Sunday 06/05/2001 15:33
Subject:

Hello.

What a shit few days. At least Juliette's OK, though apparently she's heading home. Some trouble with her mother. Yas says that she won't be back but Sarah says she's returning next year. Who knows?

It's all quite quiet, actually. Yas – who's been very supportive over this whole thing, by the way – is always at her computer studying for the upcoming exams – she's committed. Unlike Ruby, who is always out partying like revision is unnecessary – I haven't seen her since that argument, by the way. She's keeping out of my way. Too right.

Good news on the sporting front though – with foot and mouth crisis 'subsiding', maybe we'll watch that Ireland game soon.

What a fuck-up this year has been, eh?

Cal

JULIETTE

Waking up was so weird – I was in a bed with tubes and beeping and, and then I couldn't remember what had happened. Mummy and doctors and nurses and policewomen – all these people asking me about the fall, making strange accusations, saying things ... and I couldn't remember a thing. It was really weird.

Eventually, I got to speak to Ruby, who was so lovely and understanding. Made a change from Mummy who was so *stifling*. It's just the way she is – the way she's always been. But after being away from her for a while – well, it was so much *worse*, you know? I just wanted to get out of the bed and leave. Did you know she even rang the university and told them I was leaving? Of course you did. Luckily, policy is that you need to fill in a form and I said I'd have a leave of absence until next year. They signed it off – it took them aaaaages though. But luckily they signed it. So I can go back. Which I'm obviously going to do. I don't even have a choice not to now – the way things are at home.

But I'm jumping ahead, as usual. Mummy left me alone that day while she went to my corridor to pick my stuff up. She said she didn't want me to overexert myself over the next few months, but I knew she just wanted to keep me away from the 'drug haven' of university. Ha!

Anyway, that day – Smithy rang me. It was lovely – she was lovely. So caring, so thoughtful – she told me to write or ring whenever I needed, whatever I needed. She was there for me, she said – she's the first person that's ever said that that I actually believed, you know?

Then Mummy came back from our corridor and – as you know well – it all went wrong. She started accusing me of straying from the Lord, first with drugs and then with homosexuality. She preached Leviticus et al at me for aaaages – it was the worst scolding of my life – and I've had a few! But how had she even found out?

YASMINE

Callum had spent the previous evening drinking with Matt and Paul in the kitchen, something relating to a fight he'd had with Ruby, accusing her of leaking his secrets to the media. Unfortunately, what I'd hoped would be a cathartic experience for Callum seemed to have had a deeper impact, like poison slowly seeping into the cells of his body, killing them off one at a time. He was less attentive, his interest in sport (which had thankfully been dampened over the previous weeks) resurfaced with a vengeance, and he became consumed by his studies, refusing to leave the building.

After an intense yoga practice, I convinced Matt and Paul to accompany me on a walk to the poorly stocked Costcutter on campus. We were making our way back to halls, past the outdoor drinkers basking in the sun outside the Union, when I noticed the boys staring. I followed their gaze to two hyenas, their cruel shrieks sending frozen Karma down my spine.

'Something funny?' I asked them, directing my query at Ruby.

The three of us stood close in solidarity and watched as she took out a cigarette from a grubby, cheap, blue packet with her unkempt, dirty nails, lit it, inhaled, and purposefully blew smoke in our direction.

'We're celebrating Juliette being alive,' she said.

I felt the blood drain away from my face and willed the adrenalin, now pumping through my body, to replace the loss. I felt my throat seize up. Strongest amongst other random thoughts was the fact I hadn't finished my story, my legacy to the world.

'Is she alright?' I asked, as passionlessly as I could muster.

'She's alive. Not really OK. Her mother's here. She's creepy.'

'Did she tell you what happened?' I asked again,

rephrasing my earlier question so as to disguise the significance of my enquiries.

'She doesn't remember anything,' she said.

'Nothing?' I exhaled as gently as I could, letting relief flow into my lungs and from there to the rest of my body.

And now the pixie spoke. 'We might never know what happened. Some trauma victims never get that bit of their memory back. That's what my mother said. She's a doctor.'

We all regarded this vessel that held an improbable mixture of vital and useless information.

'I'm sorry,' I said, 'but I need to furnish Callum with supplies before he starves. He's hiding from the press who are after him.'

'I would probably eat some of that food too, if I were you,' Ruby snapped at me. I kept walking away from her vulgar tongue, holding my breath until we were out of view to avoid submitting to the pressure to snap back.

◦

The next morning, I was prepared. I knew I had to get Juliette away, to ensure she had other people and places surrounding her so her memory wouldn't be triggered into recalling what happened on that fateful day. Therefore, when I heard her mother unlocking her room, I opened my door and introduced myself. I then took a deep breath and told her what she deserved to know, the truth about her daughter.

Mirrors

JULIETTE

I had finally been allowed to go home – the drive down was insufferable – and once there, Mummy overreacted as usual and effectively kept me prisoner. She even 'retired' my mobile phone. 'For my own good'. What? Doesn't that sound like her? I've never been particularly good at theatre. Oh, you don't like the sarcasm? Sorry.

Yes, obviously, we came to Church. Against my will. This time, I didn't want to hear what you all had to say. It was difficult enough having to deal with my issues alone. Then, on top of that, I had the memory loss, the headaches, the leg in a cast.

But Mummy didn't care. She was on a crusade. 'Save us, O Lord our God, and gather us from among the heathen, to give thanks unto thy holy name, and to triumph in thy praise.'

Hmm.

Please don't look at me like that. You may all have been well-meaning but this ... this was effectively kidnapping. Like those crazy cults you hear about in the US. No, I wanted to work things out on my own – I was *determined* to work things out on my own.

So I made a plan. And I'm glad I did – it led me here, now, and – for the first time in a long while – I'm happy. So – despite what I put people through to do it – I'm glad I did.

YASMINE

As I opened my mouth to speak, I processed the magnitude of the words escaping. I realised that, although it was my duty to inform this woman of the true character of her beloved daughter and the effects of her actions, I had to do so without jeopardising my character. She had smiled at me and knowingly listened as I introduced myself.

'Pleased to meet you, Yasmine,' she said, in the slow manner used by women who have spent very little of their life interacting with unfamiliar faces. 'It's so nice to see that Juliette has made some good, sincere friends. I was worried about her.'

'We've all been worried about her. Especially given her recent, erm, digressions.'

For a moment, I felt that I had overstepped some invisible boundary between self-interest and murder, as the old lady grasped her chest manically, but I then realised she was feeling for the small silver cross sitting, predictably, around her neck. As she touched her aged fingers to the metal, its coolness seemed to pierce through the panic and her breathing slowed to an acceptable rate.

'Digressions?' she asked me, gently, imploringly, her eyes boring through mine so fiercely that I felt myself taking an involuntary step backwards in case this woman could see into my mind.

'Oh no, I just meant ... Have you met her girlfriend?'

'From church?' asked the poor, innocent lamb.

'No her, erm, girlfriend girlfriend. Her lover? I'm sorry for saying anything,' I said quickly, having realised that my attempt at putting distance between myself and Juliette might actually have the opposite effect if she ever confronted this hunched, yet undeniably powerful and mesmerising, figure. 'Please forgive me.'

'I forgive you my child,' she said, distractedly, the tears pooling, and returned to Juliette's room, shutting the door behind her. She left me standing there, consumed by guilt at having broken such terrible news to such a sweet old lady.

○

Everything was finally in place: Juliette had gone, Ruby had quit spending any time in halls, and Callum had begun to return, slowly but surely, to his attentive nature. It was under these optimistic conditions that Callum walked into my room, threw his arms around me and whispered in my ear.

'My dad's visiting. He needs to get away and, as there's a press ban on campus ...'

'I'm sorry, darling, are you saying he's coming *here*? Where will he be staying?' I asked, to clarify intentions.

'In my room. Just for a few days. I was hoping I could stay in yours. I didn't think that would be an issue.'

Images of Callum reading my unfinished story which, under optimal circumstances, would never have to be read by anyone other than me, flooded my brain.

'Darling, we're into exam season and …'

'Fine, don't worry,' he said sharply, and walked out abruptly.

❯

The next day, Mr Hayden-Quinn appeared in our kitchen and seemed particularly pleased to see me, something which served to reassure me of the feelings of his son.

'Yasmine,' he said, with a warmth I hadn't experienced from an adult since childhood. 'Thank you for putting up with my son during this tough period in our lives.'

I smiled at this man, whose strength and influence tore through his evident pain.

'You have a wonderful son,' I said, meaning every word.

CALLUM

Friday 11/05/2001 10:13
Subject: Re: RE:

Hello.

This week's been a little full on.

Dad's just left – he's going home 'to talk' – otherwise known as prising that bottle out of Mum's unyielding grasp. But we'll see how things go. We need to put on a united front, etc, etc.

Enough on that – I'm sick of it. And a little confused to be honest. Dad had it out with Ruby – it was craaaaazy – just after the Champion's League semis on Wednesday, actually. She was in a foul mood and stomping about the kitchen and she woke Dad up and he got up and he lost it and they had this massive shouting match and woke everyone up. But it really got me thinking. She's still claiming innocence and she's just NOT THAT GOOD AN ACTRESS – I've been surrounded by them all my life, I should know, right? But then again, if it wasn't her, who was it? No one else KNEW. I'm so confused.

Keep safe.

Cal

Sunday 13/05/2001 17:42
Subject: Re: RE: Re: RE:

Hello.

My life is getting stranger and stranger. I don't know how I feel about anything or anyone anymore. Argh!

Matt had this chat with Ruby yesterday and he's also convinced she didn't have anything to do with the tabloid fiasco. Which got me thinking about how I'd been treating her – if she's innocent, actually. I feel awful.

So, yesterday, the boys decided to watch the FA

Cup final in the Union and I joined them – Yas was sat typing at her desk as usual and wasn't interested and, anyway, I needed to get away. So here we are, at one of the tables by the side of the screen, when I see this girl – well, the back of her, actually. She was dressed as a schoolgirl and wore stilettos – great ass, great figure. She had this impressive tattoo just above her ankle – with surf flowers. A number of large sporty guys kept going up to talk to her but she was ignoring them, I thought. I was staring, I know, but the next thing I knew was Paul elbowing me in the ribs.

'Don't let Yas catch you leering like that,' he said.

I didn't get it. I just replied with 'looking, not touching – she won't mind' or something along those lines.

Then I realised Matt was looking at me strangely. He opened his mouth and floored me with 'Really? You think Yas wouldn't mind if she caught you drooling over your ex like that?'

Seriously – I couldn't believe it! High heels, short skirt, pigtails, TATTOO. What happened to her? But sure enough, after a while she turned so I could see her profile and it was her – Ruby! It was awful – I didn't know where to look.

And then this guy – this tall, black, handsome chap walked up to her and you could tell he wasn't like the others – she didn't ignore him or shrug him off or anything. He got his arm round her neck and they were laughing. It really hurt. Why does it hurt? I'm over her, she's over me. So why does it hurt? Yes, I know – I should stop being such a girl. Like I didn't have enough problems in my life!

Cal

RUBY

The vodka bottle was half empty. I stared at it and hoped it hadn't been full when Smithy'd started drinking. *I've had enough of friends being rushed to hospital.*

'What's going on, mate?' I asked.

'She said she's leaving.' Smithy stared at the bottle. Then she took out a fag from her pack and lit it.

I did the same. 'Her mother's a nutcase, mate. Trust me, it'll probably blow over.'

'You don't understand,' she said, so low I could barely hear her, 'she said she doesn't want to hear from me. She'll call me when she's ready to discuss stuff. That's what she said.'

'So she'll call you when she's sorted her head out. She was accused of serious drug-taking, mate. She fell down the stairs. She broke her leg. Plus, she's got a nutcase for a mother.'

Smithy looked at me. I could tell she wasn't convinced.

'It's silly, isn't it? I mean, we weren't *together* or anything. But, I don't know, I thought we had an understanding, you know?'

I nodded. *No, I don't know.*

❯

The next few days were a blur. I tried ringing Jules, but there was never any answer. *Maybe Smithy's right.*

I headed to the library to work, but I couldn't concentrate. I went out for runs but found myself thinking too much. I smoked. A lot.

By Tuesday, I was itching for something to happen. UEFA Champion's League semis. *We can do this. We can.*

I got to the Union early. Smithy was already there, drinking with The Captain. I joined in. Drag, swig, drag, swig, drag, three fingers for talking to someone outside the circle, gag, drag, swig.

Kick-off. Sanchez scored. *We can still do this.*

Half time shots.

Sanchez scored again. *Fuck.* Mendieta scored. *It's over. The dream is over.* I wept.

We were too drunk to drink and I wasn't in the mood for a drum 'n' bass night, so I crawled back to halls at eleven. It was quiet. I went into the kitchen and opened the freezer. *Pizza it is.* I put it in the oven and the bloody door slammed shut. I jumped, then froze. No other sounds. *Good – I haven't woken anyone.* I took out a plate from the cupboard. It slipped through my fingers and smashed on the floor. *Fuck.*

I got on my knees and started to clear it up. The door opened.

'Can you keep it down? Some of us are trying to sleep.'

I turned to see my idol – he looked thinner than the previous time we'd met, and a lot less friendly.

'Ruby! You little, selfish, vindictive bitch!' Sam Hayden-Quinn was not happy.

Now this I'm definitely not in the mood for. 'Excuse me?'

'My son breaks up with you so you wait – you wait! – and then you destroy our whole family unit – our whole family! My wife …'

Wow, he's a lot less smooth when he's angry.

'I explained to your, to Callum. It wasn't me that told the papers. I had nothing to do with it, mate.' *Now please fuck off and leave me alone. What is it with all of you?*

'I am *not* your mate. You little bitch!' He grabbed my arm. He wasn't strong, but the twisting motion hurt.

'Get off!' *And I thought my family were fucked up.*

'You've destroyed us! You've destroyed my marriage. You've put my sons in danger – in danger! And what for? Vindictive teenage angst.'

Oh fuck off. 'I've not destroyed anybody!' *Oh god – Matt and Callum and Yasmine are all here and they're all staring. As if Leeds getting fucked wasn't bad enough – now I have to deal with these people. Leave me alone. All of you.*

'You have, you little bitch! Bella was right. You're nothing but a gold-digging bitch. And I … I stood up for you. You …'

'Let go,' I screamed. 'You're all fucking crazy! Fuck you!' The last bit was aimed at Callum's face, as I pushed past them and ran back to my room. *The pizza can burn the building down for all I care.*

○

'Mate, you look hot!' Smithy looked me up and down suggestively and we both laughed.

'If only you weren't hung up over your, erm, ex?' *Too soon? No, she's smiling.*

'If only I were into women.'

We both laughed again, louder this time. It felt good.

'I feel a little … silly, dressed like this. The event isn't till tonight.'

'FA Cup followed by drinks followed by circle followed by Back to School. When do you expect to have time to change when there's all that drinking to be done?'

'You've got a point, mate.'

I slipped my arm through hers as we headed to the Union. *Nothing like a good all-day drinking session to get this last week out the system.*

We were late and there were no more seats, although the footie girls had a table, so we went and stood by them.

'A shot each for being late!' yelled The Captain.

This isn't going to end well. We did as we were told, then turned our eyes to the screen.

'Hellooooo!' Twinkle managed to speak and wolf-whistle at the same time. 'Looking goooood.'

I shrugged his arm off but smiled at him. 'So, little

girls do it for you? That's so wrong!'

'No, no, you've got it all wrong. Naughty schoolgirls do it for me.'

Of course. 'Well, you're in luck tonight. There's a looker for you right there.' I pointed cruelly towards a fat girl bursting out of her top.

Twinkle shook his head. 'She's not in uniform.'

'She's saving it for your session later, mate.'

The crowd roared as Ljungberg scored.

'A little overdressed for watching the game?' Toby slung his arm round my shoulders.

'I can go change into a full-length gown and go as a teacher instead if you prefer?'

'Depends. Will you be wearing anything underneath?'

Blokes. They're all the same. 'What difference does it make? I don't get naked for rugby boys that drink pints out of each other's arses.'

'Yeah,' Smithy joined in. 'I always thought that was a vicious rumour, but Dana *saw* you all last Wednesday. Yuck.'

'Well …'

Toby looks so cute when he's uncomfortable. I laughed.

'Just watch the game, mate,' I said, and took another swig of my pint.

Things were looking up. For a minute.

Prisms

YASMINE

After Mr Hayden-Quinn's departure, student life settled into a routine of studying and stress. While simultaneously hatching plans with my darling Callum to spend some of our holidays on his yacht (preferably at a faraway, exotic location) and revising ardently, I could not help but wonder what was happening with Juliette and her unreliable memory. I often found myself wishing she was still amongst us, so that I might observe her actions, monitor her moods, and investigate her thoughts. To that end, I always kept the curtains partially drawn so that I would have ample warning if any police van or campus security personnel decided to make their way toward our halls.

Then there was the concern of Juliette's sharing with Ruby. The hall grapevine (otherwise known as Sarah, whose intimate and intricate knowledge of us all was as inspiring as it was daunting) stated categorically that Ruby and Juliette were no longer on speaking terms, although the reason for this turn of events was unclear. It served to remind me that I was merely a pawn in this tale of larceny and deep psychological trauma.

I realise that I may not have time to finish my narrative, should the inconceivable yet perfectly plausible happen, so I will attempt to do so now, prior to returning to my revision notes. Over a year ago, I was caught in a compromising position with a figure of significance at school. As such, I was blackmailed into performing unspeakable and degrading tasks for the benefit of my extortionists. This included, amongst other things, allowing the thieves access to my house and the storing of stolen property relating to what the press termed the 'Kent Kleptomania burglaries'. I had no choice in the matter if I were to retain my dignity and my ability to excel in life, but I was also naively unaware of the lengths I would have to go to in order to conceal my involvement. The theft of a stolen broach from my room in the first term, and its subsequent recovery in the adjacent town, created unforeseen obstacles in a path I would not have chosen for myself.

I now find myself in a lull in the theatricality of this unfortunate reality. I can but hope that this continues, so that I need never follow through with my plan, nor need send this narrative on to anyone. If the unfortunate does, however, occur, I hope my friends and family will find it in their hearts to forgive me for my trespasses and remember me not as someone involved (however involuntarily) in the Kent Kleptomania spate of robberies, but as the individual they knew and loved.

RUBY

We lay on the grass on top of the once-pink Uni-issued bed cover. We had a bottle of Bailey's, a pack of fags, and a few ring files, notes, and books scattered about. We were studying. Supposedly.

Smithy looked up at me for the sixth time in the last hour.

'Studying sucks. I either know this stuff or I don't. How's revising going to help?'

I lit a fag. 'We just need to make sure we remember the things they want us to remember, mate. Then we write an exam and afterwards forget it all. It's like GCSEs and A-levels all over again. Nothing changes.'

'Unless we want to go into academia.'

Riiiight.

I looked at her, she looked at me, and we sniggered. I exhaled slowly, and stared out at the other buildings around us. 'I don't understand why everyone's holed up in their rooms or in the library on a day like today.'

'Holed up. Yeah …'

Oh shit, I've said the wrong thing.

'So, have you spoken to her?' she asked.

'Jules?'

'No, my mother.'

OK, so I'm not good at evading if it's not on the pitch.

'No, no, I haven't,' I said. 'Her phone's been disconnected. I'm guessing that's creepy 'Mummy's' fault.'

'I keep going over that phone call.'

Oh shit, this again. It's been weeks, hasn't it?

'Yeah?'

'About what she said. About how she's been thinking about everything – about what she's putting me through and, well, she said it wasn't fair on me with exams and that – not fair on me! Like I can think about bloody exams when she's decided to 'stop contact for a while' and to 'seek guidance from Christians', from 'people that understand'. Like I don't understand! Like I didn't have to go through all this shit.'

'You're religious?' I asked, confused.

'No, you fuckwit. I'm talking about being gay.'

'Oh, right. Right. But I don't know what we can do, mate, other than wait for her to call us. Just try to do some work. We won't be able to help anyone if we fail.'

'We can always resit.'

'That's your answer? Really?'

She pursed her lips and looked at the building opposite.

'I don't know what to do. I really like her – *really* like her. But she obviously doesn't want me anymore because I'm not a good, clean, Christian boy. I will never be any of those things.'

Don't laugh, Ruby, mate. Don't laugh. 'You *are* good and erm clean in the soap and water sense.'

'No, but what do I do? Tell me what to do!'

I started to laugh. She didn't join me so I stopped.

'I'm sorry, you're asking *me* for relationship advice? I'm living with my ex who shags his girlfriend who, by the way, is a total bitch and has it in for both me and

Jules – he shags her very loudly and makes a big deal about how happy they are together. Then there's my best male mate in halls who tried to kiss me but now no longer talks to me because he thinks that I'm a lesbian who told the papers about Callum's brother, which is ridiculous on both counts, but who cares about the truth? And let's not forget that I slept with a rugby boy. A rugby boy! And I did it more than the one time. What the fuck do I know about relationships?'

'What's wrong with rugby boys?'

'Really? Really? They're rugby boys, mate! What the fuck's the matter with me?'

'Easy, we were talking about my problems.'

She's smiling. Finally, she's smiling.

'Sorry.' I took another drag. *I have to get hold of Jules somehow. But how?*

CALLUM

Thursday 17/05/2001 15:44
Subject: News?

Hello.

How're you keeping up? Mum and Dad are 'working things out', though apparently Mum got hold of Mary's number and gave her an earful. Hope she's OK? I can but apologise for Mum's actions. You know what she's like.

On a brighter note, did you watch the crazy UEFA Cup game yesterday? Matt and Paul were in a good mood after that one! Although it's been pretty quiet around here otherwise – revision fever has well and truly set in.

Cal

Tuesday 22/05/2001 12:31
Subject: Re: Don't worry

Hello.

Been a weird week – Yas refuses to close her curtains and no longer seems to sleep at night – it's really annoying and it's messing with my sleep too. And I'm worried about Ruby – she seems to have disappeared. I'm feeling a little guilty about it all …

Ah well, glad your mum's OK. Keep safe and away from reporters!

Cal

Sunday 27/05/2001 18:09
Subject: Re: RE: Re: Don't worry

Hello.

Uni is very odd – sometimes I really think we're in this weird bubble that has nothing to do with the real world. Take tomorrow – it's supposed to be a bank holiday but it's going to make no difference whatsoever to any of us here – the shops on campus will be open, the Union will be open, life will go on as if there's no bank holiday. Existential crisis? Maybe. Or maybe just another strange event got me thinking about life outside halls – about how maybe I've got things all wrong.

It's Rube – don't laugh. I was sitting at my desk with the window open, when I heard some chatting and there they were – Rube and that girl, Smithy. And, well, I couldn't help but overhear the conversation – I wasn't eavesdropping or anything, I just happened to be there. But listening to them – it really made me think about things, actually.

Smithy was crying about Juliette and the end of their relationship or something which means – obviously – that all those rumours last term were about Juliette and SMITHY – not Ruby – which makes more sense.

And then Smithy asked Rube to tell her what to do and Rube went off on one about how she's the wrong person to ask for relationship advice because she's living with her ex – me, obviously – and how I apparently have very loud sex with Yas and make a big deal about how happy we are together. Then she said something about her best male mate in halls who snogged her but no longer talks to her because of the rumours – I can only guess that would be Matt or Paul – I have to have a word, actually. Pulling your mate's ex is not on – is it? And then she said something about having slept with a rugby boy a few of times – I'm assuming it can only be that guy I saw her with last time – and how it was a mistake. I knew something was up between those two. And – finally – she mentioned she was being blamed for the whole tabloids thing even though it had nothing to do with her. She wouldn't leave herself open to ridicule about the other things and then lie about that, would she?

So now I don't know what to think. Existential crisis all the way! But back to revision I go ... Or maybe just for a run.

Cal

JULIETTE

I hadn't realised how my being cut off would have affected Smithy and Ruby – it hadn't even crossed my mind. I was so focused on my own issues and on sorting things out with Mummy – who seemed to have lost it even more than she had after Daddy died. Besides, I thought Smithy understood – I thought I'd made it clear. I needed some time to work through my own issues in my head and I didn't want to burden her with my insecurities and constantly alternating beliefs on right and wrong. I wanted her to do well in her exams and to forget about me. And yet – selfishly – I obviously didn't want her to forget about me.

Remember that day when I came to you and asked you for help? That day when I told you that Mummy was overreacting and that I needed you all to understand that such a good feeling – that feeling I had when I was with Smithy – could not be anything other than a direct channelling of positive emotion from Him? I still believe that. You don't. You didn't support me or encourage me. 'Not forsaking the assembling of ourselves together, as the manner of some is; but exhorting one another: and so much the more, as ye see the day approaching.' Words are just words when you want them to be, yet vitally important when it suits? I can't live like that anymore. It's hypocritical and I'm sure He doesn't approve.

So, anyway, I decided to put my plan into action. I pretended I was ill and waited until Mummy headed off to Matins then rang up a Christian helpline and got a number to call. And call them I did. And they – in turn – opened up the world for me in a way I hadn't imagined. Because, you see, up until then I had really thought that I couldn't have it all – that I'd have to throw away the strongest love I'd ever felt or throw away my religion. That's not it at all – I can have both – I just can't have both under your terms.

So, the next day – while Mummy was at Matins and I knew she had her coffee morning afterwards – I headed down to Morning Prayer elsewhere. And what I found was what I'd been looking for – I just didn't know I had been looking for it – a place where everyone is truly welcome – not just in theory, but in practice too.

And that's why I'm here – explaining it all to you – today. Because I'm leaving – leaving you, leaving Mummy, leaving this stifling institution with its prehistoric ideas. But I'm not leaving my religion – you can't take that away from me no matter how hard you try.

But I'm getting ahead of myself again – there's one

last piece of the story that I need to explain, because without it, I might have lost them all for good.

Apocalypse

CALLUM

Thursday 31/05/2001 11:28
Subject: Re: Greece

Hello.

Exams have started – I hate exams.

Oh and it was Matt who almost-but-not-quite kissed Ruby – last term, when they were very drunk, apparently. But nothing happened, actually. That's what he says, and that he's sorry about breaking the ex code.

Hope all's well with you and can't wait for the summer – liking your idea of laying low on an off-the-beaten-track Greek island. Dreaming about the sunshine and babes in bikinis already …

I hate exams. That is all.

Cal

Thursday 07/06/2001 14:57
Subject:

You won't BELIEVE what's happened – I can't believe

what's happened. IT WAS YAS ALL ALONG. My fucking GIRLFRIEND!

Sorry, I'd better explain. But it's so unbelievable. It was Rube that told us – Juliette had remembered something – a few days before the accident, she'd seen Yas reading my emails. I didn't believe it – I couldn't – but Ruby wasn't making it up. IT WAS YAS ALL ALONG – she's the one that leaked the story about you to the tabloids. Ruby was really upset and thought we wouldn't believe her – which I guess is understandable since we haven't been believing her for a while – but it all suddenly makes sense: why the envelope with photos of us from school and holidays wasn't by 'The Walrus and The Carpenter', where I'd always kept them but by 'The Jabberwocky', why Yas stopped asking who I was emailing all the time BEFORE the leak. It all makes sense.

But I can't find Yas anywhere – the bitch. I need to know WHY. Why do it? Why put us all through so much shit? Why fuck up our whole family? And how could she sit by and pretend to comfort me? And let us all blame Ruby for all of it? I'm SO ANGRY. Fucking bitch.

I'll let you know when I find her – ring me.

Cal

RUBY

It took me days to work it out. *It's so obvious, I can't believe I didn't think of it sooner.*

I walked slowly up to the strange, diagonally-built, brick and glass building. I walked through the double-doors, up a flight of stairs, and round a tight, brick corridor. I finally got to the door I was looking for and knocked.

'Hello?' I held onto the papers in my hand tighter and pushed the door open. *No-one's in.*

I walked in, closed the door, ran over to the filing cabinet and had just managed to pull out Jules's file when the door swung open.

'What are you doing?' asked a voice.

Shit.

I turned and waved my papers at what was probably the secretary. 'I came to drop these off? I was asked to?' *It's working. She's looking very confused. Now slip that form into the back of your skirt, mate ... Done.*

'I'm sorry, I have no idea what you're talking about,' she said.

Shit, she's looking at the filing cabinet.

'We don't keep exam papers in there.'

'Oh no, no, no. I'm not an English student,' I said, shaking my head. 'I'm here to drop off my friend's assignment. She's ill and ...'

'What did you say your name was again?'

'Yasmine,' I said. 'I have to go. I have an exam shortly. Business. But I came to drop this off.'

I put Jules's unfinished paper, one she'd left in my room during a smoking session, down on the large desk, smiled, put on my rucksack and legged it.

When I got round the corner, I opened the file, took

down Jules's home number and then ran back into the office. 'I'm sorry, I must have picked this up accidently – it's not mine.'

'That's a student file,' said the secretary as she grabbed it off me.

'Sorry, my mistake. I've got to go to my exam.' I ran.

●

I waited till after ten to ring. Her mum would be asleep by then. As soon as the large pointer hit twelve, I dialled.

After three rings, someone picked up. 'Hello?' *Yes!*

'Jules? It's Ruby.'

'Ruby? Shit – Mummy's coming down. Give me your number – quick – and I'll call you tomorrow.' I told her and she rang off. I sat back on my chair and lit up.

The next day, I sat at my desk and looked at the clock. Ten, eleven, midday, one, two, three, 3:11, 3:12, 3:13 … The phone rang.

'Jules?' I hadn't even looked at the number.

'Hey! Long time!'

'You OK? What the fuck is going on?'

She laughed. 'Mummy's got me on lockdown. She's taken my phone and of course we don't have internet here. It's the dark ages! I'm stuck in the house like some naughty child. She caught me sneaking out of the house and thought I was meeting 'debauched homosexuals'.'

Good impression of your mum. 'Were you?' *Ruby, mate!*

'No. I went to church. Just not my church, you

know? Long story. How's Smithy?'

'Not happy at all. She's pining. You shouldn't have dumped her just before exams – could have made something up about recovery or something.'

'Dumped her? I didn't dump her! I just needed to work through everything.'

Oh, great. 'And?'

'And I'm OK with it. I just need to work out what I'm going to do about the entrapment situation.'

'Get your mother sectioned?'

'Ha! Maybe. Anyway, enough about me. What've I missed in the last month and a half?'

'Drinking, more drinking, even more drinking. Oh, and some smoking.'

'I'm serious!'

'Well, Smithy's been pining, Callum and his dad are mental, Yasmine is …'

'What's Callum's dad got to do with anything?'

'Don't you read the papers?'

'No, of course not – no need for that in my household! Dark ages, remember? What happened?'

'Callum's got a half-brother his mum didn't know about. She does now. Which is somehow my fault. Who knew?'

'Your fault? How?'

'They blamed me for everything. Oh, Jules, I really miss you!'

'Blame you for what? What did you do?'

'Nothing! I didn't do anything, mate. Callum told me the story while we were going out. He used to email his brother all the time. And I've been landed in it somehow because, supposedly, I was the only one that knew.'

'You and Yasmine … '

What? 'What?' I asked.

'I caught Yasmine reading Callum's emails. Well, I'm pretty sure they were Callum's emails – they certainly weren't hers.'

'Oh, fuck. Yasmine?'

'I'm just telling you what I saw. But would she really hurt Callum like that?'

I bit my lip.

'Mummy's back. Look – we'll talk soon. Tell Smithy … Say hi to Smithy for me.'

The line went dead. I brought the phone down to my lap and stared at it. Then I heard Callum and Paul talking on the stairs. Their voices faded. I opened my door and raced after them.

'Callum, wait! I need to tell you something! Callum, please! It's Jules …' The panting tackled my voice to the floor. *Fuck. I need to stop smoking.*

'Rube? Everything OK?'

Matt, Paul, and Callum all stopped and stared at me.

'No, mate. We need to talk.'

'Really?' Callum's left eyebrow shot up. His eyes made fun of me.

'It's Yasmine.'

'Maybe you two would like some privacy …' Matt began to back away.

'No! It's Yasmine who told the papers about David. Jules saw her reading your emails. I just spoke to her and she told me – Jules I mean.' *Why are you all looking at me like that?* 'I, I just thought you should know, that's all. What, what Jules saw. I thought you should know.'

'What kind of …?' Matt started with a lot of macho anger and now it was my turn to step back.

But Callum put out his hand and stopped him. 'The Walrus and The Carpenter,' he said.

Lewis Carrol?

'Of course! You haven't been in my room recently, have you? But Yas? Why would she do this to me? Yas? Yas! Fucking bitch!'

He sped off back up the stairs and Paul followed. *What are they on? Who cares? At least Callum believes me and doesn't think I'm some crazed loon.* I turned and walked to the lake. I found the bench and sat down.

'Mind if I join?' Matt sat.

I hadn't realised he'd followed me. *What do you want?* I took out a fag and lit it. I looked at him. His face said he wanted peace, so I shook the packet at him. He took it.

'Look. I'm sorry. About everything. Callum's my friend and …'

I nodded and held my breath. I felt myself on the edge of crying, but didn't want any bloke to see me do it.

'Ruby, I …'

Say it, mate! Just say it, whatever it is.

He didn't continue, so we just sat in silence. I finished my fag.

'I've got to go,' I said, and walked off towards Smithy's halls.

JULIETTE

Ruby called me – how she found my home number, I've no idea – but she did and we spoke. And then, when I put the phone down, it all came flooding back – the 'accident'. Only – of course – it wasn't an accident. It was Yasmine.

I'd been going to the toilets and she'd been heading out and dropped her bag and all this jewellery fell out. Well, I helped her – as you do. And then I saw it – unmistakeable. I mean, anyone would have recognised it – it was the crowning glory of the Kent Kleptomaniac hoard – the emerald in that absurd sun setting? And then I looked at the other pieces and they looked familiar too – I'd just been reading up on the subject so it was impossible that I'd made a mistake, you see. I looked up at her – I was scared, shocked, angry. So I confronted her. It was awful. She spat blasphemies at me and then shoulder barged me so I went tumbling down the stairs. It hurt, then went blank. I don't remember anything but falling. Falling, and the pain. But she must have been the one that put the cocaine and all the other stuff in my pocket. I certainly hadn't!

Anyway, I rang that police officer right away – the one that had given me her number. I should've rung Ruby but I didn't think … How could I have thought? I was trying to make sense of everything. How was I to know that it wasn't over?

YASMINE

Juliette has remembered and I must be on my way.

I wanted my side of the story to be heard. I didn't try to kill her, I had simply been on my way to return the items to their rightful owners by post and, if unlucky, face the consequences, be they expulsion, jail, or loss of my darling Callum. It all occurred as a result of an accident, whereby I simply knotted my legs and tripped, scattering items all across the carpet. That's how fine a line there is between doing the right thing and facing charges for attempted murder.

Juliette and I struggled over an item of jewellery that she had recognised from her obsession with the Kent Kleptomaniac burglaries and, as we both pulled, she twisted her ankle and fell down the stairs. I ran down after her, terrified, but she wasn't breathing, or so I thought at the time. I'd killed her! Guilt plagued me, but I couldn't be found with a body, not given everything, which is why I proceeded to cover my tracks.

I always knew that possibility of failure existed, as I knew that I would be unable to face the consequences of my actions, nor survive while plagued by guilt and embarrassment. And so I have decided on a different path, a romantic end to a life once so full of promise. I'm heading down to Cornwall, to the ends of England, to take a few pills I procured from an acquaintance in our halls of residence, then throw myself off one of those majestic cliffs. I will give myself to the ocean, which will then have the power to decide whether to give me up or keep me in its depths forever. I hope my mother, father, and Callum will be able to forgive and survive the onslaught of pain that I have set upon them with my actions, both past and present. Please, forgive me.

Aftermath

CALLUM

Friday 08/06/2001 09:16
Subject: Re: RE:

It's really fucked up here. There's police everywhere – they've been here since yesterday – on the hunt for Yasmine. But it's not about her disappearance, it's about the KENT KLEPTOMANIAC. I know! The girl I've been dating for months – for MONTHS – the press are going to have a field day. Fuck!

Sorry I know I'm rambling but it's all so weird. They won't tell us what it's about, either. Just keep asking me questions about jewellery and her lifestyle and money, actually. It's so frustrating. I want to kill her – she's done nothing but fuck my life completely.

And I still have exams to be getting on with. This has been a shitty few days.

Give me a ring?

Cal

Sunday 10/06/2001 08:49
Subject: Fw: Forgive me

Hello.

Thanks for the moral support – I've needed it, as I'm sure you worked out from listening to my rant! But things have become even more fucked up since yesterday and I don't know what to think anymore. Yas sent me the weirdest thing – I think it's a suicide note – well, a suicide email. I've forwarded it to you so you can tell me what you think – but please keep it quiet coz the police said not to share, but fuck them, obviously. It came yesterday, with an attachment, a strange piece a prose about the last year – she's been behind EVERYTHING. And I walked right into her bullshit, actually. And as for Ruby … How will I ever make it up to her? How?

So, what do you think? Has she seriously killed herself? What the fuck?

Cal

Saturday 09/06/2001 03:40
From: Yasmine Law
To: Callum Hayden-Quinn
Subject: Forgive me

My darling Callum,

You will no doubt have heard the myriad of accusations floating about. It is not what you are being led to believe, although I am not entirely innocent of the charges. I have attached my account of the last year, so that you and everyone else should know the truth.

Alas, I can no longer live with the guilt and embarrassment and I am sending this to you as a final farewell. I will be heading out to the cliffs shortly to end a life I no longer desire to live.

I hope you can find it in your heart to forgive me for all the undue suffering I have caused you and your family.

I love you always,

Yasmine xx

Wednesday 20/06/2001 11:31
Subject: Re: RE: Fw: Forgive me

Hello.

Exams are over, the press and police have fucked off and life returns to normal. Yeah, right! I've never heard a more absurd phrase in my life. Return to normal? What does that mean? I'll tell you what it means – whoever coined the term had never suffered or been through genuine shit. My ex – no, I can't think of that bitch as my girlfriend – has killed herself and I've fucked up my life, my family, my friends, my exams – if this doesn't qualify for extenuating circumstances, I don't know what will. I can't believe Yas killed herself, you know. It's so fucked up. I should quit and leave this God-forsaken place. I don't know anything anymore.

On a marginally brighter note, we've all pooled

together a bit here in halls – Juliette is still gone, of course, but Rube's started hanging around with us a bit again. As have some of her friends – they're pretty cool, actually. Rube's been really good – it's like all the shit never happened. I'd forgotten how COOL she was. We shared a hug yesterday. It was long and warm and tight and she smelt so goooooood. No – get your mind out of the gutter. But it made me realise that I still care for her, actually. I don't know how she feels. It's been such a weird year, after all. But maybe something good can still come out of all this craziness? Too soon?

Cal

JULIETTE

And it wasn't over. Not yet. We had to deal with police, statements, discussions, even Mummy couldn't stem the flow of people and events. I got a new mobile phone, spoke to Ruby and Twinkle ... But I couldn't bring myself to call Smithy – I just couldn't do it. It helped that every day seemed like an endless flow of movement – one day ran into the next and there was constant excitement.

Where's Yasmine? Tell me the story of how she pushed you down the stairs again? Are you sure it was the same gems taken by the Kent Kleptomaniac? How could you be sure? Isn't that an unhealthy obsession in crime? Isn't literature supposed to be about fiction and not about applications to real life? And so on and so forth.

Endless!

Then I got that email through from Yasmine. It was addressed to 'Dear Jules' – yeah she actually called me Jules! Can you believe it? Like we were buddies or something. I kept telling the police that I wasn't sure it was her – she *never* called me Jules – she wasn't even my friend! Anyway, her email said something like 'Dear Jules, I apologise profusely for all the pain and suffering I have caused, and my guilt has led me to suicide.' Frightening stuff.

And it came with an attachment – the most fantastical, self-congratulating, self-serving account of events. She clearly fancied herself as a writer but she's so over-the-top and verbose and … I felt sick. She tried to twist everything into a pious 'I had no choice in the matter' narrative. She even alludes to accomplices to her Kent Kleptomaniac persona. I don't believe a word of it, not one word. She – sorry, I'm getting a little impassioned, huh? Sorry.

'Be not over much wicked, neither be thou foolish: why shouldst thou die before thy time?' Why indeed? She should pay for her sins, not take the easy way out. Oh, listen to me! – I'm straying from the point again.

The only reason I brought this whole thing up is because it was the final straw.

RUBY

We lay on each other in the grass, and stared up at the smoke rising from our lips and fingertips. Smithy lifted her head off my stomach and propped herself up on her elbow.

'Dude, this is fucked up.' She shook her head.

'I don't know; she was pretty much teetotal – that was a whopping big clue right there.' Matt exhaled smoke then lifted his fag to his lips again. 'My Nan always said you can never trust a teetotaller. Is that a real word? Teetotaller?'

A synchronised shrug went round the group.

'Does smoking really help?' Callum looked disgusted as he stared at my hand.

'You're welcome to have one.' I tossed my pack at his head.

'Nope – it's disgusting.' He tossed it back, but smiled at me.

'I can't believe she's really killed herself.' Matt gently tugged at my big toe.

'Has she?' I asked. *Why are you all looking at me like that? Are you not all thinking the same thing?* 'I mean, do we know for sure?'

'It's not really her style, is it?'

Glad someone agrees with me, Matt, mate.

'Surely she's too precious to take her own life?' *What? Too much? You all know I'm right, so don't look so shocked.*

I rolled onto my stomach and took out another fag. I

started twirling it between my fingers.

'You think she's alive?' Callum took a swig of vodka.

'You think she's dead?' I countered. 'Yeah, right.'

'Maybe.' Matt stared out towards the row of trees separating us from the car park.

'I don't think so. It's out of character.' I lit another fag and inhaled.

'You know what's out of character?' Callum said. 'Her admitting to everything – getting the others kicked out, spreading rumours about Ruby, telling Jules' Mum about Smithy …'

Smithy gulped loudly.

'I think it's precisely *in* character,' I said. 'I mean, think about it. Things were bound to come out – and they have. The tutor told the police about the first term – I heard him. And Sarah said Yasmine had told her about me kissing Jules. She probably suspected Jules' mum would tell her who blabbed about her being gay …'

Smithy gulped again. I replaced the cap and rolled the bottle of rum towards her.

'Yeah, you're right. Gives her a chance to tell her version of the story – make herself look good.' Callum nodded as he spoke.

'Does she look good?' I laughed. 'That's not how I read it.'

'I haven't read it!' Matt and Paul both shouted.

We laughed them, although it wasn't loud or heartfelt.

I exhaled smoke. 'You didn't miss much. Just a load of waffle about how she did everything she did out of lack of choice or the goodness of her heart. Because 'people deserve to know'.'

'Good accent.'

Cheers, Callum. Good abs, by the way.

'Still haven't read it though.' Matt looked glum.

'I'll forward it to you,' I said. "People deserve to know'.'

'She really fucked Jules about, though.' Smithy bit her lip and squeezed the bottle in her hand.

'Jules will be fine. I spoke to her – she sounded fine.' I smiled at Smithy, but she shook her head.

'She's not fine about me, though.'

'Sure she is, mate. She just needs some time.'

'More time? Like how much more time?'

I shrugged. 'Maybe god can tell you, mate. Ask him. Or her.'

Smithy threw her pack at me and hit me square in the boob.

'Yeah, what was that about you going to church last term?' Callum flipped onto his stomach to look at me.

Boo, no more abs. Wait, what did you say, mate?
'What?'

'You know, last term – you said you were going to church.'

'With Jules – yeah. That was a really weird day. Top Ten, definitely.'

'Every single one of my Top Ten weird days have been this year. So much for uni being the best days of your life.' Callum shook his head, then took a swig from a can of Stella.

'Well, there's always next year?' Matt laughed.

We drank to that.

●

The sun went down. We rolled up the blanket and took it inside with a plastic bag full of cans, bottles and fag packets. I went to my room to get a fresh pack.

'Rube?'

Callum stood in the doorway, but not like he used to. His body was slumped, his hair flat, and his eyes half closed. He looked drained.

'You OK?' I asked.

'Not really. But thank you. I just … I wanted to say I'm sorry. About it all. About everything.'

Yeah, I'm too drunk for one of these conversations.

'No worries, mate.'

'No. I've been …'

'It's OK.' I don't know what came over me. I gave him a hug. He held me tight.

It was the strangest feeling. My body told me what my mind had been hoping for such a long time but hadn't believed. The signs were all there: my pulse was even, his strong smell of sweat under the deodorant just stank, his abs felt uncomfortable, and my fingers, toes, and spine felt nothing.

I stepped away from him and smiled. He smiled back. *He looks like your average bloke. Has he always looked so average?*

'Thanks,' he said.

When did I stop loving you? How? I wanted you so badly and now ... nothing. And I'm drunk. Surely I should want you now that I'm drunk? Can I be that over you? Is that even possible?

He put his hand on my arm. 'Everything alright?'

'Yes,' I said. And for the first time in a long while, I meant it.

Epilogue

JULIETTE

The final straw, yes – the whole thing with Yasmine made me realise that there are few good, kind, *honest* people in the world, and that I owed it to myself and my God to love them and care for them and be open-minded to the beauty of the world.

But you have always been there for us – since Daddy died, at uni when I was in my coma, and … and I really appreciate all that. Please don't think that I don't – I do. And I really appreciate you listening to me today. I really need you to be there for Mummy because I know she won't take it well. But I can't live my life like this anymore – there's a huge, beautiful world that God created out there – waiting to be discovered. And there's the love of my life out there too – waiting for me. So what if she doesn't fit your ideal? She's right for me. Perfect.

She's been there for me through thick and thin – kept sending me emails even though I never responded, always asking about me, giving me the space I need. So I'm going back to her now. I'm leaving, obviously. You probably won't have me back anyway.

No, no – please don't protest. It doesn't matter. It really doesn't. Do you understand what I'm saying? I'm in love. I'm happy. I have options. Yes, for the first time in my life, I actually have options! So I have to go now – back to uni, back to Smithy, back to the real world. And who knows what happens after that? Fear of the unknown is underestimation of His strength.

Wow it's late – sorry for keeping you so long. Goodbye, Edward, and thanks for everything.

CALLUM

Monday 25/06/2001 13:05
Subject: Re: Sailing boat sorted

Hello.

This has been a crap term – a seriously crap term. But Ruby's been awesome over the last few weeks. So cool. Makes the whole thing a little better, I think. She's even promised to help me out with studying if it all goes wrong. After all that's happened, she's still here for me. What a girl!

I'm really looking forward to the summer now – I need to get out of this place. Bad karma and all that. Can't wait – home on Saturday and then only two weeks until beach time – bring on sunny Greece!

Cal

Saturday 30/06/2001 20:10
Subject: Re: RE: Re: Sailing boat sorted

Hello.

I'm home! And I didn't fail! Bonus.

It was quite sad leaving, actually. Saying goodbye to everyone. The boys are working over summer so I probably won't see them till next year. How strange is that? You live with people for most of a year then don't see them for months. Weird. I didn't even see Rube before I left – she was sleeping or away from her room. I also think she might still be frightened of Dad. But anyway – I did it. What you said. I left them for her – I mean, what else would I do with them, right? And they were hers, after all. Even if there isn't any hope …

See you in two weeks!

Cal

YASMINE

Author Note

Yasmine Law was a member of the notorious Kent Kleptomaniac ring which ravaged the county over the summer of 2000. She wrote an autobiographical account of her fateful last year studying at university. She was never caught, choosing instead to take her own life by jumping from the cliffs of Cornwall. Her body was never recovered.

RUBY

They had all left early. I'd heard them but hadn't been in the mood to get out of bed.

I looked around my room. Everything was packed into a suitcase, four boxes, and two bags. *Not bad.* I took the last box and headed to the kitchen to pack away my cooking supplies.

I opened the fridge. Someone had left two beers there, so I took one out, opened it and took a swig. Then I bent down and opened the cupboard. I lifted all my pots and pans into the box. As I rearranged them, I saw a blue envelope in the frying pan. I pulled it.

It was attached to a small box and I took that out too. I turned the card over. It had 'RUBY' written along the front. *Callum's writing.* I stuck my finger under the already opened, and then re-sellotaped, flap and ripped.

The card was one of those plain ones, with a painting of a rose in front. I opened it. On the right, it had 'Happy Birthday. Love, Callum' written in blue pen. On the left, there was a longer message in black ink. I brought it closer to my face to make out the less clear handwriting.

'Dear Rube, I'm sorry about everything – especially sorry I never gave this to you on your actual birthday. Thanks for being there for me these past weeks. I hope we get to catch up in the summer and in the meantime – enjoy your present.' I brought the card even closer to my face to make out the smudge at the bottom. 'Love and stuff, Cal'.

I sat down on the chair, pulled the ashtray towards

me and lit a fag. Then I opened the box. I smiled.

It was a pair of earrings. I lifted one out. It caught the sun and a thousand prisms of light hit the wall. *Shit. Diamonds!* I'd never had diamonds before.

I took another drag and replaced the earring. *I guess these are the ones that Yasmine found. Surprised she didn't steal them!* I sniggered at my own joke.

I pushed my weight to the back of the chair, balancing on its two back legs. I inhaled. Exhaled. Watched the smoke rise up to the ceiling. I smiled at the wall. A summer of sport, sun, and visits to see the girls awaited.

Acknowledgements

Does anyone ever read the acknowledgements? Really? OK – here goes then.

I always thought books were, well, effectively, a one-(wo)man job: you write it, it gets published, end of. But reality is far from that.

Reality is having a seed of an idea and watering it every time you find two seconds of spare time, despite a child clinging to your leg and wiping snot on your last clean pair of jeans that fits while the other one screams in their Moses basket, all because your γιαγια once inspired you with tales of her writing poetry while sitting watching goats being herded.

Reality is asking for helpful feedback from your long-suffering and wonderful husband, and him coming up with 759 comments and/or suggested changes (after it had been edited) while you weep into what you thought was a decent semblance of a draft manuscript.

Reality is having your beta readers (thank you, Daniel Yakovee, Alexia Terzopoulou, and Joel Glover) read your book and pick up the loose threads and unravel them (OK, so they also lauded the feelings of nostalgia it evoked, but I'm focusing on the negative here).

Reality is having your very helpful and encouraging publisher say 'they really are hideously dislikeable, aren't they?' about characters you've (OK only sort of) tried to make marginally likeable.

Reality is having the warm and supportive book blogging community (you know who you are – my publisher wouldn't let me insert my spreadsheet here) make you feel very ill and extremely nervous as you send them your book to review because you really, really, really don't want to let them down.

Reality is having your lovely and well-meaning mother (thank you, by the way) begging to read your book and threatening to send copies to relatives that you know will most wholeheartedly disapprove of every single character and act in this book.

But thank you, all of you. Because, without you, *Lost in Static* wouldn't exist.

Christina Philippou's writing career has been a varied one, from populating the short-story notebook that lived under her desk at school, to penning reports on corruption and terrorist finance.

When not reading or writing, she can be found engaging in sport or undertaking some form of nature appreciation.

Christina has three passports to go with her three children, but is not a spy.

Lost in Static is her first novel.

Writing Round the Block – https://cphilippou123.com
Twitter and Facebook – @cphilippou123